THE RISING OF THE 14 THE SHIELD HERO

Aneko Yusagi

Come on! Isn't there anyone who can take me?

Our very first day attacking Q'ten Lo, and look at you! Celebration or not, you're drinking too much, Sadeena.

He's right, Sadeena.

Oh my, if it isn't little Naofumi and little Raphtalia! Come now, I'm not doing any harm. Like you said, this is a celebration!

Not doing any harm?

You've already drunk everyone under the table.

Which is exactly why I'm looking for new challengers. We hardly get the chance, Raphtalia! Join me. They've even got some famous "Tanuki" wine around here.

I certainly can't afford to get wasted and make a fool of myself.

Please! You can only find this stuff here. Don't miss out!

Wow. Wine you can only drink in Q'ten Lo?

That's right! It's made using one of Q'ten Lo's most closely guarded secrets. Come on, little Raphtalia. If anyone needs to boost their tolerance, it's you. I've got big hopes for your future!

Pass. I'm more likely to die before gaining a tolerance for anything you drink.

Oh, but I want to drink together!

Very well. Looks like this is where I step in. We don't want anyone to die of alcohol poisoning.

Well said. You handle this, Mr. Naofumi.

A challenge! I'm not going to lose to you.

I'm really starting to worry if we'll make it through the fighting ahead.

Bloodline of the Emperor
Raphtalia

Monster Girl
Filo

Former Water Dragon Miko
Sadeena

Like a little sister. Like a big sister.

Like family.

Love. Trust. Fatherly.

Pet?

Rivals?

Master.

Friend.

Friend.

Favorite.

Affection.

The Shield Hero
Naofumi Iwatani

Jealousy. Expectation.

Blind Girl
Atla

Sister complex.

Little sister. Big brother.

Hakuko Boy
Fohl

盾の勇者の
成り上がり
Relationship
Diagram

Table of Contents

Prologue: Prologue: Planning the Q'ten Lo Invasion...............6

Chapter One: The Sealed Orochi....................30

Chapter Two: Sharing Power-Ups...........................56

Chapter Three: The Cursed Ama-no-Murakumo Sword...........79

Chapter Four: Tailwind..............................88

Chapter Five: Information on the Enemy............................107

Chapter Six: Use of Life Force................................119

Chapter Seven: A Terrible Sense of Direction...................143

Chapter Eight: Big Sister.......................172

Chapter Nine: The Miko Priestess of Carnage......................188

Chapter Ten: Shield Power-Up Method.....................217

Chapter Eleven: A Brief Return Trip....................233

Chapter Twelve: Past and Present.......................243

Chapter Thirteen: The Past Heavenly Emperor..................290

Chapter Fourteen: The True Terror of Monsters..............329

Epilogue: Dusk.................................346

Prologue: Planning the Q'ten Lo Invasion

"I'll start by reviewing the current situation. First things first . . ."

It was the morning after celebrating our victory, and I had gathered everyone at the house in Q'ten Lo's port town in an attempt to decide what to do next.

Our venue was in a general state of disarray. The most likely cause was the celebrations from the night before, which had included much drinking and singing. Perhaps due to this being a nation much like Japan, I was reminded of the mess left behind after Japanese people had finished with their silly spring "flower watching."

"Owww . . . my head . . ." Everyone other than my friends was looking pretty unenthusiastic.

"What's with you guys? I thought you wanted this rebellion? Raphtalia leading the charge, you said! Was that all just talk?" The energy on display the night before had completely drained away, leaving people looking pasty-faced and sickly.

"Can I g-get some water?" one of the men groaned.

"This is all Sadeena's fault. She's the one who challenged them to a drinking contest," Raphtalia said.

"Is that so?" Sadeena replied.

"T-the rumors were . . . all true. The talk of so many lives lost . . . to drinking with the priestess of carnage . . ." Her latest victims could barely croak out their side of the story. Indeed, they all looked ready to die—any moment, just drop dead. Four of them had scurried off to puke, and they hadn't come back yet. Seriously, did they all have hangovers? Were these guys really going to cut it?

It seemed a good idea, for now, to skip those who had just joined us here and decide what to do with the companions I had brought with me.

Q'ten Lo was suffering under the canker of corrupt politicians, placing a terrible burden on the people. The ones who made the attempt on Raphtalia's life had apparently done so under the influence of the pus that passed for the leaders of this nation. Our advance into Q'ten Lo had therefore brought plenty of those sympathetic to the revolution out of the woodwork. Their long years of suffering were perhaps the reason why they basically threw a parade the moment we captured the port.

The resulting partying was still going on, in fact, with a general clamor of enjoyment ringing out from beyond the building's walls.

"She's one loved by Dionysus, that's for sure. We

thought she was just still out there, somewhere, drinking."

"Of course, it all makes sense. She travels with a monster, after all, one who eats the source of a brew so foul even the god of wine would run from it." Why was everyone looking at me? Was it really so sickening to them that I would eat the rucolu nut?

"I just don't understand why you call me a monster. Really, I can't think why," I grumbled.

My name is Naofumi Iwatani. Originally from Japan, I'm currently the Shield Hero in this parallel world. Well, it might be more accurate to say that I was summoned to this parallel world and had the role of Shield Hero forced upon me.

Taking into account everything that had happened to me recently, in that moment I was in the middle of contemplating once again just how differently the Shield Hero gets treated, simply depending on the country.

Before I get into that, though, I should probably explain about the world into which I've been summoned. Here everyone has a level, just like in a video game, and by defeating things like monsters you can earn experience and increase that level. The world is built on a foundation that anyone familiar with modern Japanese games will have no trouble understanding, including other elements such as stats. It's even possible to check such things as the details of your abilities just by concentrating; overall, it's not far off the mark for someone to think that I basically got summoned into a video game.

Taking that too literally, however, can also lead to misunderstandings.

I was summoned to this world in order to fight a disaster that threatens to destroy it, called the Waves, and to keep this world safe. As one perhaps overly familiar with works about a "chosen hero" and being "summoned to another world," this all started out as a pretty ideal situation for me, but guess how long that lasted? As it turns out, the country that did the summoning, Melromarc, also had religious reasons for thinking the Shield Hero is basically the devil himself. That led to me getting caught up in all sorts of plots and conspiracies. And although this may sound strange coming from the one it happened to, it resulted in me becoming one bitter and twisted individual.

Let's take a moment to consider what might have happened if instead I'd been summoned to Siltvelt, a nation that worships the Shield Hero. Siltvelt is a nation populated by races of what they call demi-humans and therianthropes. If I'd been summoned there, well, I would definitely have been treated as a god, given all due respect. But how could I forget all the nobles of the land bringing in women to form my own little harem, each more desperate than the last to be blessed with a divine child?

Which would you choose, pray tell, between being framed for a crime you didn't commit and cast out, penniless and alone, or being little more than a stallion at stud for the rest of your exhausted days?

Me, well, I don't want either of them. No way. I'm also really starting to hate the kind of story that I now have to live in.

In any case, I've made it through my fair share of plots and dangers, and here I am.

"How utterly deplorable," commented Atla.

"For once, we agree," was Fohl's reply. The two of them were still looking over the decimation wrought by the drinking.

These two were slaves that I purchased and both part of a race called "hakuko," which was apparently quite elite in Siltvelt. At a glance, Atla just looked like a young girl. Inside, though, there beat the heart of quite the warrior. For example, her putting a most persuasive beatdown on some hotheads in Siltvelt was still fresh in my memory. I might have wanted to comment on that incident to her, but it had all turned out okay, so for the moment I was staying quiet.

According to the leader of Siltvelt, anyway, her personality was the very epitome of the spirit of that nation. Considering the extreme loyalty that she showed me—and we are talking super extreme here—I personally found that a little hard to believe.

Fohl just got thrown in when I picked up Atla. No, hold on. That's not right.

He started out playing the role of the good big brother, tending to Atla as she suffered from her sickness, but after her recovery she started driving him to his wits' end. In actual fact to start with, I thought he was the one I'd get more use out of, so I paid for Atla in order to get him. As it turned out, she ended up being the stronger of the two, although, credit where credit was due—he was working to close that gap.

He could use a white tiger therianthrope form now, and you know what, he'd even grown a bit taller too. Although the conditions remained a mystery, it seemed he could even undergo a full beast transformation. That definitely sounded worthy of investigation.

We had to come through Siltvelt in order to reach Q'ten Lo, and the pair of them had been a big help during that journey. I wasn't quite seeing it myself, but they had been pretty big in Siltvelt. They'd definitely have work there leading the nation even once my duties were finished and I was "happily" back in Japan.

"You two are still minors. If someone enticed you two to drink, I'd give them a piece of my mind," I told them.

"Mr. Naofumi could ask me to drink poison, and I'd finish off every last drop!" Atla sounded like some kind of cultist.

"What!" Fohl turned on me. "You plan to have her drink poison?"

"Use your head! Of course not!" Man, that I even had to say it. This was how it always was with these two. "Anyway. Where's Itsuki and the others?"

Itsuki Kawasumi, the Bow Hero, was summoned here from a different Japan than the one that I came from. Just like me, the poor guy had suffered his fair share—another one of Witch's victims. In fact, thanks to her machinations, Itsuki's head was still a major mess. He definitely needed some treatment, but seeing as he could still fight, I was still making good use of him.

"They went with Rishia to check out some writings on Q'ten Lo. They should be along soon," Raphtalia explained. Fair enough. Probably not a problem if they weren't here. Rishia was serious enough that she wasn't going to let anyone in her charge lose themselves in drink. Right now, that also included Itsuki, but in the past that same Itsuki had treated Rishia pretty badly.

After that, with her abilities in battle reaching their full potential, Rishia defeated the corrupted Itsuki after he fell into darkness and persuaded him to come back to the light. Yes, I know. She sounds more like the hero here, doesn't she? She'd been lying low a bit recently, but originally she was more of an intellectual type than a fighter. For my part, I've come to rely on her considerably in terms of both her personality and abilities.

"You need to get these hungover men back on their feet first, anyway. We don't have time to waste. You do understand the situation?" Seriously, why did they think all of this was happening?

Raphtalia. My connection to her was the start of all of this.

Raphtalia was akin to my right hand, someone sworn to fight alongside me. When we first met, our relationship was a little different—that of slave and master. Now I'm more like a father figure. The cause of all this was more recent than that, anyway, when I put Raphtalia in a miko outfit in a village that I govern. She wore one like it in the world that Kizuna came from, and it suited her so well I made her wear one again.

The problem was, ironically enough, that it was an outfit with special meaning in Q'ten Lo, the homeland of Raphtalia's parents. On top of that, it also turned out that Q'ten Lo had been keeping tabs on Raphtalia all her life, the nation's agents quietly watching from the shadows, doing nothing but observe even during the harshest misfortunes that she faced. Dressing her up, anyway, ultimately led to them making the utterly insane declaration that they would continue to send a succession of assassins until Raphtalia was successfully killed.

I'm not open-minded enough to just let something like that go. Raphtalia had actually come to have a pretty high priority in my life. After all, when I was at my very lowest, she was the only person who had come to my aid.

So I decided to make those Q'ten Lo bastards pay— to get the guys who gave the order to kill Raphtalia. Direct action had seemed best, and so that's why we were here invading the country.

Not that just getting here had been easy. Q'ten Lo wasn't surrounded only by the ocean, but also by a powerful barrier. During our attempt to gain access to a trading vessel out of Siltvelt, assassins attacked us on the open sea. We managed to drive them off, but out of the frying pan and into the fire—Raphtalia, Sadeena, Gaelion, and I promptly got sucked down into the ocean by the Water Dragon defending the waters of the island. The dragon ended up helping us out though, and we managed to land first in Q'ten Lo.

That led to us meeting with Raluva, the mayor of the port and representative of a resistance against the Heavenly Emperor, the sort of king of this land, and in turn we defeated the corrupt officials who were treating the port like their own piggy bank.

Other things happened along the way, such as meeting the master of the old guy from the weapon shop, but I won't go into that now. We were still in the middle of taking down the imbeciles behind this mess and had plenty of better things to be doing.

The main issue was the existence of this ruler, the Heavenly Emperor, who was a relative of Raphtalia. Apparently, the only way to stop the stream of annoying assassins was to defeat this blowhard and prove that Raphtalia is the one who should be in charge. Therefore, we were now planning to advance our forces from our newly acquired base of operations, this port town.

Luckily for us, the current Heavenly Emperor of Q'ten Lo had implemented a ridiculous edict against harming living things, dishing out punishment to anyone who killed monsters. This meant he had lost the faith of the people and the country was ripe for revolution. The perfect opportunity to implement a little regime change.

The explosion of the people's dissatisfaction was

clear, just from the intense celebrations still going on after our victory.

"Kwaaa!"

"It looks like the festivities are still going on. Maybe I can go and have some fuuun!" Filo chirped.

"Kwaa, kwaa, kwaaaa!"

"Bleh! Master likes me best!" Filo went on.

This exchange came from the garden, where Filo and Gaelion were staring each other down. Filo was a bird-type monster called a filolial, which developed in special ways when raised by a hero. Her current form was that of a blonde-haired, blue-eyed young girl with wings on her back, but that wasn't her true form. She actually looked like . . . Let's called it what it is: a crazy ostrich-like thing, round and fat with powerful legs. Something like that.

All of that from a prize I won from an egg lottery that I took part in on a whim.

She's been a little down on her luck recently, but having been reunited a short while back with Fitoria, queen of the filolials, she'd received various blessings as a result. It looked like she'd had a considerable boost to her fighting power.

Gaelion, meanwhile, was a dragon—a race that has never got along well with filolials.

He normally spent most of his time in a seemingly just-born-baby-dragon state. But at crunch time, he turned into a big dragon to fight. "Multiple personality" didn't quite fit the situation, but he had two different consciousnesses inside his body.

One was the baby Gaelion, the true owner of the body and the one currently in control. The other, hidden personality, the father Gaelion, could be called out as required and was once a dragon zombie I fought. Anyway, Gaelion has both of those inside his body.

I'm his owner, but he's being raised by one of the slaves from my village, a girl called Wyndia. At that moment, though, Wyndia was putting her all into biological research in Siltvelt alongside Rat, an alchemist from Faubrey, which was why Gaelion was currently with me.

This beastly pair, Filo and Gaelion, were really useful if something needed squishing, but they also didn't get along at all and were always bickering and fighting, which means it was business as usual and should be fine to leave them to their own devices.

"My point is, if we don't decide our next move quickly, our current opportunity may slip away," I said.

"You're not wrong," Raphtalia agreed.

Then, with a painful groan and still shaking his head to drive off the hangover, Raluva, the mayor of the port of Q'ten Lo, also joined the discussion. I continued. "So here's what I need to know. Where in Q'ten Lo is this Heavenly Emperor to be found? If possible, I want to take care of him real quick and just bring an end to all this." I spread out a map of Q'ten Lo and took a good look. It wasn't as large as Melromarc or Siltvelt, but it had a density that reminded me of Japan.

Our current location was the port on the west side.

"The current Heavenly Emperor is here, in the city that's also our capital." This enticing nugget was accompanied by a finger pointing to the east of Q'ten Lo. The landmasses didn't really match up at all, and so this is pushing it, but Japan-wise, if we were currently in Kagoshima, then Raluva was pointing at Tokyo—or maybe Chiba.

Yeah, forget the whole Japan comparison. I suck at geography anyway.

This revelation of our destination also had Sadeena tilting her head.

"Hold on. The capital wasn't there when I lived here." Sadeena also originated from Q'ten Lo, arriving in Melromarc along with Raphtalia's parents. She had become the "big sister" to everyone in the village, someone everyone relied upon, and in particular played the older sibling role to Raphtalia.

She was also a fiend when it came to drinking, often dragging others down into the depth of drunkenness.

Then there was her personality, that of an overly cheerful airhead. To be quite honest, she annoyed the hell out of me. Strength-wise, though, there was no telling the depths of her abilities. An eastern-style beauty with the ability to turn into a killer whale therianthrope.

"When the current Heavenly Emperor came to power, the capital was moved from the one the previous emperors used. That's why I think we should stay by occupying the territory now known as the "old city." It's well-positioned and should make a big contribution to our subsequent activities."

"Pretty bold, leaving all that tradition behind." Raluva nodded in agreement at this comment from Sadeena.

"There were a lot of opposing opinions, but the policy was forcefully pushed through. The new capital is still under construction in some places," Raluva explained.

So all of this, as well as an edict on not harming living things? It looked like this guy didn't have a clue, except maybe where to find the next pothole to put his foot in. Even things in Melromarc were going better than this.

"So the real reason for the move was, what? Lining his cronies' pockets?"

"Ah, well. The opinion of a certain wicked woman who was intimately involved with the emperor before the last one had a large say in things. The climate in the old capital was bad for her skin."

"That sounds suitably suspicious. Surely she's the one pulling the strings behind all this?"

"Yes." Raluva nodded at my comment. "The wicked Makina is the one who really sits in the seat of power." Hah, I was right? If things were this corrupt, no wonder the people are so keen to see Raphtalia as the true Heavenly Emperor.

Then there was the old city. A place that was no longer the capital, due to that same corruption.

"There's another reason for aiming for the old city. There we can also perform the rituals of the Heavenly Emperor for Raphtalia." Geographical matters were one thing, but I didn't quite follow the logic of this statement.

"Look, sweet little Naofumi's eyes have glazed over. Let's see, that means it would allow little Raphtalia to use the same blessings that our enemy has been using. If things go well, then we'll be able to use that power too," Sadeena explained.

"Yeah, okay. I see it now." The sakura stones of destiny emit a barrier, inside which the four holy powers were weakened and anyone who received blessings of the Heavenly Emperor is powered up. Then Astral Enchant could also be used to further boost the stats of those inside the barrier. That meant that we'd also be able to perform this skill.

"There's a place in the old city to appoint a new Heavenly Emperor. If Raphtalia performs the rituals there, she should gain access to those powers."

"Sounds like we march on the old city first, then." The current Heavenly Emperor had moved to a new city in the east, after all. He must be a real imbecile to give up such an important location.

In either case, this looked like a good move. There was still so much we didn't understand about the situation too. Best to sniff out a few more things first. This also sounded like the perfect time to try and get some information from the Water Dragon's crystal ball that Gaelion had absorbed.

"To the plan, then. Affirming our current situation, our only current base of operations is this port."

"I'm sure that, with word of our chasing off those in charge and our declaration of the opposition, it's only a matter of time before liked-minded comrades start to appear from neighboring villages and towns," Raluva said.

"Good." That was definitely something. "We don't have time to sit on our hands though. Let's start planning for other strategies too."

"Sure. We have to get our village back on its feet—and there's the next wave of enemies to think about," Raphtalia reminded me.

"I know. I'm certainly not planning on spending the rest of my life here." On that note, I spread out some paper next to the map and illustrated my proposals.

"Our first option is, faced with the slog of capturing an entire nation, just charge right in, take down the Heavenly Emperor, and put an end to this." Based on information from Sadeena, the emperor was never going to stop attempting to harm Raphtalia under any circumstances, other than the complete destruction of this nation.

That said, it wasn't like we had the time to dig and lay siege, either. So this plan would involve quickly silencing the boss behind everything.

"The issues here would be the strength of our enemies and the disadvantages faced by our weapons." I was referring to the unique technique possessed by this nation, a technique that weakened the four holy powers—including, of course, the power of my shield—and putting heroes such as me at a serious disadvantage.

This nasty technique not only nullified our own power-up methods, but also powered the enemies up, making it difficult to brute-force anything with just high levels and abilities. While we did have access to weapons that would alleviate their nullification of our power-up methods, that still left them with their own meaty power-ups. Attempting to strike deep into the heart of the enemy camp carried a serious risk of just getting our asses handed to us.

"That definitely sounds like one of your plans, little Naofumi," Sadeena said.

"Just a bit lacking in practicality." It would definitely be best to avoid taking a risk and getting wiped out. "I'm also thinking about having the old guy's master make some weapons." We'd already had some powerful weapons that he made in Q'ten Lo. He was a hardcore letch too, basically Motoyasu II. He also knew techniques unique to various nations though, so maybe he would be able to create something to pry an opening. He was currently holed up in the forge along with the old guy.

Still, while it was worth spitballing it out, there were just too many unknowns to risk the old blunt-instrument approach.

"You've got it all worked out, Mr. Naofumi. You are a god! You'll show Raphtalia's relatives who the real god is by delivering a divine smackdown!" I guess maybe that was true back in Siltvelt. I ignored Atla, anyway. I don't have the time to deal with her right now.

"Next, option two. This is the one where we gather those sympathetic to our cause under the banner of Raphtalia and take the nation. We call in more traders from Siltvelt to load up on supplies and bolster our forces. If we can bring in others speaking out against the current Heavenly Emperor's policies, we can probably win a lot more easily than the first option—it will just take more time."

"This isn't easy to decide, is it?" Fohl stood, arms crossed, deep in thought. I'd originally pegged him as a muscles-for-brains type, but maybe I was wrong?

"The very idea of taking a nation makes my heart pound! We should deploy the full might of Siltvelt to take them down, as a display of your true authority!" Atla, for her part, seemed quite into the idea. If her thinking was a little barbaric, well, it wasn't the first time for that either.

"So we want to end this quickly, but there are too many unknowns for us to infiltrate their capital safely," Raphtalia stated.

"That's the short of it," I agreed with Raphtalia. Chopping the head off the snake would surely solve this problem, so it was tempting to try, but it would also be like walking into a fog of uncertainty.

"Rafu?" Our group was now joined by a yawning, tottering Raph-chan. This little cutie was a shikigami—a familiar—created from Raphtalia's hair. A monster, I guess, that looked a bit like a raccoon-dog and a bit like a badger? More craziness, anyway. I admit I had a soft spot for her and was far more willing to spend a little more love on her than the two critters still staring each other down in the garden. She had all sorts of useful skills and could be really valuable when the excitement started.

That said, she hadn't taken part in the battle of the previous day.

"I did think of taking the fight right to them, but with all the problems the people here are having, I think the stoic approach might be the best one," Raphtalia said.

I was in agreement with Raphtalia. Thinking further ahead, having the people of this nation under my control would also bolster my forces when facing future waves.

"It just looks like it's going to take a bit of time." Just defeating the enemy wasn't enough, after all. You had to completely break them. Otherwise, even if you did defeat their leader, you still couldn't claim to rule the nation.

It reminded me of a revolution Itsuki once participated in, in a nation neighboring Melromarc. The revolutionary forces did manage to defeat the king and occupy that country, but the people were still starving, meaning in the end nothing changed.

It's important to see through to the truth, in all things.

That said, if corrupt politicians were the cause, chopping the head off—literally their heads—may well appear to be a solution in this case. But would simply draining this particular swamp really make things better?

"This is only our second day here. It might be too soon to commit to any of this stuff."

"Another good point."

"That said, we also can't leave it too long. Keep in it a corner of your minds, everyone."

"Roger that."

"Raluva, I'm going to need you to prepare our defenses. Taking into account that news of our occupation is going to spread, it'll lead to a pretty big counterattack. Whether we wage an all-out war or try to end this quick, we should expect such an attack to come." I probably didn't need to spell this part out, to be honest. I certainly didn't place myself ahead of specialists in the area of tactics.

"Of course, Hero!"

"Last but not least, let's have Raphtalia take part in a parade today, dressed in her miko outfit. That should help boost morale a bit." We also currently lacked both combat strength and an awareness of our cause, so this looked like a great chance to have the newer of the two Heavenly Emperors put on a bit of razzle-dazzle. It didn't hurt that Raphtalia was a standout beauty too, perfect for fanning the flames of national pride.

For the sake of our future plans, it was time to present her to the people, loud and large—the new Heavenly Emperor, here to defeat the current monster and his policies of evil.

"So that's what this all comes down to. Any particular reason you see the need to show me off in that outfit?" Raphtalia asked.

"Because it suits you." That was hardly declaration enough. The facts were, Raphtalia simply looked too good in that miko outfit. It wasn't just the cut of the clothing or those sleeves, but the emanation of an overall, highly mysterious appeal. Perhaps that was proof of her being the Heavenly Emperor?

"Rafu." Raph-chan certainly agreed with me. I'd have to try making a miko outfit for her too, when I got a moment.

"Do I have to remind you that none of this would have happened, Mr. Naofumi, if you never dressed me in that miko outfit?" she reminded me.

"That's neither here nor there. There were people just sitting by and watching you suffer. That fact alone is enough to warrant all of this." I wasn't seeking to shift responsibility. I just couldn't forgive them for treating her like that.

"Very well . . ."

"Raphtalia. I'm so jealous of the clothing that Master loves so much, so envious!" Atla told her.

"If you want to wear it"—Raphtalia looked wearily at Atla—"it's all yours."

"Playing it cool, aren't you? Brother! Isn't there a special outfit for hakuko to wear?"

What were they even fighting about? And dragging her brother into it too.

"Yes, there is! I'll acquire one as soon as possible!" Ah, Fohl was holding back a smile. Maybe he was happy to be called on? It was rare to see Atla ask him for anything. It might have been the first time since she was sick.

"I'm going to send Master into fits. You'll see," she went on.

"Good luck with that."

What a pain these two were. Seeing Raphtalia dressed in her miko getup sounded like just the remedy I needed.

"Nuh?" Gaelion suddenly stopped fighting with Filo and turned to look out of the garden.

"Hummm?" Filo displayed a similar reaction.

"Ra-rafu?"

"What's going on?" I directed my question generally at the three critters, and then at almost the exact same time, there was a sound. Far away, but very big.

Something like an explosion.

Chapter One: The Sealed Orochi

"What was that? The townsfolk finally taking things too far?"

"An odd sound for that, I think."

"I'm sensing a strange flow of life force."

Expediently enough, Filo was already in her filolial form, so I climbed onto her back and looked in the direction of the noise. It looked like a cloud of dust was rising from the mountains just outside the town. We passed through there after arriving in Q'ten Lo, if I recalled correctly.

The place with a burial mound.

"W-what was that noise just now?"

"Sounds like someone's having fun." It was Rishia and Itsuki, back from their search and wondering what was going on.

"It can't be. It simply—!" Raluva was at a loss for words, staring toward the burial mound.

"Hey, kid!" Now the old guy from the weapon shop and his master came running up.

"Man, our enemies aren't holding back. Looks like they want to maintain their status here at any cost." The old guy's master shaded his eyes with his hand, also staring off, semi-exasperated, toward the mound.

"You know what's going on?" I asked.

"Nothing I'm sharing! A bigshot who won't even make a harem? Anything I know would be wasted on you!" Gah, this guy! Talk about a pain in the ass!

"Master, can you please give him a break?" The old guy grabbed Motoyasu II's head with one hand.

"Owwww! Erhard, quit it!" I definitely wasn't letting Raphtalia anywhere near this guy.

"Mr. Naofumi? Could you please stop stroking my head quite so hard? I'm not Raph-chan!" Raphtalia said.

"Rafu!"

As I clicked my tongue and showed him me stroking Raphtalia's head—mainly out of spite, I admit—Sadeena realized what was going on and picked up the slack.

"Maybe, then, you big handsome blacksmith you, you'd like to tell me what you know?"

"Of course, most lovely lady. I'll tell you everything!" Seriously! Motoyasu II indeed, he was a complete and thorough upgrade! "A monster that caused serious damage to our country long ago is now sealed in those ruins. Of course, sealed by the Heavenly Emperor of that time."

"Yeah, when we passed by, Sadeena mentioned

something like that. So the monster wasn't defeated?"

"Maybe I remembered it wrong. I thought that was just a cenotaph?" Sadeena said.

"This place being what it is, only a few people know the truth," he went on. Hmmm. So was it a monster that actually existed to protect the world? Like the Spirit Tortoise?

"The reason they sealed it, keeping it here in this place, was to enhance the barrier that separates Q'ten Lo from the outside world—one of the gods defending this land, if you want to think of it like that."

"And that's really what it is? A divine protector?"

"Those corrupt officials thought so, at least." A case of passionate believers, was it? But Raphtalia's family line apparently took the top spot, even over some divine protector. They really were willing to do anything, anyway—including breaking the seal on a monster. "That's not the only problem mixed up in all this though."

"Go on, then. Try me," I said.

Rising to the challenge, Motoyasu II scratched hard at his head, pointed toward the ruins, and muttered.

"Just a little while ago, our current Heavenly Emperor—that little shit with his ridiculous love of monsters—went around to every sealed site and placed sakura stones of destiny and blessings at each one.

Making things easier for the gods protecting us, that was the official line."

"Is he soft in the head?" I exclaimed. The guys we fought yesterday had been quite tough enough, thank you very much! And he'd placed the same blessings on monsters that once caused damage to this nation? What was this moron thinking? It didn't take a genius to predict the disasters that might be caused if even just one of those monsters was revived.

Well then. Now I saw why the Water Dragon was opposed to the Heavenly Emperor and lent us aid on our approach to this country. There was no way having this crazy crackpot in power was good for the nation as a whole. This whole thing was starting to feel as unpleasant as the business with the Tyrant Dragon Rex. There was desperation in the air, like they didn't care if everyone went down together so long as they were in charge when it happened.

They also clearly considerably underestimated the threat that we had posed. Then we actually showed up and quickly got them on the ropes. That was likely to make anyone a bit loopy.

That said, my abilities were diminished because of the curse, and we were also facing enemies with the power to weaken my shield, meaning I couldn't fight at full capacity. I was starting to get a bit sick of the situation suddenly turning against us.

But hold on. Maybe we could use this. Use the fact they had freed a sealed monster against them. What if, for example, one of Raphtalia's first deeds as the new Heavenly Emperor was to defeat a dangerous monster set loose by her political opponents? How would that look to the people? The gap between the current administration, with their contemptuous neglect of the people, and the revolutionary forces who fought for the sake of those same people would only be highlighted further.

One thing I could say about all this corruption: it gave us no shortage of material to use in our attack.

"Kwaa, kwaa, kwaa!" Gaelion grew large and I climbed onto his back. With his ability to fly, he seemed the fastest choice.

"Enough talk. Let's get over there! Speed takes priority, so you follow behind as fast as you can, Filo. If you can beat Gaelion then I'll ride you next time!"

"Whaaaaaat! I'll do my very best!"

"Ah, wait for us!"

"Let's get moving."

"Come on. I don't know if you'll be much help, but we're going too, brother."

"Count me in!" Raphtalia, Sadeena, Atla, and Fohl

all followed along too. Of course, Raph-chan was right where she belonged, in my arms.

"Itsuki, you guys take Filo and come along too."

"Of course."

"Feeeehh! Very well! We can hardly claim to be justice if we give up now!" Rishia joined in.

"And we'll be running away, then," said Motoyasu II. "Dear ladies, if you do get in trouble, I recommend using the corpse of this idiot to shield your escape."

I swore to make him pay for his comments. Later, though.

"Let's move." The lethargic Itsuki joined Rishia on Filo's back.

"What? I have to carry the bow guy as well?"

"Kwaaaa!" Ignoring Filo's dumbfounded cries, Gaelion gave a roar of victory and took to the skies.

"I'm not losing to a dragon!" That's the way, Filo. She started out, running across the rooftops. This would be a good race! If things went her way, Filo might even win.

"Kwaaaaa!" Gaelion started flapping his wings in earnest, and the race was on. Oh yeah. Pitting the two of them against each other was definitely going to be faster.

"Here we go!"

The ground cracked, and the monster sealed inside

revealed itself. Its red eyes started searching around for prey. Its mouths were full of sharp fangs, with tongues periodically flickering out like licks of flame. It also had an organ called a "pit," which it used to detect temperature and locate its victims.

"It's a hydra. Yes, this won't be an easy battle." This analysis from the father Gaelion. I guess that was one name for it, but personally—as a dragon with eight heads, no less—to me it looked more like the Yamata no Orochi from Japanese mythology. In either case, this was the creature that climbed free from the burial mound and turned its gaze toward us. On its back it had a carefully tied sacred festoon and something that shone with a soft pink light.

As we faced it down from the air, the Yamata no Orochi–like monster—the "Sealed Orochi"—started to intimidate us, throwing out a multiheaded hiss.

"From the looks of it, it's been fitted with both a sakura stone of destiny and sacred festoon of blessings, providing a pretty big power-up," I said. Along with that threatening hiss, it also spat some poison in our direction. With a grunt, Gaelion flapped and avoided the missiles. Still, the creature was in the center of a sakura stone of destiny barrier, which weakened the four holy powers, and then had blessings on top of that. Which meant what? We had to approach it across terrain in which the power of the heroes was weakened and somehow finish it off?

That wasn't going to be easy.

"If we don't keep it busy the port will suffer damage," I declared. Backing off, and perhaps giving up on attacking us, Orochi now started toward the town. It may prioritize attacking us if we got in close and bothered it, but for now it seemed happy to target the general population. That was very dangerous.

"You know what? A bit of damage will make the nation all the angrier."

"Mr. Naofumi!" Raphtalia scolded.

"Okay, okay. We can at least put up a fight with the sakura stone of destiny weapons. We don't have a choice."

"Oh my," Sadeena exclaimed.

"This will be quite a tough one." Still. Time to take this thing down. "Come on! We can do this!" I shouted.

However, in the moment before Orochi reached the town and we faced the thing down, it was stopped by some kind of wall.

"W-what now?" I wondered.

"Little Naofumi, there." Looking in the direction that Sadeena was pointing, I saw a sakura lumina glowing brightly, creating something like a wall.

Sakura lumina were plants native to Q'ten Lo, very much like sakura cherry trees, but convenient for being able to do a variety of things. Perhaps, then, they had defensive abilities against larger monsters?

"Hold on. I sense the power of a dragon. Maybe the Water Dragon is helping us out?" father Gaelion told me.

"That sounds promising," I said.

"It looks like just a matter of time before it breaks through though." Indeed, the resistance of the barrier was visibly weakening. I guess we had to use this time to get ready.

Gaelion landed, and as I climbed down, Sadeena started to turn into her therianthrope form.

"In either case, we fight, right?" she said.

"Yeah. If we don't stop that monster somehow, we'll never be able to take this country." But still, taking on a monster equipped with anti-hero gear? Why did my battles always place me at such a disadvantage!

"We'll deploy the Sakura Sphere of Influence right away," I said. We'd use our new power-up skill, Sakura Sphere of Influence, to enhance our allies while also casting some support magic. The issue was that this was still placing restrictions on our weapon power-up methods.

A little testing had revealed that we were unable to use Sakura Sphere of Influence unless the barrier from the sakura stone of destiny—the sakura destiny sphere—was also active.

"Shooting Star Shield! Air Strike Shield! Itsuki, you've already registered your sakura stone of destiny weapon, right?" I blocked some attacks from the Sealed Orochi even as I asked the question.

"Yes. All taken care of." His voice was lifeless, due to the curse, but he responded without question to commands. If he selected the correct power-up method and used it well, he'd be able to handle this situation. Indeed, his lack of distractions might actually make this version of him more convenient.

"Then fight with that weapon. Any others will definitely be nullified."

"Understood." How about if Itsuki fired from outside the barrier? But no, the arrows themselves would still end up inside. Duh.

"If Astral Enchant has been cast on that thing, this isn't going to go smoothly." If all of these monsters were being linked together and powered up, this one might be more powerful than even the Spirit Tortoise.

"That wouldn't be an easy thing to pull off. If they'd managed that, any defensive capabilities the town may have would have surely been wiped out in an instant," Sadeena said.

"Good point. Anyway, we have the new skill Raphtalia learned to remove that kind of problem."

"Shall I go in first, then?" Raphtalia promptly offered.

"Yeah, go ahead. Even if we can't take down this sakura destiny sphere thing, you should still negate the blessings. Can you?" I asked.

"Yes. I think so."

In any case, we just had to concentrate on the enemy in front of us.

"I'll do my best too," Filo promptly offered.

"Kwaaaaa!"

"I'll do my part," Sadeena chimed in.

"Me too." Filo, Atla, Fohl, and the others also displayed their resolve. I hoped they could handle it.

"One more thing, you guys. If you get close and feel your strength flagging, drop back a little."

"Ah, well, the weapon shop guy gave me this back there," Filo explained.

"Me too." Each of them had weapons in their hands and on their legs made with sakura stones of destiny. Apparently, they had the ability to lessen the nullification of the hero's protection. For a moment, the support of that old guy warmed even my shattered heart. He made these so quickly, after all, thinking ahead to keep us safe for something just like this.

"He told us we'd need them in the times ahead."

"That we should keep them with us in order to not fall behind."

"Kwaaa!"

"Hold on. No one told me!" Atla looked confused for a moment and then promptly grabbed Fohl from behind. Clinging to his side, she proceeded to try and pry free the gauntlet fitted on his hand.

"A-Atla? Guwah! S-stop that—what are you playing at?"

"Brother, you have to give that to me."

"What happened to the one you got?"

"That pervy old goat sickens me. He clasped my hand with his sweaty palms when he gave me the item, and so I tossed it away. I don't have time to go back and get it." So Motoyasu II had gone personally to give Atla hers. No wonder she'd thrown it away.

"He came to me too," Filo chirped up. "But it was so sparkly and pretty I kept it!"

"Brother! Hand it over."

"A-Atla, quit it—" Just looking at this scene, in complete isolation, and she could appear to just be a little sister begging her big brother to borrow his favorite toy. Fohl actually looked pretty happy about it.

"Oh my," Sadeena exclaimed.

"You two, seriously," Raphtalia began.

"We don't have time for these games!" I shouted. Seriously, none of them were mentally prepared in the face of the enemy. "Atla, if you haven't brought your weapon with you—" Hmmm, good question. The brother or the sister? The weapon was a gauntlet though. Atla wasn't going to work well with that. "Taking the capabilities of this opponent into account, Atla, you can stay in the back. No complaining. Don't take anything out on Fohl, either."

"Gah! How humiliating. All thanks to that letch," she said. I understood how she felt, I did, but in this case, she was clearly in the wrong. That said, she generally fought barehanded, so there was a high probability she wouldn't have brought it with her anyway.

"If you don't like it, maybe you should pay a bit more attention to fighting with a weapon equipped in the future." Weapons were imbued with various effects. Fighting barehanded provided no such benefits, so having Atla carry a weapon with some kind of effect might be worthwhile.

"If those are your orders, Master, then I'll equip one in the future!"

"You hang back then, Atla. You can defend Itsuki and Rishia."

"I'm on it!"

With that, then, we formed up to face off with the Sealed Orochi. Having so many hotheads in the party wasn't always a good thing.

Filo ruffled up her filolial feathers, threatening the target. Gaelion said she was a type of dragon, right?

"Enough chatter! Let's take this thing down! Sakura Sphere of Influence! Attack Support!" A barrier with a cherry blossom pattern appeared, centered around my feet, and the thorns created by Attack Support flew toward the Sealed Orochi. When those thorns passed through the barrier they were transformed into five cherry petals and proceeded to bind themselves around two of the Orochi's heads. The creature gave an angry hiss.

"Time to strike!" Filo shouted.

"Kwaaa!"

Filo and Gaelion both flew in, still competing to be the first into anything, and slashed into the two bound-up heads with their claws. Both had pretty decent abilities, and with power equal to any special attack, they tore their respective heads right off the creature's body.

"Doesn't look like it's got much in the way of defense," I commented.

"Vitality, though, it's still got in spades." Atla provided this analysis from the rear. Perhaps agreeing with her, Raphtalia also nodded. That was also the moment both of the heads Filo and Gaelion tore off immediately regenerated. Yeah, the father Gaelion had classified this as a hydra.

"Raagh! Huh?"

"Get me in there." Fohl, now in his therianthrope form, grabbed onto the charging Filo and used her speed to close in. He used the impact of his descent to land on and squish one of the heads and then immediately fell back. He was really getting ferocious. He'd definitely been on a roll recently.

In any case, the heads were regenerating with such speed they definitely didn't feel like the beast's weak point. Do all of these Spirit Tortoise–like monsters have regenerating powers?

"Rafu." Raph-chan was sitting on Raphtalia's shoulder, her fur standing up. It looked like she was providing some kind of magical support.

"Aim for the body! That seems more likely than the heads!" I yelled.

"Sure thing." If that didn't work, we'd have to try something like destroying all the heads at the same time. In the next instant, though, and with a metallic sound, a barrier shaped like a hexagonal prism appeared centered around Orochi. So it was definitely the body.

"Raagh!"

Not to be outdone, Filo launched a flying kick, but she just bounced off the barrier. "It's super hard!" Hissing again, perhaps enjoying the compliment, Orochi's many eyes flashed red and then it started to spit fire.

"Second Shield! Dritte Shield!" I already had Float Shield active. By standing at the head of the party, this allowed me to draw all of the enemy attacks to me.

"Hmmm. It's absorbing some of the Dragon Vein power. It would be foolish to spend too long fighting this thing." Father Gaelion offered this advice even as he flew up close and nipped at the heads I was keeping occupied, in an attempt to distract them.

"I know, Gaelion. Hey, Sadeena!" I yelled.

"Count me in, sweetie! Finally time for us to have some real fun together!"

"Lose the innuendo! Gaelion, we need your help too." Getting the support magic Descent of the Thunder God active and pressing our attack seemed like the best move here.

"Arrow Rain! Eagle Piercing Shot!"

"Hengen Muso Throwing Technique! Rolling Spin!" That was Itsuki and Rishia providing some support fire for Filo as she fought bravely against the eight heads of Orochi on the front line.

The hexagonal prism on its back provided protection just like the shell of a turtle. Any attempt to get in close to kill it was also blocked by the barrier. It basically had double walls protecting it.

"I'm going in too." The skill Raphtalia had learned appeared to nullify the protection of the sakura stone of destiny and was definitely going to prove convenient. I'd also got a useful new skill, which was really going to help out in the coming battles.

"Okay. On my signal, we strike together!"

"We're with you!"

Rather than talking, though, I should have been concentrating on my magic. Since Gaelion joined us we could now use cooperative magic much more quickly.

"Descent of the Thunder God!" This particular spell was a hero-exclusive skill based on Zweite Aura, which increased all abilities. Combined with lightning magic, a specialty of Sadeena, it at least had an effect more potent than high-ranking Drifa. It definitely got another hiss out of Orochi. Raphtalia was closing in with the heads, and the beast started breathing poison, fire, the full works at her.

"Raagh!"

"Haaah!" Filo and Fohl took care of the attacking heads while Itsuki and Rishia continued their supporting fire.

"Drifa Chain Lightning!" Finishing her incantation, Sadeena joined in to launch magic against Orochi. Raphtalia gripped the hilt of her scabbarded sword, and then swung the blade toward the head that Filo was already engaging.

"Supreme Ultimate Slash of Destiny!" The attack itself was little more than a simple sword slash. The trick to this technique was the attack also being able to cancel any protections cast on the target. The only difficulty was that Raphtalia needed to be able to see the protections placed on her target. Being able to break the curses placed on me or Raphtalia herself, well, that would be asking too much.

It produced more hissing, anyway. Orochi started spraying flaming counterattacks.

I took the brunt of those attacks and used the counter effect of the sakura stone of destiny shield to activate Blossom Blaze. Being close to me during this effect had been shown to provide additional strength. A little speculation on my part, perhaps, but I also believed it to alleviate interference from other sakura stones of destiny.

"Filo! Hit that shield again, will you?"

"On it!" At Raphtalia's direction, Filo quickly closed in with the barrier and kicked it again. The barrier gave a powerful shudder, and then a ying-yang symbol appeared on it and surrounded Orochi. As though being crushed by a weight made of magic, that symbol started to press down on Orochi, the creature writhing and hissing in confusion under the pressure.

A few more moments and all eight heights started to scream.

The ying-yang symbol eventually faded. The heads wobbled back up, slower than before but still spitting angrily at us.

Seriously, this was one tough reptile. Reptile-thing.

"That's temporarily broken the sakura stone of destiny's protection!" Raphtalia exclaimed.

"Right, everyone, pile on!" I shouted.

"Okay!"

"My time to shine!" Atla rushed recklessly in, launching a preemptive attack on Orochi. Gah! "Raaaaagh! I say raaagh!" She attacked one of the heads, and it immediately stopped moving. Wasn't she paying attention though? That wasn't the weak spot!

"Oops! I need to target the body, right? I'm coming!" she said.

"Atla, do as you were ordered and stay back!" Fohl yelled.

"Brother, don't stop the attack now!" Fohl and Atla moved to strike at the body, bickering as they went.

"I'm coming too!" Filo headed in after them.

"Hmmm?"

"Oh my."

Not to be left behind—in fact, ahead of all of them—Raphtalia dashed in close to the body and unleashed her own skill. "Stardust Blade!" With a series of meaty thunks, each special attack struck at the body. Orochi convulsed just a little, and then all of the heads dropped to the ground and it fell silent.

What? We'd won? That was pretty easy.

"More a worm than a snake," Itsuki offered from a little distance away.

"You said it. I was expecting a bit more of a fight," I announced. Pathetic was what it was. Absolutely pathetic. The start of the fight made me think it was tougher than this.

Even as I had that thought, Atla started to back away from the body, eyebrows furrowed.

"Everyone, I think we should run away now."

"What's going on?" I asked.

"It's giving off a strange reaction. Like . . . the same

reaction as those people who blew themselves up."

"What! Everyone, get out of here! Now!"

"Okay!"

"Waah!"

At my command, everyone fell back from the Orochi corpse. The next moment, that same corpse swelled up and then exploded in a shower of poison. That alone was enough to break the barrier protecting the town and also create a noxious fog in the vicinity. My party and I only just got out of the way in time.

My Shooting Star Shield could hold off the poison for now, but what about after that? It wouldn't be long before the spreading fog started killing the townsfolk. I wasn't really one to care about the unwashed masses, but losing any of what little fighting strength we currently had would definitely hurt.

More than anything, though, we were looking at a sealed monster, an explosion, and now poison. This string of events was our chance to mobilize the people of Q'ten Lo, and the new Heavenly Emperor being the one to end this threat would be a great start to her career.

"Filo, can you use some wind magic to blow that poison cloud away?"

"I'll certainly give it a try!" Filo immediately spread her wings and started an incantation. "Drifa Tornado!"

The fog was lifted by Filo's magic and blown in the opposite direction from the town—but it wasn't enough to disperse it completely. In fact, while it had thinned out, we might have only succeeded in spreading it over a wider area.

"Nuh?" Then Gaelion gave a cry of surprise and whispered to me, "I fear we are facing quite a troublesome beast here." A moment later, and with a foreboding rumble, eight fresh Orochi heads peered out from the burial mound. They even appeared to have more lustrous scales than before.

"What's going on here? Didn't we just kill that thing?" I said.

"It was what you might call a clone. A copy. It won't be that easy to defeat the real monster," father Gaelion replied. That explained why it had been weaker than I expected. A freaking copy! And a copy that had still blown up and spread a thick poison when defeated? Talk about a pain in the ass. Why the hell did they have to go and set this thing free? If it did manage to defeat us, just how were the Heavenly Emperor's goons planning on stopping it?

"It's even been buffed a bit too," I said. I was seeing more and more reasons why they had no choice in the past but to just seal it away—hah, I was even starting to think the Tyrant Dragon Rex might make a cute pet.

"Is there nothing we can do?" I asked.

"There's one quick approach, perhaps, which I think you'll be a fan of," father Gaelion offered.

"Tell me."

"That's still a dragon, give or take. You know a little about the biology of dragons, correct?" I did—ah, of course. He was talking about it having a core somewhere that we had to remove.

"That's why I called it a copy. If we can obtain that core, it will be reduced to an empty shell. There's still a chance it might revive a few times, but this seems like the fastest way."

"Which means the real Orochi is down where that thing is coming out of the burial mound and we'll have to keep the copy occupied too?"

"Correct."

"And if we get the core? What next?"

"I'll have to suppress it."

"You can do that? Weak little Dragon Emperor."

"Heh."

What was that laugh for? His weakness was the very reason I was worried. "It wasn't so long ago that Ren kicked your tail, remember?"

"If we're only talking about a core, it should be easy

for me to suppress it," he said. Hmmm. That hardly inspired confidence.

"Okay then. Let's split up into two parties: one to fight the copy and keep it pinned down and another to go in and fight the main body." I did a quick headcount. It would be best to keep the copy from heading to the town, or the damage—and body count—would quickly start to climb.

"I feel like I might be best suited to pinning it down?"

"About that. Something has been bugging me since the fighting started." Sadeena actually put her hand up to speak.

"Yes? What?"

"I thought Orochi was targeting us, to start with, but doesn't it look more like it's only targeting either the town or Raphtalia?" A good point. In the instant Raphtalia closed in to attack, all eight heads had immediately focused on her.

"So what? Raphtalia is like the Heavenly Emperor, meaning the beast is turning its grudge on her?"

"I don't like the sound of that," Raphtalia said.

"We could try and stop the copy then, but if it's targeting Raphtalia, then we probably can't do much," Sadeena said.

"If the copy is targeting Raphtalia," Rishia offered,

"we should probably have her fight it, right?"

"If the main Orochi has the same capabilities as the copies, though, we won't be able to nullify its protection without Raphtalia," I said. The handling of the sakura destiny sphere really was a pain.

"It also depends just how tough the real Orochi is going to be." It was a fair bet it would be tougher than the copies, at least.

As the discussion continued, backup arrived from the town.

"That's a fair boost to our combat power. Maybe now we just keep it in place with sheer numbers?" Rishia suggested.

"Yeah, I think so. While they're doing that, we'll head into the burial mound and fight this real Orochi, then," I said. I quickly imparted the details of the operation to our reinforcements, which included Raluva and the contingent from Siltvelt.

"Itsuki and I would be better fighting the copy, I think?" Rishia said. I gave her proposal some thought. We didn't know what the situation would be like inside the mound, and Itsuki and Rishia worked best when providing support from the rear. Not to mention, it made sense to have heroes in both parties.

"Very well. Rishia, you and Itsuki work together to

stop the copy. Do your best not to finish it off, but just buy us as much time as you can."

"Master Naofumi, what should I do?" Atla asked.

"You don't have a weapon, so you take the copy. Fohl, that also means I'll be expecting more from you."

"Hmph! As you say, of course," she said. Atla didn't look happy about it, but it was definitely best to keep her back. "Brother! You'd better not let me down!"

"Gah. I know, I know!" They both sounded so much like each other, truly brother and sister.

"What about me?" Filo asked.

"With me."

"Great! I won't let Gaelion show me up!"

"So let's get to work!"

With everything decided, we split into two groups, and I started with mine toward the looming burial mound.

Chapter Two: Sharing Power-Ups

Checking behind for a moment, I saw that the reinforcements from the town, Itsuki, and Rishia were putting up a good fight against the Orochi copy. It wouldn't be easy to play for time instead of just finishing it off, after all. That task would have been easier if I stayed behind, but if the real Orochi did turn out to be more powerful, they would definitely need me.

Even as I considered the situation, I looked over the half-destroyed burial mound. There was definitely an evil presence emanating from the place, a flow of some kind of magic. Was this something someone who had learned the Way of the Dragon Vein could feel?

"It looks pretty ominous in there," I said. What was this Heavenly Emperor fool thinking, taking pity on a creature like this?

"Rafu."

"Geh! You're right, the air is foul!" Raph-chan and Raphtalia were both spluttering, indicating just how bad the situation was. We needed to finish this quickly.

"Still, our only choice is to go inside," I maintained.

"We're right here with you." Nodding at Raphtalia's

reassurance, I took the lead and we started into the burial mound. The interior looked ready to collapse but appeared to have been some kind of stone burial chamber.

"Is the main body in here?" I asked.

"The flow of power indicates so," father Gaelion said. Indeed, even I could feel a strange flow of power periodically flowing through the space. So was this the Dragon Vein corruption I'd heard about?

"It's gradually eating into the barrier protecting the nation. If we don't finish it off quickly, the other seals may break too." This too from Gaelion. Desperate or not, was there no limit to the idiocy of these idiots? They were going to destroy everything their people had protected for generations. If all the sealed monsters revived, the country would wipe itself out.

It might be better if we just made a run for it.

"It started before I left, but I can't believe how corrupt this place had become," Sadeena was saying.

"Tell me, what kind of history does Q'ten Lo have? The Heavenly Emperor has, what, been treated as a national treasure down the generations?" I asked.

"I don't know all the details, but it's been around for at least as long as Melromarc and Siltvelt," Sadeena replied. Wow. I was amazed they made it so long.

"Huh? What's that?" There was some text written

on the wall of the stone chamber. Even better, I could read it! It looked like the magic text I saw on the Cal Mira islands.

"Is there another hero inscription here?" I traced over the letters with my fingers while reading them. "Shield Holy Weapon . . . power-up method!?" Why was this here?

The letters suddenly started to shine, and the gemstone on my shield started to shine too. It definitely seemed worth reading some more. It wasn't all that long, anyway.

"What is it?" Sadeena asked.

"I'm not sure why, but it says something about 'Shield Holy Weapon power-up method' and then some more text here on the wall. Can't you read it?" Everyone there with me gathered around and took a look at the writing.

"Nope. I can't read it." That counted Raphtalia out.

"Me either. Is that the language of your home country, Naofumi?" Sadeena had no luck either.

"I sense magic." That was all Gaelion was good for.

"I don't know much about magic, so I can't read it either." Fohl had much the same reaction.

"Hmmm?"

"Filo, I'm not expecting anything from you. Don't

worry. Anyway, I'm going to read it out." I cleared my throat. "Holy Shield power-up methods. Number one: share the power-up methods from other holy weapons and vassal weapons." Gah! That's what we were already doing! In fact, Kizuna had also said something very much along those lines to Raphtalia. The rest of the text was just further details on the same topic, and kindly enough the same text even proceeded to appear under Help.

But what was the point? Showing information we already knew was pointless at this juncture!

"It's meaningless if this is just information we already know," I said.

"Maybe it's just here to make sure you haven't missed out on it?" Raphtalia offered. In any case, it might prove useful if Ren and Itsuki could read this language. I'd have Itsuki take a look at it later.

At that moment, we discovered a vertical hole glowing with a purple light. Perhaps triggered by our arrival, the stone chamber started to shudder and shake.

"It's below here?" I asked.

"Looks like it. Hmmm, this place has a pretty interesting structure." Gaelion, as analytical as ever.

"What's so interesting about it?"

"It was created to siphon away the power of the

one sealed here, no doubt about that. At the same time, however, it also works to maintain the barrier while not letting them loose but also not killing them. It even has repair functions, allowing it to operate, theoretically, forever. This is some pretty incredible technology right here."

"A timeless seal?"

"That would be an apt description. Free from idiotic outside intervention, this seal would have lasted for an eternity."

The purple glow allowed us to see down quite a long way. There was something down there, shining. It also looked like there was water seeping out from the hole.

"The underground water and Dragon Vein have a deep connection? No, hold on." Gaelion indicated something inside the hole. It looked like, well, the skull of something? "The body of the Orochi from the time it was sealed has already rotted away. The breaking of that seal has led to a merging with the Dragon Vein via the media of the core."

"So where's that core now?"

"Right there," Gaelion stated, indicating a spot at the bottom of the hole where purple smoke was pooling, like some kind of miasma.

The next moment, cracks spread through the entire

hole, widening it considerably, and then water gushed out.

"A cunning plan. It's using the copies to buy some time while the core creates a new body."

"Cunning? More like a pain in the ass." A torrent of water was now pouring out, quickly reaching our waists.

"We can't hang around here. Sadeena, grab hold of the Shield Hero and his companions. We're about to get washed out!" Gaelion yelled.

"Oh my!"

"Washed what?"

"Filolial, you watch out too!"

"I can swim!"

Even after Gaelion gave his advice, the water gushing from the hole started to swiftly sweep us away, leaving more than a few of us spluttering as we went. Why was it, I lamented, that coming to this country had seemed to involve so much water?

Even as I had that thought, and even as we struggled against the flow, Raphtalia, Raph-chan, Fohl, and I, all held by Sadeena, were washed back together the way we had just come.

That's how strong the current was.

All of us, Filo and Gaelion included, were blasted out of the burial mound together and fell through the air. Just before we crashed into the ground, Gaelion spread his wings and caught us.

"Phew. That was a close one," Gaelion remarked.

"A big waste of time too," I commented, somewhat bitterly.

"Don't say that. There, take a look. Here comes the main body." Gaelion indicated with his head, just as an Orochi that looked perhaps three times the size of the copies emerged by destroying the burial mound completely. "That purple light at the base of that Orochi is the core. This isn't going to be a pushover like that copy either! It's still growing, absorbing Dragon Vein power."

"Which means we need to take it down quickly," I said.

"That's right. Although I won't stop you if you do want to do the noble thing and at least wait until it is fully exposed," Gaelion replied.

"What good would that do us? So it's like a Demon Dragon?"

"That was only the surface of the Dragon Vein, but yes, something like that. The issue is the scale. It's receiving power from the other sealed monsters, and it's got a troublesome sakura stone of destiny too."

"So let's get to work. Swift and minimalistic, such as how little Naofumi likes it," Sadeena announced.

"That's right! Even if you've left this nation behind,

you don't want this monster tearing it to pieces, do you?"

"No, I don't think I do. Not to mention, we're meant to be taking over, so it would be a shame if this nation was wiped out before we got that chance." This was all for Raphtalia, for my village, and for our future. "You can count me in, then! I'll do my best!"

Just as I was about to get some support magic going, my shield responded again.

Provide target with power and trigger beast transformation?
Yes / No

Okay. This was an ability housed within the Shield of the Beast King, a piece of gear I obtained in Siltvelt. The conditions to trigger it remained unknown, but it appeared to allow those among my companions capable of transforming into a therianthrope to perform an additional, more powerful transformation. When I previously used it on Fohl, he had turned into a powerful white tiger.

I hadn't really counted on Fohl for battle stuff up until that point, but this boost had made him really strong, and he'd fought alongside Atla to take care of the monsters we'd faced in Siltvelt.

What would happen, then, if I used it on Sadeena, who was ranked high for strength among my companions?

"Sadeena."

"What is it, sweetie?"

"It looks like I can command you to transform."

"Oh my!" She had a massive smile on her face. I didn't like it, but still, there was seriously no other choice here but to use it.

"I'd rather use it on Raphtalia, if possible."

"I can't turn into a therianthrope, and I don't want you to do it on me anyway."

"Why not?"

"Because I don't want to turn into something like Raph-chan!"

"Rafu?"

Heh. That was exactly what I wanted to see. Or a more therianthrope-like Raphtalia, maybe? Like one of those round little raccoon-dog statues? I was sure she'd look so cute.

"You're thinking something distasteful, aren't you?" She'd cottoned on, of course.

"Never! Come on then, Sadeena!"

"Yes, yes!" This was a bit like a skill though, so before she was transformed by it, I decided to have her activate the other magic first. "Sakura Sphere of Influence!" With that done, I activated the beast transformation support.

A flurry of cherry blossoms suddenly appeared, centered around my shield, and flew toward Sadeena. Sadeena was enveloped, just like when I used it on Fohl, turning into a sphere of light and rising up into the air. Furthermore, the nearby sakura lumina, which looked broken and withered, also started to give off some kind of light, coming together to provide protection. Then the light surrounding Sadeena scattered, and a massive killer whale appeared, with a sacred festoon and all.

"Oh yes, this is incredible! Such power flowing through me! What is this? Naofumi's love?"

"Stop saying weird stuff!"

Sadeena had turned into her killer whale form but simply started to swim elegantly in the air as though it were water.

"I think I heard the Water Dragon too. There's nothing I can't do right now." With that proclamation, Sadeena deployed a whole sequence of magic circles and then launched her assault on Orochi.

"Hmmm. How does it go again? Like this?" She had to ask herself? How obtuse could you get! "Thunder God! And Sea God!" Thunderclouds rapidly formed in the air above Orochi, dropping the largest thunder strike yet. This was immediately followed by a vast tidal wave appearing in front of Sadeena and rolling over the monster.

Talk about an all-out attack.

"I also experienced such a transformation. Was it something like that?" Fohl inquired, observing the ragingly one-sided assault launched on the main body by Sadeena.

"Yeah, I guess so. You were like that in Siltvelt, Fohl."

"Incredible! I'm always messing up. So uncool. But even Atla only had good things to say about that transformation." Wow. He was more self-aware than I'd given him credit for.

"We shouldn't just be standing around watching!" Raphtalia shouted this caution and then dashed in to aid Sadeena.

"I'm with you!" Filo got moving too.

"You won't outmatch me! Graaaah!" Ah, Gaelion had switched personalities again.

"Everyone is so excitable. Let's join the pile on," I said.

"S-sure thing!" Fohl shouted.

The Orochi hissed horribly, certainly not backing

down. Then each of its eight heads started spitting its own unique breath at us—fire, ice, poison, the works.

"I won't allow that! Air Strike Shield! Second Shield! Dritte Shield!" As I unleashed skills to create shields, the effects of the Sakura Sphere of Influence caused cherry blossom shields to appear and block the attacks. The petals withered with each attack they blocked, but they provided wide-ranging protection from Orochi's attacks.

Hold on. The petals weren't breaking down? They were actually pretty tough! My abilities, severely compromised by the curse, appeared to have substantially recovered—no, suddenly increased!

What was going on here?

The only thing I could think of was the power-up method text from the burial mound. Could it be that the power-up method I'd been using until now hadn't been sufficient? It felt like the multiplier behind the enhancement had changed.

"Naofumi. Little Naofumi?"

"What?"

"I've been observing it closely, and the weak point does seem to be the same. There, where the body is glowing," she said.

I muttered to Sadeena to take out some magic water and soul-healing water and restore the power expended during the beast transformation support. Weak spot, she said! A pinpoint attack there would mean having to dodge through the attacks from the eight heads, and even then it would be difficult to hit—

"Raphtalia!"

"Ready!" Just as when she fought the copy, Raphtalia took up the Supreme Ultimate Slash of Destiny stance in order to nullify the enemy's blessings. The Orochi gave a hiss—Raphtalia was clearly its target.

"Not today, pal!" The transformed Sadeena dropped a thick bolt of lightning, floating in the air between Orochi and Raphtalia in order to keep them apart.

Okay, I admit, the image of Raphtalia with her sword raised and Sadeena, wreathed in lightning, protecting her, struck a super geeky chord with me, not to mention that Raphtalia was wearing the miko outfit that I had put her in.

Of course, I also stepped up and blocked the Orochi's attacks.

"Right! Attack Support! Shooting Star Shield!" I tossed the Attack Support at Orochi, sealing off its movements.

"You guys! Buy us some time!"

"No problem!"

"On it."

"Atla has been on my back, after all! I'm not going to give any ground to this monster!" With that, Filo and the others swept aside the attacking heads, creating a large opening.

"Now I can make a chance to attack! Supreme Ultimate Slash of Destiny!" Perhaps becoming more familiar with the attack, Raphtalia launched her slice toward Orochi's barrier faster than before.

With a clash, however, the sword bounced off.

"What!"

"That should've been a hit. A clean hit!"

"Mr. Naofumi," Raphtalia said as she returned to me, "it seems the Orochi has realized that my attack will break the barrier created by the sakura stone of destiny, and it's creating its own barrier to prevent that." Now that she mentioned it, the pillar of light from the sakura stone of destiny and the purple light appeared to be mixing together. So another barrier, not present on the copies, was protecting its weak spot.

"Can we destroy it using the Hengen Muso Style?" I asked.

"I don't know why, but my attack didn't work. Physically breaking it is going to be difficult," Raphtalia said.

The Orochi hissed, as though in agreement, and then the revived heads all fixed on Raphtalia at once and attacked with multiple breaths.

I stood in front and took the brunt of the attacks.

"Guwah," Raphtalia spluttered.

"Are you okay?"

"Yes. I'm—okay."

"Rafu." Raph-chan stroked Raphtalia's back as she coughed. Just that seemed enough to naturally relax her breathing.

"It's not the same as the copies, is it?" Sadeena ventured.

"Looks that way. A real pain." I took a moment to glance at the copy, which was rampaging close to the town. Even if we defeated it, this main body would just bring it back. But was it worth taking it out again and making this fight easier to win, even if that meant fighting a total of sixteen heads?

"So the problem is that purple barrier? That's the issue," I stated.

"Yeah."

The big problem was that barrier. Raphtalia could deal with the sakura stone of destiny, but the purple barrier clearly had completely different conditions. Honestly, it just made me want to scream! Just how much hassle did these sakura stones of destiny have to be? It was almost as though they'd been created specifically for fighting heroes, although the Q'ten Lo Heavenly Emperor seemed to think of them as nothing more than devices for powering up abilities using a special ceremony.

Such thinking had led to this dangerous situation, clearly.

"However, little Naofumi, there is one thing. Based on my intimate observations—"

"Spit it out."

"There is a moment when that purple barrier appears to weaken." As a former hardcore gamer myself, it wasn't hard to imagine that defeating an opponent like this would require multiple conditions to be fulfilled. They never would have sealed it away in the past if they couldn't work that much out. Now it sounded like Sadeena had realized it too.

"When I attacked and took out a few of those heads, the density of the barrier appeared to drop a little," she went on. So the heads regenerated quickly after being destroyed, but that also weakened the barrier. If Hengen Muso Style attacks couldn't break it, it was natural to think that there had to be some other conditions involved. If we couldn't just muscle through with raw power, then we had to do this the proper way.

"So killing all the heads at once will bring down the

barrier. Sounds like a pain!" I grumbled.

"They revive so quickly the timing is going to be crucial."

"You said it." To be honest, I was really starting to feel like it would be best to have Itsuki and the others join us here and all attack the heads together. After killing them all at the same time, Raphtalia could neutralize the sakura stone of destiny on its back and then we could finish it off.

"Sadeena, in your current state, how many heads do you think you can kill at once?"

"Having received your love, my dear, I'm invincible. If you use that, what was it called, Attack Support to bind them, little Naofumi, I should be able to account for no less than four!" Four, then. That wasn't bad.

Raphtalia needed a little charge time in order to unleash the Supreme Ultimate Slash of Destiny. That wasn't going to change, even with the Sakura Sphere of Influence. No, okay, it would probably take a bit longer without it, in which case, we needed the remaining heads to be handled roughly by Filo, Gaelion, and Fohl—one a piece. My job was defense and interrupting enemy attacks. One more attacker would be nice, but unfortunately Raph-chan was busy protecting Raphtalia.

"Let me," Filo offered brightly. "My timing is

greaaat!" With that she struck the Haikuikku pose. Ah, great idea. Filo could probably handle two heads with Haikuikku.

"I can move longer than before too."

"I'm counting on you."

"No problem!"

"Then Raphtalia will destroy the second barrier and blast that core out of its body."

"Okay! I'm ready when you are!" Good, then. Everyone was ready. Time for action!

"Attack Support!" I unleashed Attack Support and tied up three heads. Then Sadeena dropped a massive bolt of lightning.

"Here we go! Thunder God!" The Orochi writhed, hissing and spitting into the air as though to resist Sadeena's attack. That wasn't enough to stop her, however, not to mention that my Attack Support was doubling the damage.

"I don't think so! Applied Chain Lightning! Successive Thunder God" Thick bolts of lightning struck the bound heads, and the electric shock even paralyzed the body. Then Sadeena twisted in the air, bending the lightning to send it through another head before it flew off into the sky. Quite the party trick.

Good, then. She took care of exactly four heads, as promised.

"Kwaaaaa!" Gaelion matched the timing of his attack, charging in, breathing fire, and smashing another head.

"I'm doing my part too!" Fohl was going hand-to-hand, dropping an ax kick on another head and taking it out. He was really starting to pack a punch.

"Jingle-jangle! Haikuikku! Take this!" Filo tossed in her morning star and then immediately charged in with a high-speed spiral strike, crushing a head in an instant. She then maintained Haikuikku and kicked the final head with all of her strength. Wow. Filo was one step faster than anyone else in this fight. Then again, she'd always been pretty fleet of foot. She said Fitoria had given her a boost across the board, and she certainly was fast. Just her basic stats placed her as a close match with Raphtalia too.

"—!?"

With all the heads gone, Orochi's body started to convulse, and the purple barrier around it vanished.

"Raphtalia, now!"

"This is the one!" Raphtalia dashed in and swung her sword at the sakura destiny sphere. "Supreme Ultimate Slash of Destiny!" With that shout, she slashed down at the sakura destiny sphere, then returned her blade to its scabbard.

"Rafu!" Then Raph-chan, still on Raphtalia's shoulder, tossed out a ying-yang-like sphere that quickly swelled up to enclose the entire Orochi.

"Phew. I managed it, but that wasn't easy," Raphtalia exclaimed.

"Now the protection has been removed?" I asked.

"Yes. But that isn't the finishing blow. We need to press the attack!"

"You've got me for that!" Sadeena offered.

"I'll purify the Dragon Vein at the same time!" Gaelion also focused his power to finish the Orochi off.

"In this closed-off land of the Heavenly Emperor, let the clean flow of ideals wash away the old regimes, with the desire to save the world transformed into power! Dragon Vein! The purifying power of the sea! Wash back this filthy tide!"

"I, Gaelion, order the heavens and order the lands! Diverge now from all physical laws, become one, and spit forth this blighted puss. My power, the protection of the spirits! Purify the land!"

"Great Sea God!"

Sadeena and Gaelion completed their spellcasting, rising up into the air while water swirled around them, and then plunged toward Orochi as though dropping in freefall.

"Uwah!"

"Waah!" Filo and Fohl, surprised by this downward charge, beat a hasty retreat.

"Kagura Dance of the Sakura! First Formation! Blossom!" Just ahead of Sadeena and Gaelion unleashing what was presumably the finishing blow, Raphtalia and Raph-chan got off a second attack of their own. Cherry blossoms danced in the air alongside the sword attack. Then a metallic clash rang out, and at the same time, something was sent flying out into the air.

What was it? The dragon core? Something else?

Then Sadeena and Gaelion's attack landed, blowing the remaining body away.

"That was close!"

"You said it. I know the timing was important, but I almost got taken out too!"

"Looks like you still managed to get out of the way." Fohl glared at me for that comment. "I guess you can complain to them later, anyway. At least we're all alive for you to do so." Raphtalia's Descent of the Thunder God had still been in effect too, allowing her to get off that additional attack of her own.

Not to mention the boost my own abilities appeared to be experiencing. At the least, I'd managed to keep up with Raphtalia's speed.

"We won!" Sadeena, back in her demi-human form, leapt out from the spraying waters and stood, back to the group, shouting at what little remained of the Orochi.

"Kwaaaa!" Gaelion was showing off too, striking a victory pose of his own. We definitely needed to up our teamwork or it was only a matter of time before friendly fire took someone out.

Checking behind us, I was treated to the sight of the Orochi I had left to Itsuki and his team also dispersing into mist. It looked like we'd really pulled off the kill.

"Little Naofumi, it seems we've managed to purify the one rooted in the Dragon Vein too."

"That's pretty hot stuff. You seem full of energy too, even though you just came back from a beast transformation." Based on the Fohl example, beast transformation support seemed to cause considerable physical exhaustion. Fohl, at least, had been so worn out afterward that he could hardly stand. Sadeena, on the other hand, looked to be in pretty good shape.

"Oh, I'm completely wiped out, I assure you."

"You really don't look it."

"He's right. I bet you could go another round or two!" Raphtalia gushed.

"You think so?"

As we chatted, the fighting finished, Atla and the

others came dashing over.

"Master Naofumi! We did it!"

"We do seem to have had some measure of success," I admitted.

"But hold on? I still sense an impure presence." Then Atla turned to look in the direction of the whatever-it-was that Raphtalia had sent flying right before the final blow. I'd been wondering about that myself.

"Raphtalia. You knocked something out of it, right?"

"Yes? I believe that was the Orochi core, just as we originally planned?" Ah. Right. That had been the plan. All the craziness of Sadeena and Gaelion in action had pushed it out of my mind.

"Kwaaa!" With his own growl, Gaelion flew off in the direction of the presumed core.

"I don't think we can leave something like that lying around. Mr. Naofumi, let's go check it out as well."

"Yeah, good idea." After checking to make sure Rishia, Itsuki, and the contingent from the town were also with us, we headed in the direction the Sealed Orochi's core had been sent flying.

Chapter Three: The Cursed Ama-no-Murakumo Sword

Ahead of us we found, sticking from a patch of barren ground, something that had definitely just dropped from the sky. A sword.

From where it was stuck into the ground, a purple encroachment was spreading.

"A sword?" I said. That's exactly what it was, a sword with a white blade and something very much like the core embedded in the middle of the handguard. If the monster was like Yamata no Orochi, it would make sense—from the perspective of Japanese mythology, at least—for it to spit up a sword. I might have understood if this was a drop, but it looked like the sword was actually the core.

"We should dispose of this quickly. It's already polluting the ground in an attempt to revive itself," Sadeena recommended.

"Kwaaa!"

"Well, that's why we have Gaelion. He can take care of the core, I'm sure," I said. It was a dragon-type monster, ostensibly, so if we took care of the core, that should shut it up for good. Then Gaelion placed his mouth on the core-like decoration and was flicked away with a snap.

"Kwaa!"

"So what? It's too corrupted?" Sadeena asked.

"I knew he wasn't up to the task," I said. Truly, when it came to the crunch, Gaelion always seemed to drop the ball. "In any case, we need to pull it out and deal with it—but it looks like just touching that thing is going to curse you." It certainly looked pretty suspicious. My own body was still suffering from the pollution of a curse, and so just getting close to the core was throbbingly painful. Like my skin was burning, perhaps. I narrowed my eyes and checked it out.

Cursed Ama-no-Murakumo Sword.

That the appraisal didn't even work properly proved it was a particularly high-capability weapon. I'd never expected to find this particular weapon, one of the three fabled divine items of Japanese history, here in this other world, although that was just how my shield chose to translate it for me, and so it was surely a different weapon altogether.

"Feeehhh. W-well, if it's a sword, how about having

the Sword Hero take it and deal with it?" Rishia suggested. Give it to Ren, perhaps? Would it be safe to give him gear that looked so obviously cursed? That said, it also felt like a waste to just leave it stuck in the ground. Not to mention, the Orochi might revive itself again if it was left unchecked.

I could also place it inside the shield, of course, but I was scared of creating a second Demon Dragon incident.

"Hey! It looks like you defeated it!" That was when the old guy and his master—Motoyasu II—turned up.

"First the Spirit Tortoise, now this. You guys sure know how to put on a fight. I was watching from a distance and it was still amazing." The old guy was giving me a thumbs-up, and I returned the gesture.

"Thanks. I mean, all I really do is defend," I admitted.

"Oh no, I don't think we would have won without your powers, little Naofumi." Sadeena offered that compliment. She'd been watching me more closely recently. That said, after deploying Air Strike Shield and the other support, it wasn't as though I was just sitting on my hands. If I had any regrets, it was maybe that I couldn't contain the movements of the Orochi a little more.

"So what are you doing out here now?" the old guy asked.

"Right, well, we chased after the core that flew out of that monster and found that it's shaped like a sword and looks cursed. So we're just trying to decide what to do with it." With that, Motoyasu II took a look at the sword stuck in the ground and checked it over.

"Wow. That's quite the weapon. So that's the body of the beast?" Then, most foolishly, he grabbed the hilt and pulled it out. A cloud of purple miasma rose up and swirled around Motoyasu II. So he'd just gone and gotten himself cursed? Ding-ding, round two. What was he, soft in the head? Even as I cursed him—verbally, this time—in my head, I raised my shield, ready to fight the monster all over again.

"Shut it. Enough wriggling," Motoyasu II shouted at the clattering sword, and the miasma around it dispersed.

"Huh?"

"Yeah, this baby is cursed. You can't hope to use it."

"Says you, after just snatching it up. Are you okay?" I said.

"What are you jabbering about? I'm a blacksmith! How could I do my job if weapons started cursing me?" Was it really that simple? I looked at the old guy, but he just offered a shrug of his shoulders.

"Most impressive, Master. Being able to hold that sword," the old guy admired.

"Hah. A blacksmith getting cursed means he's small fry, at best. Holding it in such a way as to not get cursed is easy." Oh crap. Was I going to have to rethink my impression of him as a skirt-chasing dope? It was starting to look like he really knew his business.

"Can you at least stop it from going on another rampage?" I asked.

"Me? Like I care." The old guy's master went to—what, put it back in the ground?—as though nothing had happened.

"Please, can't you do something? If that monster appears again, it really will be terrible for all of us." Reading the situation well, Raphtalia begged the old guy's master, hands clasped in front of her.

"Very well, young lady. I will do whatever I can to prevent that," he said. Goddammit, this guy!

"Old guy, can't you do something about that sword? Like that letch did?" I asked.

"Sorry, kid. Looks like I'm just small fry. I do want to reach that same level one day." For me, the old guy was already the very best. Anyway, it looked like it couldn't be helped.

"We're up, Erhard. We've been called on! Let's reforge this sword so it has no problems!" Motoyasu II announced.

"I'm here with you, Master. Kid, you guys help as well. I think we're going to need some pretty tough-to-find materials for this one."

"Yeah, it does look pretty high spec. It'll provide you experience for making weapons too, so we'll help," I added.

"Thanks, kid." In the end, then, the sword that appeared upon defeating Orochi was placed in the care of the old guy and his master.

"What else, then? Any damage to the town or around there?" I asked.

"Part of the port was destroyed, but only a handful of people got hurt. That's also thanks to the Heavenly Emperor, the Shield Hero, and your retinue," Raluva replied while checking the town. Good, not many people hurt. That laid the foundations for inciting the people to join our cause further down the road. "However—in the vicinity of the burial mound, we're looking at serious damage and some remaining pollutants, meaning it'll take quite some time to return that to normal."

"Then we'll have to give up on it," I said. It wasn't as though it was an important location. "In any case, there's no justice in a nation that would unleash a sealed monster on rebel forces. Don't they have any idea of how much damage the people might have suffered?"

Raluva and the others from the town nodded in hearty agreement at my words.

"We are going to impart these facts immediately, not just to neighboring settlements but the entire country. If we make good use of this, we should be able to rustle up some collaboration from others who take issue with the policies of our nation," Raluva said. I looked over at Raphtalia. This was it, then. We'd come this far. Now we had to go through with it.

"Please, do so. It seems we're the only ones who can hope to stop these people." That was exactly what I might have expected Raphtalia to say, but it also wasn't quite the push we needed—it was likely to leave some people decidedly unincited.

"She's right! There's no justice in a Heavenly Emperor who'd do something so heinous! He and his cronies couldn't care less about the happiness of the regular people! You men, you women, are you really okay with that?" I continued to lay it on as thick as I could, and as loud as I could, firing up Raluva and the others. Perhaps hearing this steeled their resolve, because their eyes looked deadly serious and they replied with one voice: "As the Heavenly Emperor commands!"

Thus, Raluva and the other Q'ten Lo revolutionaries got over their hangovers and swore allegiance to our cause once again.

"I'm not going to be too harsh on you, but you like this kind of thing, don't you, Mr. Naofumi?" Raphtalia commented to me, somewhat exasperated, as she looked over Raluva and the others.

"When you're doing something in the name of great justice, a little exaggeration feels good," I admitted. We were justice, punishing evil. That kind of feeling was great for boosting morale. After all, everyone wanted to be the good guys, not the bad guys.

"A nation that worships Raphtalia! What a nightmare." Ata couldn't resist an opportunity for a smarmy comment.

"I'm not asking for any of this. For some reason, once I get this miko getup on, people pray to me, that's all. If my father and mother weren't involved, I would have run from this, I assure you."

"Whatever." There was no convincing Atla. "You did well though, brother!"

"Y-yeah, I did! Atla! I did my best!"

"Which also meant I was unable to do much for Master Naofumi. I won't forgive you for that, brother!"

"Whaaaaaat! Atla!" She was even on his case when he did well. That was completely unreasonable. Fohl really didn't have it easy. I almost felt sorry for him.

"One other thing, Shield Hero," Raluva ventured.

"Yeah?" The revolutionaries were looking at Filo, who was currently in her filolial form. She was just coming back from collecting the morning star that she threw at Orochi.

"Huh?"

"Something I noticed when you went into battle—"

"Something about Filo?" I said.

"A talking filolial—that is, a girl with wings. She's one of your companions, correct?"

"Yes! Filo's name is Filo!" Filo chirped. It looked like Filo and Gaelion had been facing off again.

"Yeah, she's a filolial. A race that develops in a unique way when raised by a hero. Why, do you need something from her?" I asked.

"Actually, yes. A white filolial with a cherry blossom pattern? We may well be able to use this to our greater advantage." I looked at Filo too. In that moment, though, I had no idea what the Q'ten Lo contingent was talking about.

Chapter Four: Tailwind

In the subsequent days, leaders and others in authority from the surrounding settlements came to ask to join our forces. It seemed they agreed that freeing a sealed monster in order to drive us out was indeed going too far.

Of course, those in power tried to explain it away by saying that the seal simply broke on its own due to our arrival. But due to the Heavenly Emperor placing blessings on the monsters, and his order not to harm living creatures, such claims were met with distrust.

Some did still believe them, however, and came looking for a fight. When they saw the filolial Filo at the head of the revolutionary forces, however, their morale drained away and they posed no threat.

"Master, they are all just running away again," Filo said.

"I noticed." I hadn't been sure about it myself, to start with, but it seemed there were all sorts of myths and legends in Q'ten Lo, and we were taking good advantage of them. Filo's presence seemed to act as some kind of test of faith.

"Rescue the divine bird from capture by the heathens!" some of them shouted.

"Oh? Looks like some of them have a bit of energy after all," I commented.

"I'll do my best!" Filo offered brightly.

"Let's do this!" Some enemies still did charge in, but it also meant they were now divided between two purposes—to take Raphtalia's life and to capture Filo.

For her part, Raphtalia was now capable of disposing most of the blessings relating to the sakura stones of destiny. When we did encounter those blessed with Astral Enchant, she was able to use her Supreme Ultimate Slash of Destiny and immediately shut them up. Looked like they'd give out blessings to any old weakling.

So things were going well. The revolutionary forces were expanding apace, made possible, most likely, by the ready acceptance of the people for a new Heavenly Emperor. It only helped matters that the reputation of the current Heavenly Emperor was in the dirt, what with continued releasing of monsters sealed close to points we advanced along. We had fought numerous other sealed monsters already. Defeating them always provided some kind of weapon. Of course, these weapons were also always cursed.

Taking stock, at that point in time, we'd already

found the sword, some claws, a spear, and an ax. Just how many of these things had been sealed away, honestly! We'd even taken to sending scouts ahead to capture the ones trying to break the seals.

Things among the Heavenly Emperor's forces were falling apart, seriously. It made me feel like asking whether they really cared. As for why the enemy was trying to capture Filo—

"Master. Why do they want to come for me?" she asked.

"Ah, that's because one of the animals the Heavenly Emperor we're facing wants to protect is the filolial, and the sakura lumina is a symbol of national power."

"So?" That wasn't enough for Filo to quite grasp the concept. I needed to try and explain things in more detail.

"So, Filo, both your race and the pattern on your body are important symbols to this country. Indeed, they have divine connotations. That means, the deeper the faith of those we fight, the harder it is for them to fight you." Like the family crest animals from the Edo period in Japan—I was thinking of dogs, for some reason, but something like that. Yeah, my Japanese history sucked too.

What this meant overall, then, was that the more

loyal our opponents were, the harder it was for them to try and hurt Filo.

"Hmmm. They want me? I don't want to be put on display again!" It looked like Filo had finally worked it out, and the trauma from her experiences in Kizuna's world was coming back to haunt her.

"It's fine. Even if they do get you, they aren't going to treat you badly. Not at all."

"Really?"

"That said, if you do get captured, you won't be able to see Melty."

"No!"

"Anyway, Filo. Stay in filolial form for a while, if you can. In this nation, that'll make almost as large a contribution as Raphtalia in her miko outfit."

"Which means what?" Raphtalia asked.

Well, that we had to make use of it. No choice there. It would be interesting to see just how deep a grave the Heavenly Emperor would dig for himself. Apparently this whole protection order had started with his obsession with filolials. Dogs in Japan, bizarre bird creatures here. Seemed legit.

And so our progress continued. Until—

"Finally caught—"

"Hey, it's been a while."

S'yne joined up with us.

We had met S'yne in Zeltoble, the land of merchants and mercenaries. She was a vassal wielder from a different parallel world to this one. The world she originated from had apparently already been wiped out, and so she was now riding the waves, that terrible disaster that links all parallel worlds, from world to world. I had requested that she check out Siltvelt along with Wyndia and that group, because she had detected the scent of a certain force there with which S'yne was fatefully opposed.

I'd also left her in charge of the village, just in case.

I kind of remembered her mentioning she would come if we needed her—but she had likely been blocked by the barrier and unable to transfer in. I'd felt a bit bad about it myself.

Then S'yne grabbed onto me.

"W-what do you think you're playing at?"

"Yes! Hands off! Hugging of Master Naofumi isn't allowed!" Raphtalia and Atla both vented in surprise.

S'yne had taken something of a liking to me.

However, perhaps due to the damage to her vassal weapon when her world was wiped out, her voice had strange skips mixed into it and so she couldn't communicate well. So we had attached a tool with a translation function from one of her foes to a familiar doll and used that to converse with her.

Perhaps the familiar also contained a pseudo-personality, because it spoke pretty fluently.

The familiar had started out looking like Raph-chan and Sadeena in her therianthrope form, but after I complained that a Raph-chan that spoke normally was just freaking me out, it had been remade into a doll of Keel's therianthrope form and now talked like that.

It was more polite than the girl it was based on too.

I wondered what that mischievous little puppy was getting up to back in the village.

The original Raph-doll, by the way, ended up in pride of place in my room. Just in case you were wondering.

In any case, S'yne just wanted to protect me, and she'd developed a habit of showing up even when the timing wasn't that great.

"Calm down, both of you," I offered to the still prickling girls before turning to S'yne. "But however did you get here?" Raphtalia was fastidious and Atla jealous, after all. I needed to calm them and then talk to S'yne. In the least, transfer-type skills couldn't get into Q'ten Lo, this nation so closed off from the outside world, and I'd left Siltvelt and the village under her protection.

"You take so many risks—"

"You take so many risks, Mr. Iwatani, so we arranged for a ship in Siltvelt."

"Ah, so the ship following ours arrived?"

"Yes."

"This time—"

"This time, she wishes to aid in defending you."

"Somehow things have kept coming up, haven't they?"

That said, it was thanks to S'yne that we made it close to Siltvelt using a transfer skill. That was a big point in her favor. Without that, we'd probably only just be rolling up into Siltvelt around now. That had saved us so much time. She'd really done more than enough, overall.

For S'yne, though, that clearly wasn't enough.

"Well then, now S'yne has caught up—" The issue was, to be honest, we weren't really having that tough a time of it anymore.

Raphtalia was now capable of shutting down the enemy's blessings, after all, and the sakura stone of destiny weapons gave some leeway in nullifying their enhancements. We just needed to carry on like this and we were going to win.

"Yet she still wants to protect you." Hmmm. She really was showing serious devotion. I guess I could keep her close until she was satisfied. Although she could only transfer herself, I'd taken advantage of her ability to get around so easily numerous times too.

"Okay, I'm sold. You can protect me for as long as you like."

"Very well—"

"She offers her agreement." I'd had this thought before, but even though she skipped, S'yne was quite the chatterbox. From her appearance, I first thought her more the brooding type, but it looks like I was wrong.

"Hmmm, the scent of a powerful enemy."

"Are we about to get ambushed?" I turned to look at Atla, as it seemed she had sensed something.

"I'm talking about this new rival for your affections, Master Naofumi."

"Who? S'yne" S'yne herself was tilting her head in puzzlement. Looked like that wasn't the case.

In any case, we met back up with S'yne and continued our conquest of Q'ten Lo.

As we expanded our territory, we also found the time to go hunting.

Of course, our primary objective was, what? To increase public security, I guess?

"Q'ten Lo really does have a unique ecosystem. The experience from hunting here is pretty good," I commented. Monsters seeking to do harm to the people were attacking villages, but they couldn't be turned back. They were expanding their habitat, and that space also had to be reclaimed—but with the order against harming living creatures, it also wasn't possible for people to hunt them. Talk about an illogical mess. Were they managing to hunt some of them away from the watchful eyes of those in charge? When I asked about that, I was told that a culture of informants and betrayal had been lovingly fostered, and taking the risk just wasn't worth it.

Therefore, the forces that joined our side were being sent to hunt monsters and then providing some of the defeated monsters to us as materials. The monsters in Q'ten Lo were quite like traditional Japanese spirits: sickle-wielding kamaitachi and eldritch foxes. Stuff like that.

"You know, you're right." Sadeena's lightning wiped them out in seconds, making this a smooth and simple process, but they did provide plenty of experience. In terms of strength, they could probably be beaten at around level 50 without hero enhancements, but the obtained experience was equal to that from much stronger monsters. In game terms, this was an efficient grinding spot.

"They aren't that different from the monsters fought at sea," Sadeena commented.

"Really?" I hadn't done much offshore fighting, but that did remind me; after Sadeena's level had been reset, she went alone to the sea and had raised her level considerably.

"If you want, I can give you some special tutelage, little Naofumi, just one on one. Not the first time I've made such an offer."

"Yeah, I remember." If I went out hunting on the ocean with Sadeena, I was pretty sure I'd get dragged off somewhere crazy. Just too scary to risk it.

"Sadeena, please keep your focus on fighting."

"Well said. But if there's any opening, they will strike at you, little Master Naofumi."

"Is that for you to say? If you've got time to talk, keep hunting."

It did feel like a while since we'd done this.

"That reminds me—"

"That reminds S'yne, she arranged in Siltvelt for Ratotille and Wyndia to collect monster materials for the Shield Hero," S'yne's familiar informed us.

"Wow, that's a big help." Developing the village was slowing down the work of releasing my shield. There was no reason not to accept these monster materials from Q'ten Lo. I'd have to give some of them to Itsuki and Ren later too. If I went hunting with Itsuki, the hero weapons would rebound off each other, so he was off with Rishia.

"This is the best they've got?" Fohl finished off another monster and looked over at me.

"You're working harder than Atla. I'll give you credit for that."

"Huh."

"Brother! Don't get carried away just because Master Naofumi said something nice to you!"

"Wh—!" Now she was jealous because I praised him for doing his best? Completely unreasonable.

"Then I'll just fight harder! I'm not losing to Raphtalia or my brother!" With that, Atla ran off.

"C-count me in!" Fohl sounded pretty happy. Was that really all I had to do? I think I was getting the hang of handling those two. If I gave a little praise to Fohl, that pushed Atla to try harder.

"What's this? A hunting challenge? Then I won't be left behind!" Sadeena announced.

"You're doing fine. Including your use of magic, I think you're hunting the most, Sadeena." Perhaps due to originating here, Sadeena had defeated the majority of the monsters we faced.

Increasing general safety in the vicinity through hunting like this also purchased the gratitude of the towns and villages we had occupied.

"Thank you so much! The revolutionary Heavenly Emperor and her retinue are doing wonderful things, reducing the damage caused by monsters," they would say.

"I don't think we can change the entire ecosystem quite that easily, but you should be okay for a while," I would offer in return. Turning a blind eye to the havoc caused by monsters and even punishing those humans who fought back? What was this moron thinking? Such actions had definitely given the people plenty to think about.

A few days passed in this fashion, and we were able to take control of a third of Q'ten Lo. It hadn't even been long since we arrived, so I was surprised at this speed myself. It felt like we were making even better progress than the other plan, to just sneak in and take the head of the enemy Heavenly Emperor.

"It reminds me a bit of our escape journey in Kizuna's world." This being a Japan-like nation, there were a lot of similarities. "I mean, give or take the presence of the sakura lumina and whether or not it's a Japanese-Raphtalia land."

"Rafu!"

"You're still going on about that?" Raphtalia grumbled.

"Hey, there are statues that look like Raph-chan everywhere! I can't help it if this seems like a wild Raphtalia theme park!"

"You like what you like, little Naofumi, I'll give you that," Sadeena chimed in. I didn't just like it. I was seriously thinking about taking at least one of those statues home as a souvenir.

"As we get closer to this old city, though, I'm seeing more that look like Filo."

"Me too. Statues of this divine bird that the Heavenly Emperor has put up. That look like Filo."

"They say her coloring doesn't exist?" Was Filo really such a rare specimen? She'd only cost me 100 pieces of silver!

"She's not completely unique," Sadeena replied, looking at Filo, "but the legends and tales passed down in each region actually differ a little from real filolials. For that reason, Filo's appearance and coloring are absolutely perfect." She was a filolial raised by a hero, after all.

"Do you think maybe Fitoria came to this country in the past?" Not a bad guess on my part. If they'd been exposed to her in the past, pictures might still remain and were changed to white and pink due to the coloring of the sakura lumina flowers.

"I can't hear Fitoria's voice," Filo chirped up. Sometimes Fitoria was watching us through Filo. It looked like that wasn't happening at the moment though. Maybe due to the barrier around the country?

In any case, the form and coloring of Filo were definitely causing all sorts of problems for our opponents.

"It looks likely we won't meet Kizuna and them again. If we do, though, it might be fun to bring them here." Even Glass might show her face. It would be great to show them all a nation with Raphtalia in charge. Glass's skill, Reverse Snow Moon Flower, would fit right in.

"The scenery is definitely worth seeing." I did catch myself, sometimes, wondering if they were all doing okay.

As we were making our way back, feeling pretty good, we happened upon that pervy moron Motoyasu II trying to pick up a girl.

"Ah! My lady, would you like to have some tea with me?" Seriously, just who was this guy?

"Geh!" As we closed in, the girl he was targeting bowed her head at us and made a run for it, and he turned to face us.

"Where's the old guy?" I asked.

"Hah! You think I can't shake Erhard off?"

"Look, if you go around wasting money, we'll have

to tie you up!" Motoyasu II just gave a cackle and flashed some Q'ten Lo currency. Showing off his wealth, was he? I snatched it out of his hands.

"Hey, that's mine!"

"Only because you lifted it from the old guy's coin purse, right?" This goat looked like he spent money fast and loose, meaning seeing him with such coin was certainly suspicious. He'd apparently worked up quite a series of tabs all across the port town. Indeed, to my comment at how he obtained these riches, he looked askance and started whistling. I knew it. I'd return the coin to the old guy later.

"Anyway—" I checked the party I had with me. He'd only get a kick out of it if I had women handle this. "Fohl, Gaelion, take him away."

"Kwaa!" Gaelion gave a respectful nod at my orders.

"What!" Fohl sounded somewhat less pleased. As too did Motoyasu II.

"You won't let me spend any time with one of these pretty faces you've got here?" he complained. At that response, however, Fohl realized what was going on and quickly nodded.

"Very well," he conceded.

"You can go off and have some fun with Atla once you get back," I said.

"We won't be long."

That reminded me, in a shop back there they were selling ornate hairpins, and he'd been eyeing them closely. He was planning on buying one, for sure. I'd given him enough spending money to afford at least one of them.

"Kwaa!"

Gaelion pinned Motoyasu II's arms behind his back, placed his jaws onto his neck, and they started walking.

"Dammit! You let me go! I thought that even if that shield brat did catch me, at least he'd have some of the cuties he hangs around with dispose of me, but this is a total sausage fest! Don't tell me, he swings both ways?"

"What are you rambling about!" Man, there was no helping Motoyasu II. Did he really love women that much?

"I'll stay with you even after my brother comes back, Master Naofumi," Atla offered.

"No, you go and spend some time with Fohl."

"I don't want to." She was a pain too, to be honest.

"Seriously—"

"Huh?" S'yne was pointing at Motoyasu II while showing off her weapon. Right, of course. She'd had sakura stone of destiny shears he made, right? They had a copy ability. They'd started out as two sakura stone of destiny swords, right? S'yne was looking at the shears, captivated.

"She says that he has real skill," S'yne's familiar translated.

"I never said he didn't." Just as the old guy had said, Motoyasu II did quality work at remarkable speed. His stock of sakura stones of destiny had been used up, meaning those we were using as shields were now the last of them.

"Rafu?"

"That reminds me—" S'yne began.

S'yne pointed at Raph-chan and said something. Recently the sound skipping had been getting even worse, meaning we couldn't communicate at all without the stuffed toy. It made me worried that maybe her vassal weapon was breaking down too.

"She's asking about what's happening with the giant Raph-chan doll?"

"Hmmm—"

"Excuse me? Are you planning on making something? This is the first I'm hearing about it," Raphtalia asked. Ah, right. I'd forgotten to say anything to Raphtalia about this.

"I'm hoping that maybe we can make Raph-chan a bit bigger. It came up that maybe S'yne can use one of her special attack skills to create an emergency familiar," I explained. Apparently she had a skill that allowed for control of giant dolls. I was thinking of allowing it, with the condition of not allowing it to speak.

"I'm vetoing that one!" Raphtalia shouted.

"Rafu? Rafu, rafu!" Raph-chan was watching the conversation and cutely tilted her head.

"Enough hijinks, anyway." I forcibly changed the subject. "Let's turn to the HQ in town and plan our next move."

We then returned to the largest building in the town.

"You need to train too, don't you?" Raphtalia said. Yeah, don't remind me. I hadn't exactly mastered the Hengen Muso Style yet. I really wanted to buckle down and get some training done, but with all these problems popping up all the time, I just couldn't find an opportunity.

"I think battles would go a lot more easily if you could acquire some Liberation-class magic," she said. The one time I had pulled that off, with Ost, had also proven to be the only time. I felt so close it felt like it was right there, but something—something was still missing. I just needed to get closer to that feeling.

In any case, it was definitely magic that I wanted to obtain before the eventual Phoenix battle.

Chapter Five: Information on the Enemy

Amid this chatter, the heads of the revolutionary forces had all arrived, and so we started our meeting on our future policy.

"The old city is right there for the taking. Once we reach it, the fighting should turn further in our favor," one of them announced.

"You said that before," I replied. It was the location where we could perform the rite to officially make Raphtalia the next Heavenly Emperor.

"Once Lady Raphtalia can cast those blessings, each fighter affiliated with our forces will be worth a thousand of the enemy," he went on.

"Sounds good," I remarked.

"However, there's one potential issue. Records from past conflicts suggest that barriers created by different sakura stones of destiny will repel each other. We can assume the enemy is going to be pretty desperate in trying to stop us."

"It's still a good move on our part. We can remove something which until now has been a permanent fixture of their defenses. I mean, Raphtalia's nullification of their blessings is already starting to render them meaningless." If we were careful about their gear for nullifying the power of the hero weapons, we could probably just strong-arm them now, making things much easier overall. The only annoyance had been that, until now, it had been unique to our enemies.

"Still. Casting aside such an important base and setting up a new capital in the east? What was he thinking?" I guffawed.

"Well, the east also has some geographical advantages and was used in battles to decide the next Heavenly Emperor in the past, so it's not such a big loss for him," he explained. Hmmm. Everything was still getting mixed up in my head with Japanese history. I was starting to see the old city as Kyoto. That looked like a pretty good comparison, actually.

What can I say? I kept going back to what I knew, even if the shape of the nations were quite different.

"The fact we've proceeded so quickly is because we're so far from the capital. Once we take the old city, that's when the real fighting starts," Raphtalia said.

"In either case, we do the same thing. Carry on, just like this," I stated.

"S-sure—" Raphtalia nodded, but she had a troubled look on her face. She was worried about all of this fighting happening because of her.

Come on, shake it off! Yes, we were the invaders, but they were the ones starting this insane stream of attacks to take Raphtalia's life, and they were the ones who were never going to give up!

"They don't have any intent to negotiate a ceasefire, do they?" I asked.

"No. It seems most of their leaders consider us pretty easy to handle," the revolutionary said.

"Are they seeing what's actually happening here?"

"I think it's because they underestimate Lady Raphtalia, thinking her to be of a diluted Heavenly Emperor bloodline. This is all because of the foolish methods of Makina, that poisoning witch who stands behind the Heavenly Emperor."

"She's come up before, hasn't she? Is she really that inept?" Everyone assembled in command nodded as one at my question. Even those from Siltvelt.

"She was a missionary, coming originally from Siltvelt in order to spread word of her beliefs. The Heavenly Emperor before last—that is, Lady Raphtalia's grandfather—took a liking to her, and as his concubine she then started to have a say in political matters. Eventually, she came to hold the reins of power."

"While she came from Siltvelt, she doesn't have a

shred of patriotism and placed a heavy tax on trading."
Uwah. She sounded like a real piece of work. Siltvelt
clearly didn't care for her either.

"There were even mutterings that she was involved
in the assassination of the family of the Heavenly
Emperor, but there was no proof. She's now the only
remaining one behind the Heavenly Emperor."

"They say the moving of the Heavenly Emperor's
base of operations to the east was also at the word of
Makina. The airs in the old city don't agree with her,
apparently."

"So what? The current Heavenly Emperor is her
child? Her grandchild?" I asked.

"No. Makina's children were also poisoned, assas-
sinated. So it seems unlikely she was the culprit."

"I hate to say it, but it sounds like this would never
have happened if the family of the Heavenly Emperor
hadn't been wiped out," I commented.

"Mr. Naofumi." Raphtalia gave me a solid glare. Still,
this vicious old bag would still have had an issue if the
royal family came to an end and isolation was abandoned.
It would also be obvious to her that she would quickly
be ejected if the distantly related Raphtalia ended up
sitting on the throne. Hmmm, well, who knew what the
current moron of a Heavenly Emperor was thinking.

"She often belittled me. I remember her well. And she's still in control of the nation?" Sadeena hissed. So Sadeena knew her too?

"The other problem would be the miko priestess of the water dragon." Ah. Sadeena had been the previous miko, or something like that, right?

"A miko priestess, blessed by the Heavenly Emperor? She's going to appear as a murderous assassin, you can bet."

"Oh my." The former miko to hold that position, Sadeena, spoke up.

"As the previous priestess, then, what do you think? Now the water dragon is on our side, how does that affect things?" I asked.

"She must be pretty mad about it. I guess? Like, she's been totally betrayed by the god that she believed in. You know, something like that." She spoke as though this was all someone else's problem. "If she's been blessed by the Heavenly Emperor, though, the current miko must be pretty hot stuff. I never got blessed like that." Wow. That was an interesting tidbit. What might it mean? Considering the way the current Heavenly Emperor was carrying on, anyway, she probably didn't have anything to be jealous about.

"You must have some information on her," I said.

"Y-yeah. The current miko priestess to the water dragon is known to be the younger sister of the previous miko," the revolutionary leader said.

"What was that?" Sadeena tilted her neck, a shocked look on her face. "That's the first I'm hearing about this. Those two had a sister for me?"

"Those two," she said. That spoke volumes about how close she was to her parents.

"She was born after the previous miko was cast out. However, there's not much other information available about the miko village, so that's about all we've got. What testimony we have suggests they raised her pretty harshly, seeking to fill the miko position with an equal to the one who held it previously," he went on.

"Those two always did try so hard," Sadeena lamented. Once again, a bit of a sad way of phrasing the birth of a sister. Now I was actually getting interested in her family situation.

Hmmm, this was taking me back. I was feeling something similar to the feelings I had about my own younger brother. He had been better in school than me and bore the burden of our parents' expectations as a result.

"The sister should always surpass the brother," Atla chimed in. Gah, just ignore Atla. She'd distracted me. Right now, I needed to prioritize Sadeena's sister.

"So she's intended as a replacement for her superior sister?" I said. This was sounding like one twisted family. Still, her star had to be fading, betrayed by the water dragon.

"It's said she continues to work incredibly hard, pushing herself to match the power of the previous miko."

"Hmmm." When I calculated back, she was probably close to Raphtalia in age. I definitely needed to get more details from Sadeena.

"In terms of experience, I'm thinking Sadeena has the edge there?" I remarked.

"In regard to feats of arms and work for the nation, the previous miko is definitely superior. But in regard to divine rites, she has some superior aspects—so it is said, I should say."

"Oh my."

"For example?"

"Well, she identified that the oracle miko and priests serving the Heavenly Emperor were trying to trick him and successfully got them removed. Now she's known as one of the few true oracles in the land."

"Oh, how wonderful. The miko following me is an oracle?" Sadeena said.

"Which means what, exactly?" I could never be sure of the rules here.

"It's something miko or priests can be. Like, a special ability, right?" Sadeena explained. Even she didn't seem quite sure.

"Correct. Here in Q'ten Lo those with the abilities of an oracle are treated with great respect, but it wasn't among the powers of the previous miko."

"Apparently it lets you hear the voices of your ancestors, stuff like that. It's an ability that many miko and priests serving the Heavenly Emperor have. Back then, you know, it did bother me that I didn't have that ability myself," Sadeena continued.

"Wow. So it's like being able to see ghosts?" I asked. I could do that by putting Raph-chan on my head! Hah!

"They can drink alcohol and go into a special type of trance, allowing them to make use of powers they don't normally have access to. It allows them to invoke exceptionally powerful cooperative magic alone. Apparently," Sadeena said. That did sound pretty awesome—but it didn't sound like seeing ghosts.

It was also odd to me that Sadeena didn't have any ability.

"Sounds like a load of make-believe to me. Like, they drank too much, shook something loose in their head, and the magic just happened to work out," I jabbed. Alcohol had properties to restore magic power. There were also those who could somehow slip into a type of rampage state, providing a conscious boost to their power.

"That all sounds very fishy to me too." Raphtalia's brow furrowed as she commented.

"Rafu?"

"I agree with Mr. Naofumi," she went on. "Surely they're just going off the rails after drinking too much."

"Look at you two. You sound exactly like Raphtalia's father," Sadeena said.

"If someone of the bloodline of the Heavenly Emperor said so, then it sounds totally legit," I replied.

"Hearing that does put my mind at ease," she mentioned.

So what was she? The perfect miko, possessing some kind of suspicious power that Sadeena didn't have? Still, listening to these leaders of Q'ten Lo talk about it, this new miko had apparently proven herself to be a match for Sadeena.

Something else was bothering me. Raphtalia. She'd started to become as suspicious as I was. That sort of made me happy and also sort of made me sad, as though I had sullied her somehow. In that moment, I understood exactly how Fohl felt.

"Why are you looking so sad, Mr. Naofumi?" she asked.

"Well, I guess this can also be considered progress?" I replied.

"Did I say something odd?" she said. I'd really brought her up to be suspicious. Maybe I need to reflect on that a little. Not that I believed things so easily myself.

"Anyway, these are the people we're fighting against," I stated.

"Yes. Please be careful."

"I can't wait!"

"I hope they're willing to listen to reason," I remarked. We could pray that the miko, at least, was actually aghast at the corruption consuming her nation and willing to help us. That she didn't think the water dragon had betrayed her but rather was going along with it from the shadows.

"In any case, we just have to carry on. We just have to do this." To be honest, there were simply too many people trying to join our forces, and even just making a list of them was proving close to impossible. We were really riding this tailwind—a wind only blowing, of course, due to how idiotic the opposing Heavenly Emperor's forces continued to be.

"I was expecting to have to besiege some castles, things like that, but so many of them are just opening the gates for us after collapsing from the inside." The people, and even the governors, didn't want a war, and yet those above them were releasing sealed monsters—a tactic that was only losing the trust of those below them. How anyone could be so dumb, I really didn't know.

All they had to do was hunker down, draw things out, and as we also had the waves to think about, it would have forced us to take far more risks than this.

"Anyway, at least for now, there doesn't seem to be anyone among the enemy who can oppose the combination of Raphtalia and Filo. That might change if, for example, Sadeena's sister shows up," I declared.

"All well and good, little Naofumi, but it's also true that things are going to get a lot harder up ahead," Sadeena cautioned.

"I know. We can start by getting through this old city."

"Indeed. There's all sorts of places there, including spots dear to Raphtalia's parents, so it's definitely worth a visit."

"That does sound worth seeing." Raphtalia sounded unsure though. Yes, there might be trouble, but learning about Raphtalia's roots could only be a good thing. This could all ultimately lead to Raphtalia taking charge of this nation, if she so desired, once the world was finally at peace.

"Right. We're going to train until nighttime and then hold a night parade in order to further spread the glory of Raphtalia. Atla, once Fohl gets back, you go shopping with him. That's an order."

"Bah! I hope that blacksmith gives my brother the slip, forcing the poor fool to chase him into the night. Then I can have Master Naofumi all to myself," she snapped. I didn't like seeing a younger sibling wishing for the downfall of their elder. Definitely not as someone with a younger brother myself—even if he'd been pretty preoccupied with external appearances.

In any case, we ended the meeting and started our training.

Chapter Six: Use of Life Force

I'd recently been training a little each morning, but it had been a while since I'd gone about it so seriously. During the training, Itsuki and his party had also returned and so joined in.

I was reminded that Rishia had quite the mastery of Hengen Muso Style. Maybe I should have her oversee my training for a while? The old lady wasn't here, and Rishia surely had enough knowledge to at least tutor me.

I was watching Atla and Raphtalia train. Sadeena was sparring with Filo. Filo had obeyed my orders and was in her filolial form, and Sadeena was in therianthrope too.

"Haah!" Atla used both hands to unleash a concentrated burst of magic at Raphtalia. Raphtalia repelled it. I had thought it was a ball of magic, but actually, something was different about it. It wasn't magic. Life force? Could it be? Was the power flowing from Atla . . . life force?

"Come on!" Raphtalia imbued her wooden sword with power and created some kind of barrier, sending the whatever-it-was Atla unleashed flying. Wow. Why? Why, now, was I starting to get a feel for this life force stuff?

W-what was going on?

Could it be? I could get stronger *just by watching other people fight?*

Hah, and you'd be a dumbass, too, if you believed that. Just how many hits had I taken from Atla? That had to be the reason for this. The old lady had said that it would be faster if I trained with Atla. Was this what she meant? It did feel like watching her made it easier to understand.

Up until this point, I'd been learning various things for my shield, just like a game. However, obtaining abilities like this, though training, meant my own body was also developing along game-style lines, although it was a little concerning to be undergoing physical changes I didn't really understand.

Anyway, while it didn't look possible right away, with more training I should even be able to handle defense rating attacks. The important thing was to create a flow of power within myself. All this "soft" stuff was junk. I simply needed to get onto the flow of power before my opponent's attacks went wild. Creating a soft part was for beginners, clearly. That old lady could have been a bit less obtuse about it!

"Atla. Raphtalia."

"Yes?"

"What do you need?"

I called them both over and explained that I was starting to see life force. Strangely, it almost felt like I'd missed out on something. I wondered why. I'd hoped to acquire this skill through ascetic training, but now I was just seeing it, and it felt like I'd lost something.

"I'm glad to hear it."

"Shall we have Rishia take a look?"

"That's a good idea," I remarked. Rishia had been given the full stamp of approval by the old lady, so having her check me over sounded like the best idea.

"Yes?" Rishia was helping Itsuki train. At that moment, he was repeatedly striking a large rock in the garden with his fingers. Yeah, it wasn't the first time I'd seen him doing that. We'd secured plenty of life force water anyway, which I hoped would speed up the training.

"Oh? Have you finished little Raphtalia and Atla's training?" Sadeena inquired.

"Haah!" Even in that moment, she dealt with an incoming kick from Filo.

"Yeah. It looks like I've started to see . . . something from the people around me."

"Wow. Do you think I could learn that too?" Sadeena wondered.

"It would be pretty crazy if you did," I noted.

"You might not see it," Atla offered, "but you're already unconsciously making use of it."

"Oh my!" Sadeena beamed. That was pretty big information for Atla to just drop into the conversation! Was it true?

"If you could do it consciously, you'd be a formidable opponent. I definitely don't want to teach that to you," Atla remarked.

"Is that the right attitude to have here?" Raphtalia said.

"Would you teach me, little Raphtalia?"

"Ah, of course!" As this conversation progressed, Rishia came over to me.

"Right then. I'll teach you what I can of the power control my master taught me. That said, you seem to have already picked a lot of it up from watching Atla." With that, Rishia pointed a semi-transparent weapon at me. I tried my best to receive and divert the flow of power mixed into it.

"You've got evasion down, but not defense." The Hengen Muso Style probably used this power for attack and detection. Even if it was used to avoid, life force wasn't used to defend. The only method for dealing with defense rating attacks was to redirect them, not take them head-on—and if that happened, the focus was still on redirection, with no notion of standing your ground. To be honest, it looked like there were only a few techniques from this that I'd be able to incorporate into my fighting style. It could be applied to skills too, perhaps.

"Here I come. Keep a close eye on me! Air Strike Throw!" Rishia imbued a throwing weapon with power and tossed it at me. Ah! I could see the life force mixed inside it. When it hit my shield, it was conducted through it and flowed into my body. Seeing as I was still just a beginner, I used SP and magic to forcefully expel it from my body. The impact shook me. It was pretty rough.

Since starting to see the flow of life force, I'd also observed everyone around me, and there were people, other than me, who looked out of place.

One was the Bow Hero, Itsuki. Then there was Raphtalia and Rishia. Hmmm. Rishia, in particular, was really odd. To try and put it in words, she had no flow of life force. No, that wasn't right. She had some, but it was . . . weak.

When Rishia was in Muso Activation, even before I could see life force, I could see something around her, but right now her life force looked so weak. That was a bit of a mystery. I guess maybe S'yne was similar?

No, thinking about it, in S'yne's case, her weapon

was weak, but she herself had the power.

So what was going on?

The old lady had been thrilled with Rishia, saying she was a great student, so what was the meaning of all this? She had Muso Activation to enhance her own abilities.

Now that I could see it myself, I would be able to also learn a bit from Raphtalia and Rishia. It also allowed me to discover that, perhaps because I was focused so totally on defense, the flow of my own life force was abnormal. My power was focused on protection, and if I pushed it down too hard, it could even tear itself apart. It was like asking the enemy to exploit it.

Life force, then. Or I guess it could also be called the flow of magic or of power. This was good! I was starting to see why Hengen Muso Style was said to be so strong. With further proficiency, it would be useful in the future. I was also painfully aware that I was still only starting out, however.

"I said that you had no defensive form, and that's true. The Hengen Muso Style that I learned from my master has no defense, but just evasion and redirection," Rishia explained.

"I guessed as much," I retorted.

"Master said that such techniques did exist in the past, but they were not passed down. We'll just have to create new techniques for you to use, Naofumi."

"That's pretty inconvenient." So I'd finally become able to see life force, and yet it seemed I was also just getting started.

"Oh, it's incredible. Now you'll be able to try all sorts of things with Atla and Raphtalia. Mr. Itsuki should be able to do this too, one day," she went on.

"Yes. I'll do my best." Itsuki was still talking in a monotone. I hoped we'd break that curse soon. Maybe there was something in Q'ten Lo that could work on curses? I'd have to ask later.

"Right. There's still some time, so let's carry on training," I pointed out.

"Atla!" That was when Fohl turned up.

"Kwaaa!" Gaelion too. It looked like they'd finished the job I gave them.

"That old goat can find the slightest opening to slip away. It was tough to bring him back."

"He sucks. Did you think about putting the hurt on him a little? Just to, you know, keep him in place," I prodded. I could imagine that might be required.

"No, I'm pretty sure he'd still run away. Totally sure, actually." I empathized with Fohl's reply. Motoyasu II was fast on his feet and pretty strong too. Seeing him "take a break" by training with the old guy had certainly left an impression on me.

"Right, Atla, let's go shopping!" he appealed.

"No, thank you, brother. We're just at a good point with the training, so we can do that later."

"Hey, Atla! That's not the promise we made!" She was right though. The training was going well, and I wanted to continue it. But a promise was a promise. I'd make sure she went with him later.

"You should watch too, brother. Just master's teachings alone won't be enough to make you stronger." Fohl's face hardened for a moment, but then he silently sat down. All said and done, he liked fighting, too, and so didn't seem to want to put a stop to the training either.

It might not be a perfect example, but there aren't many adults who say, "Let's go have some fun!" to a kid right when they're in the middle of studying.

"Just a little more, then," he accepted.

"A commendable attitude for you, brother. Come then, Master Naofumi!"

"I'm here! Bring it!"

"I most certainly will!" Atla's thrust landed square in the center of my shield. There was a flow of life force, like a massive balloon exploding from the inside. Now I had to train to flow this through my body.

After repeated attempts, I became able to take the

blow with almost no damage. Knowing how to handle it would expand the range of applications and also increase my precision with the technique.

With this, finally, we could consider me capable of nullifying the defense ignoring and rating attacks of L'Arc and Glass. What I needed next was a way to skillfully control the flow of power.

I tried experimenting with it as a means of attack, but my lack of attack power was baked into me, it seemed, and I just couldn't get it to work. I tried launching concentrated magic into the body of the opponent, just like Atla did, but it proved meaningless. It looked highly likely that I wasn't going to be able to use it for attacking.

The life force, or magic, of the Shield Hero likely just had those properties. So I tried all sorts of things when not in a combat state.

"That's certainly an atypical style of fighting. I can't see that with my master," Rishia stated.

"Indeed. Mr. Naofumi can't attack, so we'll have to twist that power into defense," Raphtalia acknowledged.

"Kwaaa!"

"Rafu."

And so our training continued until the sun went down.

"Right, that looks like enough training," I stated.

"Yes. I think Mr. Naofumi has a decent command of it now," Raphtalia remarked.

"Not bad. Now I can put up a good fight, whatever happens."

"Well done!"

I'd definitely earned something today, managing to acquire this.

"Come on then, Atal!" Fohl was still ready to go.

"Ah, Master Naofumi! Please, save me from the clutches of my brother!"

"Atla, if you run from Fohl today, then I'll be angry if you come anywhere near me tomorrow. Okay?"

"No! Gah. Very well, brother. Whatever you need me to smash, I'll smash it!"

"What are you talking about, Atla?!" She did walk off, led by Fohl, but I had to wonder why she was such a hothead. I hoped, for once, they'd just do some normal sightseeing.

"Next, Raphtalia and the others. I think we'd better get you cleaned up first." If there was going to be a parade that night, I needed to get Raphtalia and Filo ready to be put on show.

"Sorry, but we've been doing this every day already. We really have to do it again?" Raphtalia grumbled.

"That's right. Raphtalia and Filo get priority bathing. Go wash yourselves off and get changed," I commanded.

"No problem!" said Filo with a nod, turning back into human form. "Come on, Raphtalia." She led her toward the bathhouse.

"I think I'll tag along with them," Sadeena offered.

"Sure, sure. Off you go."

"Rafu." Raph-chan also went with them while Itsuki and Rishia stayed to continue their training.

"Kwaa?"

"Gaelion, you too?" We had Gaelion along as well, treating him as a vassal of the water dragon to show that justice was on our side. He hadn't been training though, and so there wasn't any need to lavish time on him in the same way as Filo. Right? That said, Gaelion had probably cottoned on to what was happening and started to preen himself. Wyndia would probably have given him a hand, if she had been here.

Finally, S'yne. She was staring right at me.

What now?

"I see—"

"She is saying that she knows what you were trying to train. That you were attempting to open your inner eye," her familiar translated. The inner eye? That did sound like a good way to describe it.

"S'yne can do it?" I inquired.

"Something similar—"

"Something similar, but a different power, yes." Then S'yne took out her scissors and charged her life force. Hmmm? The power of the scissors was increasing, just a little. Were these the lengths she was going to keep using her weapon?

It looked like a lot of work.

The truth of the matter was, she was actually strong, but the regression of her weapon made her weaker.

"Do you want to—"

"She's asking if you want to learn the defense forms."

"She knows them?" S'yne nodded in response to my question.

"Like—" She lifted her scissors, as though defending. Hah, I was going to need a bit more than that.

"Let's actually put it into action," the Keel doll said. And with that, the Keel doll flew at S'yne. She lifted her hand, pointing at the doll, and swept her arm sideways. That was all it took to hook the doll and change the course of its charge?

"That should be—"

"She is asking if that is the basic evasion form, as practiced by Raphtalia and the others and that you can apply your own powers to."

"It sounds like what she said was quite different," I mentioned. The idea was, what? Redirect attacks using just life force? I thought I'd seen Atla do that.

"Then—" This time the Keel doll launched its own life force attacks, in the same way as Atla but incredibly weak-looking. They were flying in completely the wrong directions too. S'yne wasn't over there—and then the orbs of life force flew on a strange trajectory, adjusting themselves to fly close to S'yne. Once all of the orbs had gathered in one place, S'yne grabbed and threw them back, with the gathered single orb passing close to the side of the doll.

"Even magic—"

"Even magic can be gathered in the same way."

"That's quite something," I admitted. I didn't know this was a possibility. I'd definitely make use of it.

"There's more—after learning this—" Hmmm, it looked like S'yne had quite a lot to teach me too. I was still at the beginner stage, but it felt like I'd taken a big step forward.

"Wow. You've shown me an unknown technique." Rishia was looking over with surprise on her face. Yeah, you said it. It looked like S'yne knew quite a lot, even if she couldn't do it all here in this world.

"Right, let's get dinner before the parade tonight."

My suggestion was met with a growl from S'yne's stomach. She was always hungry. When she came to the village, she'd been looking for a meal too. I gave a wry smile and headed toward the house myself.

Filo was taking part in the parade under the condition that I make her meals, and so recently I'd been doing a lot of the cooking—although, in all fairness, the basic preparations were being done by our servants in the house.

"We've got some wonderful fish today," one of them commented, showing me fish still flipping in the bucket. It was big, like a grouper. There'd been something like red snapper the other day too. I could see Kizuna enjoying the fishing here. The fish looked ready to leap right out of the bucket. A little too lively for dinner!

"I'll just shut him up." A thrust through the head and the deed was done. Thinking about it, I could kill fish and stuff like that—although I didn't get any experience for it. "Then drain the blood—" I tried to think of what to make with it. I had skills like appraisal and poison sensing, so I could tell this wasn't dangerous. I knew the proper way to handle things like squid, as well.

Q'ten Lo was a Japanese-style nation, so the residents enjoyed things like simple sashimi. A fish this big, though, could be used for all sorts of things other than just raw slices. Some kind of stew might be good. I could broil the head whole. Steaming it might work too. I'd debone it with a kitchen knife and then boil the bones for a nice broth.

As I proceeded with the cooking, the kitchen staff in the house was all watching me closely exactly like the kitchen slaves back in the village. Raphtalia had said that they were watching my technique in order to try and copy me. Something like that.

Q'ten Lo was also a rice-eating nation, so I'd clean some rice and cook that. I checked the required flow and identified where I could leave certain tasks to my helpers. Having fire magic was convenient too.

Still, this wasn't going to be especially interesting. I wanted to make something with a bit more flair, but what? Maybe I could use a deep pan to melt the fatty parts of some of the monster meat we had brought back with us and fry something up? Now that I had some command of life force, maybe I could use that for something? I imbued life force around the hand holding the knife and tried cutting some fish.

"Wah!" My observers let out a collective gasp. I guess they would. For some reason, I'd cut down into the chopping board. What was this, an infomercial for knives?

"Amazing. He's even cooking with the chopping board!" someone exclaimed.

"As if! Think for a moment!" The hell? They seriously thought I was going to cook with wood? Filo sometimes looked ready to eat the dishes and the table, but I wasn't going to take things that far.

Still, just a little cut and I'd used up quite a lot of life force and magic. Raphtalia, Atla, and Rishia were using this all the time. With her command of this, I was starting to see Rishia—and Éclair, for that matter—in quite a different light.

This looked like a good chance to practice with the flow of life force through my body, anyway, and I experimented in various ways while cooking.

Once I was finally finished, I took the food to Filo and the others, who were waiting after taking their baths.

"Go ahead, eat," I said.

"Thanks!"

"Time to tuck in!"

The food had been carried into a large room, and everyone there enjoyed it together. Once we were done eating, it would be time for the parade.

"Wow! Today's food is so delicious!"

"Kwaa, kwaa!" Filo's and Gaelion's eyes sparkled as they complimented me.

"They're right. This is more delicious than normal." Even Raphtalia was in concert with them.

"I'd like a drink with it."

"We've got a big event coming up. Don't drink anything."

"I know, I know!" Sadeena was clearly enjoying the meal too though.

"Delicious." S'yne too. That one looked ready to burst into tears. Being able to hear her without the sound cutting out was rare too.

"You think so?" I asked.

"Yes. What did you do?"

"Just a few experiments. It's pretty exhausting though. This stuff isn't easy."

"It looked like he was concentrating very hard," one of those who had been watching reported to Raphtalia. "If I may be a little, well, rude—"

"It looks like he's just messing around, right?" It sounded like Raphtalia was onto something. "And yet, when you observe more closely, he's actually cooking very carefully. It seems simple at a glance, easy to replicate, but that's actually very hard to do. That's Mr. Naofumi's cooking."

"That's because normally I slack off as much as possible." That was definitely one of my defining characteristics.

"What you refer to in terms of 'slacking off,' when it comes to cooking, differs from our definition of that concept," Raphtalia retorted.

"Indeed. I think Naofumi is quite an excellent chef." Itsuki could barely speak around stuffing his mouth. Him too! Still, if he was sharing his opinions, maybe he was finally recovering a bit from the aftereffects of the curse.

"I'm sure he can at least tell the difference between times it's okay to slack off and times it's better not to," he continued.

"I'm not sure he's quite on that level—and anyway, that's not the issue here. Imagine what he might be able to make if he actually did concentrate on it!" Raphtalia proclaimed.

"Hey, that's not the kind of concentration we're talking about," I said. It didn't change the fact I was slacking off either.

"What if he—"

Man, how would they react if I told them I'd put life force into it? Thinking about it now, it was like I'd poured something from my own body into the food. That could be nasty. Might even lead to food poisoning or something like that! Also, to be honest, it just didn't sound very clean.

"W-what did you do?"

I couldn't leave things like this though.

"Is there some kind of magic potion to make food taste better?" This from Rishia.

"I don't know. Naofumi might have access to such a potion though. Well?" Itsuki turned the question back on me.

What choice did I have? I'd just have to come clean.

"I tried adding some life force," I finally admitted.

"You've applied it to cooking?" Raphtalia immediately didn't look impressed. That said, they were all still chowing down. I'd thought they'd immediately say they didn't want to eat it.

"My chopsticks won't stop moving. Just what kind of magic is this?" If this was the response I was getting, I was going to have to whip up another batch for Fohl and Atla.

"It would be nice if you just agreed that I've improved," I stated.

"Delicious! Ah, that's mine!"

"Kwaa, kwaa!" Filo and Gaelion had started fighting over whatever was left. There was never a quiet moment with these guys.

"Rafu." It looked like even Raph-chan liked it, because she was eating more than normal.

Life force really was incredible.

After making it through another tumultuous meal-time, Raphtalia and Filo set off around the town at the head of a parade to reinforce their image as the leaders of the revolution. Filo had also been given a special outfit for a Q'ten Lo filolial and a carriage—a bit like a cattle cart, but different. Definitely different. Raphtalia then sat in the carriage and was pulled slowly along. Filo had been in a pretty good mood since that carriage showed up. Then Gaelion followed along behind while Raphtalia waved from the carriage's windows.

"Praise the new Heavenly Emperor!" and similar shouts were elicited from the ground. Everyone was excited to see Raphtalia. Merchants had informed me that a large volume of drawings of Raphtalia had been made and was selling well. That was one of the ways we were funding this revolution. For me, it was like I was seeing the success of my daughter every single day, and I couldn't have been prouder.

Ah, but there was Raphtalia, giving me the stink eye again. She complained each and every time about being put on display. She didn't see what was so appealing about her miko costume either.

Anyway, Sadeena and I were posted on each side of

her, for her protection. The placement of Itsuki, Rishia, and S'yne was somewhat fluid, but they were always close to me.

Raphtalia was always at the head, and then Filo and Gaelion protected her. Sometimes those who had joined us from Siltvelt, Werner and the like, also took part, although they didn't seem very happy with their placement.

Atla and Fohl weren't back yet either, now that I thought of it. How long were they planning on shopping for?

We took a slow tour of the town, anyway, and then returned to the house.

Once we got back inside, Atla was there, sprawled out, a hairpin in her hair. Fohl, meanwhile, looked incredibly happy.

"We're going back to those shops that were closed tomorrow!" Fohl announced.

"What! Not more shopping, brother!" I noticed that multiple outfits had already been purchased. He was almost using Atla as a doll to play dress up.

"Welcome back, you two," I said.

"Gah! If this was Master Naofumi, not my stinking brother, then I'd happily do whatever he asked. I've no idea what pleasure you derive from all this!"

"Rare, but we agree for once. I feel exactly as you do. At least when it comes to clothing," Raphtalia agreed. Raphtalia always had to find a way to barb her words. There was no helping it, anyway. It made them better fighters too.

"You've got it better than you know, Raphtalia. Having an outfit that Master Naofumi loves so much is something to be happy about," Atla expressed. Ah! That comment only made Raphtalia sigh about as loud as I'd ever heard.

"Anyway. We've done more than enough training and work for today. Raphtalia, you rest up. Sadeena, you guard her. Atla, Fohl, eat," I commanded.

"What about you, Mr. Naofumi?"

"I've got some things to do before bed, so I'm going out to see the old guy, places like that." I just hoped I could avoid further entanglements with his master.

"Then I'll go with you—"

"Me too!" Filo perked up.

"No, you can't. Think of the fuss having both of you along would cause. I just need you to stay here." To be honest, even though I was supposedly the leader of the revolution, everyone's attention was so focused on Raphtalia that I kinda got ignored. That actually made it easier for me to get around.

"Kwaa."

"You too, Gaelion."

"Kwaa . . ." That said, if he was in baby mode I could probably handle taking him along. If I did take him, though, Filo would get all pissy, so better to have him stay behind as well.

"I'm so tired," was her contribution. Good.

"So get some sleep. We've got an early start again tomorrow."

"Okay! I wonder what Melty is doing right now?" Filo wondered.

"Fighting a mountain of documents, maybe?" I doubted there was any need to worry about Melty. I'd heaped plenty of praise on her before we set out, but . . . the effects of that had probably worn off by now.

"Then I'll go with you, especially if Raphtalia is staying behind," Atla announced.

"No. You eat your dinner, with your brother. You haven't had a bath yet either, have you?!"

"Spending some time with you, Master Naofumi, is far more important than that."

"What are you talking about!" Fohl was quick to step in.

"Okay then, Raphtalia, Sadeena, Fohl, you all keep an eye on Atla."

"Very well. Come on, Atla. Settle down and take a rest, just as you've been told."

"Bah! I'll slip out, I promise it!" And so Atla was reluctantly dragged away by Raphtalia and the others.

Chapter Seven: A Terrible Sense of Direction

Rather than in my parade getup, I set out into the town at night dressed in clothing more suited to Q'ten Lo. Ah, but regardless of what I said, S'yne followed along behind me. Could she really not take her eyes off me for even a moment?

In any case, S'yne wasn't going to cause much of a fuss. Q'ten Lo was a nation that had demi-humans, therianthropes, and humans too. Even though there was a civil war going on, the streets didn't look that different from when they did during the daytime. I'd heard that nights in Edo were pretty quiet, people going to bed early, but Q'ten Lo looked different in that regard. The sakura lumina also functioned as illumination, keeping the nighttime somewhat bright. That faint cherry-pink light had a real atmosphere to it. It mixed with the moonlight to create an atmosphere that would definitely be really popular among Japanese people.

As to why I was heading to see the old guy, it was because I'd finally made some headway with life force. Taking the example of my cooking from earlier, there was a high possibility it could also be used when making items. It might be hard for him to learn it, but if he became able to do so, he might be able to create an even greater range of items for us. So I'd decided to go and report to him. I was thinking about that as I walked toward the forge where he was located, when—

"I'm sorry. Excuse me?" A pretty relaxed-sounding voice stopped me.

"Huh?" I looked in the direction of the voice and saw a woman standing there with a bit of a vacant expression. Still, she had quite a nice face. With her baggy clothing, I couldn't tell if she was a demi-human or human. It did kinda look like I'd seen her before somewhere, but no, this was our first meeting. Right?

Yeah, this was definitely our first meeting, but a woman who I really felt like I'd seen before was looking at me with an apologetic look on her face.

S'yne, a little on guard, reached for her weapon.

"My apologies for the question, but could you tell me where Main Road is?"

"The Main Road? That way." I was currently walking on Craftsman's Road. Main Road was, apparently, the large thoroughfare that cut through the center of the town.

"Thank you so much." The woman looked in the direction I pointed, bowed her head deeply, took three steps that way, and then, looking up into the sky, started off in a totally different direction.

"What's with her?" I tilted my head, and S'yne did too. She took a completely different turn from the one I had indicated. Had she even listened to what I said?

No matter. I'd just carry on and see the old guy.

I headed to the forge where the old guy was staying. It was the place responsible for such tasks as repairing the weapons for the revolutionaries. Of course, the local blacksmiths were also taking part, and the old guy was helping them.

Motoyasu II was pretty famous, in certain quarters of Q'ten Lo, so I thought we'd get into the forge just on the strength of his reputation. At the forge in question, people were coming and going, some permanently posted there, making weapons and armor.

Ah, there, I found the old guy.

Motoyasu II was rolling around, tied up. If I gave him the time of day, that would be the end of it.

"Hey."

"Hello? Ah, kid! What brings you here so late?"

"I was busy training during the daytime. There have been quite a few developments, so I thought I'd come to let you know."

"Erhard! It's dark out! That's the time to go drinking! If we don't go drinking, where the hell are we going to go?" After spending all day getting chased around by Fohl, he still had nothing in mind other than having fun. I couldn't help but give a sigh.

"Okay, and how are things going with that cursed sword?"

"The basic prep is all done, but I need somewhere I can get some real peace and quiet first."

"I see." Well, even if we could use that sword, the one among my retinue most likely to make use of it wasn't even here. It would be tough without Ren.

"We're planning on taking the old city within a few days. You should be able to reforge it there," I mentioned.

"Ah, my master has his own studio there. Yeah, that would be perfect. So many good experiences to be had by coming to my master's homeland!"

"I wouldn't put it past this old perv to have qualified you just to get rid of you." I directed my comment with as much venom as possible at the prostrate Motoyasu II.

"That's a distinct possibility." Ah, it sounded like the old guy had considered the same thing. But still. You only had to look at the quality of his weapons to know he had some serious skills.

"I qualified him because I'd taught him all I could! After that it's all up to him, and I'm certainly not responsible for that!" the old perv spat.

"I guess that's a good point too," I admitted. It's actually fairly similar to Hengen Muso Style. Ah, of course. I needed to let the old guy know the information I had just picked up.

"That reminds me. Old guy, can you see the flow of life force? Anything like that?"

"Like . . . what?" he pondered. I proceeded to explain how adding magic and SP—life force—to my cooking had improved its quality. That seemed like the only explanation for what had happened, anyway.

"Imbuing something with an unseen power? I understand that, yeah," he mulled.

"Okay."

"Although I don't think it's quite as clear-cut as what you're talking about, kid. There's meaning in concentrating on something though. Right?" That definitely suggested the old guy was already using it without even knowing it himself. "You also have to listen to the voice of the materials. Pressing is good, but pulling is also important." Hmmm. So imbuing with magic and life force was important, but inducing that was also a requirement.

"What about you? Know anything about this?" I

barked, turning a scornful eye onto Motoyasu II.

"Hah! That's the level you're working with? Very well. Just don't collapse in surprise when you see what I'm capable of—hot girl!" Ah, he'd noticed S'yne. I took my eyes off him for a second and when I looked back at where Motoyasu II had been on the ground, he was gone!

Somehow he was already out of the ropes and was now giving S'yne the full, slimy chat-up routine. He'd been bound on the floor a moment ago! What was he, some kind of escape artist?

"I remember you. The cutie who ordered those scissors the other day," he soothed. The age gap made my head spin! What was he thinking?

"Yeah, they are quite—" For her part, S'yne tried to respond by showing him the scissors, but the sound cut out.

"You've got such a unique voice. I could listen to it forever," he went on.

"What's this with guy? Is he senile?" The Keel doll quickly got to the heart of the matter. S'yne seemed to be asking pretty much the same question.

"You do good work. Maybe you look—"

"She is saying that, because you do good work, maybe you would look most appealing when actually doing some of it?" the doll quipped.

"Hah! If she's begging to see me hammer something, very well." Motoyasu II wobbled over to the forge. "Little lady! Just you watch this!" With that, he started to hammer the weapon that the old guy had been working on.

Hmmm. Looking closely, yes, I felt a flow of life force . . . and a larger one than when the old guy had been working.

"Shield boy was talking about, what, life force or some junk? That's the power you expend when concentrating, right? Hah, anyone can do that. Sending it intentionally into things, that's child's play," he bragged.

"R-right . . ." As the hammer rose and fell, each and every movement sparkled, and I realized that being able to see life force opened the door to seeing how skilled an individual was at any given task.

This old goat was a perverted moron at any other time, sure, but he was a genius when he got to work. The weapon was visibly starting to shine. I was right, then! This technique could also be used when making items!

"You said SP, right? That hero power? Just think for a moment if that's the same thing as life force," he jabbered. Yeah, good point. Life force water was created by extracting the ingredients from magic water and soul-healing water. If life force was a different element from magic or SP, then it made sense that whatever was drawing out the quality was also a different element.

"This is the wall that separates amateurs from professionals, beyond the imbuing of magic. Still, I have some idea of what you mean by life force. This, right?" Motoyasu II extended a wobbly hand and gathered life force to it. "I can't see it, but I feel it. You can't make any quality items without imbuing them with this. You also use this to listen to the voice of materials. Simply relying on the quality of your materials makes you a second-rate artisan!" Then the pick-up artist looked at the old guy. "I only have to listen to the sound of your hammer to know you've got some work to do there. I'm going to have to do some hammering of my own. Beat you into shape!"

"Bring it on!" The old guy also concentrated on watching his master work. Hopefully this was going to enhance his skills.

"Listen to the voice of the materials and bend them to your will. It's the same as when doing something by force. Have you forgotten all my lessons?"

"No, not at all. But I do see what you're doing." It sounded like he was following what was going on, at least. "I can't wait to get back to my shop in Melromarc and try out a load of things. I've got all these recipes in my head now!"

"That sounds great. Can't wait to see them," he responded.

"There, all done!" With a hiss, Motoyasu II plunged the heated weapon into a water bucket and then lifted it high. It was a katana. When I saw the old guy working on it, I'd thought it was a Western-style sword.

"Why's it a katana now, Master? I was just making a sword!"

"Ah? Erhard, look at the materials. It's saying it wants to be a katana, not just a sword!" Wow. That answer really made him sound like a moron. Taking the katana, the old guy looked confused about whether to look angry or captivated. "Right! That's it for work today! Let's go get wasted!" the old guy spouted.

"You've got plenty more to do," I scolded. What about the cursed sword?

"So you say. If I'm going to teach Erhard, he needs to be able to look at the materials and instill in them what he wants to make. I can't work with him if he can't do that."

"Gah." Ah, the old guy looked upset.

"If you want to proceed deeper, first you need to reach that point," he went on.

Maybe I could offer some aid here. Instilling what you wanted the materials to become was like an instinct for sensing what those materials were suited to being. So this "instilling" was like working them with a knife or tools.

It annoyed me that I had some idea of what he was talking about.

"I'm sorry. Excuse me," a voice suddenly interjected. I turned toward the voice—

"Hot girl! Ah, sweet lady, whatever can I do for you?" Motoyasu II revved up his spiel again, unwanted advances and all, and turned it on the woman who had appeared—it was the same one that had asked me the way earlier that night.

"Can you please tell me how to get to Main Road? Oh!" She tilted her head, probably recognizing me from before.

"You asked me the way, didn't you? Then took a few steps and completely changed direction," I questioned her.

"Is that so? The stars were so pretty I just got lost in them completely."

"Hold on! You're not trying to bring another beautiful young woman under your control?" the old perv interjected.

"Enough!" That was always the way with Motoyasu II. I just wanted a break from the guy, seriously. Maybe I could order S'yne to tie him up?

"Kid, I've got to make a few practice swords, so will you please watch my master?" Even as he said that, the old guy made a drinking motion with his hands. "You can handle that, right, kid?"

Okay. So he wanted me to drink him under the table? The old guy must have at least heard the rumors about me. Maybe I could just set Sadeena on him? Ah, no, I'd heard she already drowned him in booze a few days ago.

"Sure thing. I'll bring him back later. And on that note—" I turned to look at the woman with seemingly no sense of direction. "Main Road, right? I'm going to have to move to keep an eye on this guy, so I'll take you myself. Come on."

"Thank you so much." The easily confused woman gave a deep and respectful bow.

"No need for that. You too, perv. Move it."

"That's what you're calling me now? You're joking!"

"Shut it. Okay, Motoyasu II!"

"Who the hell is Motoyasu I?"

"I said shut it. Once you've helped improve the old guy's skills, we're finished with you."

"What!"

"Should I—" the woman began.

"No need to worry about anything, sweet lady," the perv reassured her. Such comments were exactly why I wanted to call him Motoyasu II. Or just perv. That seemed simpler.

"We'll get going then. S'yne, are you coming too?" I sighed. She gave a wordless nod. Time was getting on, and I didn't want Raphtalia and the others to worry. "So let's move." That was how we left the forge and headed toward Main Road.

"My lady. You have such beautiful skin. This moonlight only adds a further sheen to your porcelain beauty," the perv continued. Motoyasu II wasn't giving up on the easily lost woman yet.

"Oh . . ."

He was persistent, I'd give him that. Then S'yne prodded me on the shoulder.

"What's up?" I turned back to see our wandering new companion heading off into a side street, and Motoyasu II was heading after her—and attempting not to be noticed by me either.

"What is this, an abduction?" I said.

"Nothing of the sort. She was weaving off onto a different path, so I thought I'd better escort her," he grumbled.

"Huh? Ah, I'm sorry. I smelt something delicious and just kind of zoned out," she explained. It looked like she hadn't had any idea of what was happening. Seriously?

"That's not the way. Just stay quiet and keep with me," I snapped. Was she going to get lost at every single crossroad?

"Of course," she replied. After taking a few more steps, S'yne poked me on the shoulder again.

I turned again, and she was about to head back the way we came.

"Just keep with me! Right at the road ahead, understand?" I ordered. This woman was really starting to bug me. Was she even listening to what I was saying? I took another look, and she was turning left!

"I said right!"

"Eh? But that bug turned the other way."

"Stop following bugs!" I'd heard that people with zero sense of direction had a tendency to subconsciously focus on moving things and then take the wrong path when those things moved. Or they were drawing a random map in their heads and ended up taking the wrong street. In any case, it would be a nuisance if she wandered off somewhere strange, and I didn't want her falling prey to Motoyasu II, so I grabbed her hand and led her along.

"Oh my. How forward of you!" she exclaimed.

"Enough of that." The conversation reminded me of someone else, and I really didn't like it. This wasn't Sadeena's sister, was it? Just as I thought that, we came out onto Main Road.

"This is Main Road, your destination," I stated. I wasn't sure if she had no sense of direction or was just a complete moron, but I was never going to get anywhere with both of these weirdos trailing around behind me.

The woman looked at the people on Main Road.

"I heard there was a parade for the Heavenly Emperor," she inquired.

"That finished ages ago." So that was it. She'd been looking for Main Road to see Raphtalia and the others?

"Oh my."

"So what are you going to do now?"

"Hmmm."

"How about coming for a drink with us?" Motoyasu II went ahead and invited her to join us.

"A drink? Would that be okay?"

"It certainly would. My treat." Motoyasu II chirped up with a look on his face like one of those cartoon wolves. For her part, the woman definitely seemed interested in getting a drink. So how was this going to turn out?

In any case, Motoyasu II was going to be under the table eventually, so I just had to part ways with her when the timing seemed right.

"S'yne, I take it you're not the type to drink," I ventured. She nodded at my statement. She didn't have any interest in drink, just as I presumed. "So just keep on filling his cup. Let's knock him out quick and get home."

"She seems to understand," the Keel doll offered.

"So come on! I'll take you to my favorite little spot," he offered. With that, Motoyasu II headed into a tavern with both the easily lost woman and S'yne. Maybe he was trying to shake me, but that wasn't going to happen.

I entered the establishment too, sat down, and looked at the menu.

Gah, I couldn't read it. It wasn't the Melromarc common tongue. I guess I'd just order at random. That said, I didn't want the entire bill landing on my lap either.

"You can pay your own way?" I asked Motoyasu II, just to make sure.

"Hah! I can handle this! You've got money too, right? These two women are drinking on me, but I'm not treating you to anything," With that, Motoyasu II went ahead and ordered both drinks and food for everyone, including me.

"Okay then, I'll have this, this, and this." Our

wandering companion placed quite a hefty order herself. Did she like drinking too, then? Really, just how was this going to end?

"S'yne doesn't drink alcohol," I said.

"Juice it is then. Do you want something to eat?" he asked. S'yne didn't respond verbally, just nodded. From her expression, though, it was clear she really did want to say something.

"Here's your order," the waiter announced. The drinks arrived—along with a water barrel and rucolu fruit.

"Heh! I think this suits you best," quipped Motoyasu II, placing the bunch of rucolu fruit in front of me. So what was this? A roundabout way to tell me to get lost?

What a dick. Like, I hated this guy.

Still, I'd met his type before, even back when I was in Japan. At offline meetups for Internet games, for example, there were always those annoying creeps who found a girl they fancied and bullishly separated them from the rest of the guys. They always destroyed the atmosphere, so the best way was to humor them a little, then drink them under the table. Even better, they were also exactly the kind of guys who liked to boast about being able to hold their drink.

They were pestilent carnivores, just trolls looking to

hook up online rather than play. I always remembered their antics, anyway, and kept an eye on anyone who looked likely to cause trouble at such gatherings. Nothing was as annoying as the junk pertaining to human relationships. Another good method was to change the groups around and place them where they couldn't do any harm.

"We drink! To our meeting!" Motoyasu II announced, putting his tankard to his lips. I seized my moment to squish one of the rucolu fruit placed in front of me and add some drops to the next drink he had lined up. It was pretty potent stuff, so I adjusted it carefully. I didn't want to kill him.

"Cheers!" the confused woman said and lifted her own drink and started to down it. In fact, she was chugging it in one gulp. That wasn't particularly safe. "Phew. I'll take another."

"Yeehah! You sure can put them away! This is going to be fun!" he roared. Laugh it up, perv. Let's see how long that lasts. I just had to play along so he didn't get wind of my plan.

S'yne took her juice and started drinking too.

"So tell me, young lady. What brings you here? Where's your address? I'll see you home later, if you like," Motoyasu II inquired. He really went for the throat!

"Well, I wanted to see the Heavenly Emperor. I live in a village along the coast, to the north."

"So you have lodgings here? Where are you staying?"

"Ah, well—"

"Maybe lay off on the interrogation?" I growled. He really was a letch. That said, though, he didn't seem to have much game when it came to actually picking the ladies up. The original Motoyasu seemed better at that side of things. There was also the difference in appearance and age to be considered too.

"You can keep quiet—hey, what're you playing at?" Motoyasu II jabbed, pointing at me in shock.

"Huh?" I had picked a rucolu fruit from the bunch and was stuffing my cheeks with it. "You ordered them. They taste great, these fruits." They really did. If someone put them on the table, I was going to eat them. They were also used to brew incredibly powerful alcohol, with a really bad reputation in certain quarters.

They also had magic and SP recovery properties. It almost seemed a waste to use magic water or soul-healing water in their place. Perhaps I should be healing using these? They gave a pretty good healing ratio too. Might be worth stocking up.

The only issue was the cost.

"Hey. Don't go showing me things like that. Ugh, that's sick," Motoyasu II shuddered and put his hands to his mouth and turned away.

Hah! You had them brought to the table!

Other patrons around us had also noticed and were looking pale. Our waiter was shuddering with disgust.

"Oh, wow!" Our new, directionless friend said, eyes sparkling, "You can really handle your drink. I'm jealous."

"I've never been drunk. I also know another woman who reacted exactly like you just did," I mentioned. My suspicions flared up again.

"Amazing! Amazing! I have to try and keep up," she said. With that, she started to drink again. Heartily, it could be said. She was really getting into the swing of things! I'd thought maybe she had a connection with Sadeena, but her seemingly permanently drunk persona seemed quite different from that of my companion, so maybe I was just imagining things.

"Come on, stop talking to that weirdo and talk to me. You're from a coastal village in the north, correct? There are lots of beautiful women up there," he commented.

"There are?" she replied. Ah, so she was one of those. Unaware of her own assets. I just wanted to put an end to this quickly, anyway. I needed to wipe out Motoyasu II. He hadn't touched the drink I spiked yet at all.

"To be honest, speaking personally—" she began, ignoring him and looking at me again.

"What race are you? I'm so jealous of you being able to drink so much." In the end, Q'ten Lo was a country with a lot of demi-humans and therianthropes. There were humans, but the ratio was fairly low. One of the characteristics of this world was that no one was especially bothered about my physical appearance. What's more, some in Q'ten Lo actively concealed their demi-human traits. There were various reasons for this, including things like family standing. That was a custom not found in Siltvelt.

Maybe this woman lived close to where Sadeena had lived. That would explain their similar sensibilities, such as being attracted to people who can hold their drink.

"I'm human. What of it?" I said.

"Eh? Humans can hold their drink this well? You must have someone, a distant relation, from a race who can drink," she wondered. So that was how they looked at me in these demi-human nations. Of course, seeing as I was Japanese, summoned here from a completely different world, I could definitively say that wasn't possible. But stating the truth would only complicate things in a different way.

Ah, Motoyasu II looked pissed at being ignored.

"Being a man is about more than just drinking. Let's play a game!" he roared. With that, Motoyasu II brought out some dice. "How about some Cee-lo!" Uwah! I didn't expect that to show up in a parallel world. I looked over at S'yne to see her getting out some cards. She was the famous player Murder Pierrot from the Zeltoble underground coliseum, after all. Of course she had some cards. Personally, I preferred that too.

"Better to play with cards," I said.

"I bet this lovely lady doesn't know how. That's a point, my dear. I haven't got your name yet. What should I call you?" he pondered.

"Ah, I'm Zodia," she announced. It was a pretty venomous name. Was it my innate nature as a gamer that made it sound like just saying it would summon some terrible demon god?

"Zodia. Do you know how to play cards?" the Keel doll translated for S'yne.

"Card games? Like ones with nice pictures on them . . . maybe a little," she said.

"You mean hanafuda?" I wondered. This place really was like Japan. I only knew a little about that myself though.

"Not that old game. I play the modern version," she went on.

"Ah, gotcha," the perv said. Motoyasu II didn't sound too into it. "The hands are so complex though, and the cards are so thick. There's nothing we can use around here—" Even as he droned on, Zodia reached into the holder at her waist, took out a deck of cards, and placed them down on the table.

"O-oh!" Motoyasu II babbled.

"I have something of a taste for it." She grinned. It looked more like a serious hobby—like she had her own set of cards!

I checked the deck. Hmmm, it looked like a card version of mahjong.

"So you place them like this to create a hand?" I asked.

"Yes. You know it?" She beamed.

"Just another game like it," I said. And only a little I played in a few arcades—and maybe mini-games in other games. I'd never played it seriously. "If this is my first time, it might not be that much fun."

"It's fine. I'll teach you as we go."

"Okay, okay." With that, the cards were dealt, and we started to play. S'yne—well, she actually looked pretty confident.

"You okay with this?" I asked her. She nodded in response to my question.

"During my travels—"

"Apparently she has played a similar game during her travels," the Keel doll translated. As she wandered through various worlds, she probably learned it in a tavern somewhere.

First you get thirteen cards and then draw one and discard one. Those were the rules. It was basically mahjong. It also looked like it was going to take some time.

"As we've got some beginners here, let's use different rules using five cards—" she suggested.

"Isn't that like poker then?" I said.

S'yne started to dexterously shuffle the cards. They were similar shapes to the cards I knew, so I reckoned we could make a go of it.

"We just gotta play along with Zodia, you dolt!" Motoyasu II bellowed.

"Okay, okay. I get it. Let's go," I conceded. So we ended up playing poker with clunky playing cards that had four of the same type. At least the length of each game was incredibly short. Her plan was likely to teach us a little at a time and then transition to something a bit more serious. Honestly, it looked like a bunch of beginners barely managing to play. We played about ten rounds like that.

"It's finally getting fun!" Zodia announced, drinking

heavily between each hand. Getting a bit carried away she played a powerful hand. A straight, perhaps, if this was poker. Her personality seemed to be changing as she got more drunk. "Kabloom! Take that!"

"Heh." I had four cards of the same type, so I played them along with one other plain card. This wasn't a variant of mahjong, but poker, right? I didn't know the hands in either case.

"Oh damn. I lost!" she groaned.

"You don't know how to read the room, do you? Meathead!" Motoyasu II roared. I wasn't sure what to make of that, considering Motoyasu II hadn't played a single decent hand yet. It wasn't like he was discarding good cards on purpose either. I was starting to think he sucked at gambling too.

He was also starting to get pretty drunk.

"At least I haven't lost every single game. You're too drunk!" I jabbed.

"I'm not—not dwunk at all!" he said as his head was wobbling from side to side! It was only going to take a little more to bring him down.

"What about this?" S'yne dropped her hand, three plain cards and two with the same symbol on them. Maybe something like a full house, if this was poker.

"Both of you are so good at this! Now I'm really

having fun!" Zodia beamed. The booze was pushing her into the stratosphere. Yeah. She really didn't feel like Sadeena's sister—her sister would be a lot stronger than this.

"Moron! You hold—hold beck! Now, dwink!" That was how Motoyasu II foisted more alcohol on Zodia. I think it was about time to put an end to this.

"Thank you! I'm gonna drink this place dry!" Zodia was getting more and more pumped. At least S'yne was resolutely staying on the wagon.

"Try this—" S'yne also smoothly handed Motoyasu II the spiked booze that I'd been hoping he would drink.

"Uwah, so cute! How couwd I wesist!" Slurring his words, Motoyasu II took the proffered cup and drank it down in a gulp. "Guh!" The cup promptly fell from his fingers, and then he looked quizzically at S'yne. It would be a pain if he misunderstood, so I pushed into his eye line and pointed to myself, grinning for the full effect.

"Y-you dog! You set me up!" he shouted.

"I'm sorry, but it's about time this little drinking party came to an end." I spoke softly in order to draw him in. Seriously, why had simply going to visit the old guy led to all of this?

"Gah! At least let me collapse piwowed on a pwetty girl's tits!" he mumbled. Such gracious last words! I'd only put a few drops in, anyway, so he wasn't going to die.

"Oh damn. He's collapsed under all that drink. Let's call it a night," I quipped. A little forced? No, a lot. Still, I hoisted up the unconscious old goat. The bill—yeah, it was coming out of his pocket.

"Oh, no! I want to drink and play some more!" Zodia announced, sounding like a petulant child.

"I know you're having fun, but staying out too late will be detrimental to tomorrow," I warned.

"But I still want to play!"

"And I don't want to deal with your selfishness," I barked.

"Uh! At least tell me your name! Please! Let's play again soon. When? When can we play?" she begged. Drinking clearly turned her back into a child. If possible, I never wanted to see her again.

"If we meet again, sure. I'll pass some time with you," I groaned.

"Really? So tell me your name!"

"Sure, sure, pipe down. I'm Naofumi Iwatani."

"Ah! Cute little Naofumi."

"I'm neither cute nor little." The drunkard side of her was a lot like Sadeena. My fading suspicions rose again.

"Sweet Naofumi, then. Hahaha! We'll meet again, I promise! Ahaha, oh, the lights are so pretty!" Zodia stated and staggered a little toward us, then took Motoyasu II's other shoulder as I supported him. She was surprisingly strong.

We paid the bill and left the tavern.

"Well then. See you again soon! That was so much fun! I don't think I've ever had so much fun!" she went on.

"Yeah, sure, sure." She was close to tipping over too. Definitely not as strong as my party's resident drunkard who never got as sloshed as this.

We did have a drinking competition once, and I won, but she quickly recovered and returned to normal. It might be more accurate to say that she was always drunk.

"Uwah. I'm so hot!" she began.

"Hey! Keep your clothes on!" I yelled. Zodia started to strip, basically, so I reined her in. Although maybe I could use this chance to find out what kind of demihuman she was?

"I'll just stir up a little breeze, then. Zweite Wind!" Zodia caused a gust to blow with a pretty short incantation.

"And don't use magic in the street either!" I fumed. The strong wind picked up a swirl of dust. I couldn't handle two drunks at once, seriously.

Hold on! She still had a drink in her hand! She chugged the entire bottle in one gulp, and then her back straightened and she turned to face me. What now? I thought she was drunk, but now she seemed sober.

"Well then. To commemorate today," she said, and with that she gave me a card from the holder, or whatever it was, at her waist. The card had a gemstone set in the middle, and the image on it was pretty unique. It depicted a killer whale.

"This feels so strange. I think I've taken a liking to you. Would you become my husband?"

"What the hell are you talking about? I know someone else who often says things like that." She was like Sadeena, after all. Could she be the current water dragon's miko priestess, here undercover?

"Hahaha, are you turning me down?"

"You've got to be kidding, right?"

"I don't think I've ever felt like this, so fixated on something. I'm looking for a storybook romance, anyway, so I'll leave it at this tonight." With that, and skipping as she went, she disappeared off into a side street. Was she going to be able to find lodgings? Her sense of direction sucked so badly I honestly wondered how she'd made it to today. Perhaps all the drink had pickled her brain?

Should I really be letting her go alone?

It was a serious question, but after I followed casually after her just a little, she was gone.

"Will she—" S'yne began.

"Will she be okay?" the doll finished.

"No idea." Even if I chased her down, I wasn't sure I could detain her. Letting her walk the streets alone at night might not be a great idea, but S'yne and I already had one drunk to deal with. I'd just have to count on the relative safety of the streets of Q'ten Lo.

"Let's just get this drunkard back to the old guy and then get on home," I said.

We proceeded to take Motoyasu II back to the old guy and then hurried back to the house.

Chapter Eight: Big Sister

"Welcome back." Raphtalia greeted us upon our arrival.

"It's time you were in bed. Staying up late is bad for your skin," I scolded.

"Hah. You never stopped me in the village when I was going out to intercept Atla," she retorted. Ah, so she was annoyed by me coming back late. I should have made better use of S'yne.

"I got stuck spending time with that pervert. S'yne and I set a little trap for him."

"I don't need the details, if possible. I sent one of the servants to the old guy and heard that much, anyway."

"Ah, yeah, he mentioned that." A messenger from the house had come to check where I was, something like that. I had been on my way back at that point though, so I didn't think it mattered.

"Anyway, you go and get your rest, Raphtalia. We're going to be busy again tomorrow."

"Very well."

"In which case—"

"In which case we'll go to bed too. If you need us,

we'll be right there." S'yne entered the house and went off to bed.

"What about Atla?" I asked.

"After bathing, she ate the food you made, Mr. Nao-fumi, and then got a bit rowdy. For now, she's resting." The "for now" part worried me a little. Sounded like they'd had their fair share of fun here too.

"Big sister!" That was Fohl, and it was directed at Raphtalia. Huh? "Big sister?" Fohl was calling Raphtalia big sister now? What the hell happened here tonight?

I pointed at Fohl, and Raphtalia's reply was mixed with a sigh.

"I finally had enough of Fohl enabling Atla's spoiled rampage and gave him a bit of a lecture. This is the result," she explained.

"Okay, you're going to have to fill me in," I said. Raphtalia proceeded to give me the details.

As it turned out, there had been a scuffle with Atla after I left, because she wanted to follow after me. As always, Fohl had tried to keep her under control. Sometimes he did, but he always needed someone's help to do so.

"Brother, please. I've spent so much time with you today. Please, move aside." Atla had turned her wiles on

Fohl in order to get him on her side and then escape. Raphtalia, Filo, and Sadeena had still stood in opposition to her.

"After spending so much time with you both, I know how important Atla is to you. But just sitting by and watching your precious Atla's violent tantrums, I have to wonder—is that really the way a gentle brother should act?" Raphtalia had lectured.

"Uwah! I'm—I'm on Atla's side! She's been so kind to me today. I have to repay her for that!" Fohl had said and proceeded to take a swing at Raphtalia. But his fist didn't reach her, and instead Raphtalia landed a slap on the violent Fohl's cheek. Of course, with the modifier from the katana vassal weapon, he didn't take much damage.

"If Mr. Naofumi said something odd, I'd warn him and put him right. Worst case scenario—physically, if it came down to it," she had denoted. She wasn't wrong. Raphtalia would indeed get physical if I looked to make a mistake. The first time I used the Shield of Rage, for example. I could still remember that vortex of negative emotions. I couldn't allow them to swallow me.

Yes, she was right. Raphtalia always stopped me if I was going to make a mistake.

"But what about you? You handle your kid sister

with kid gloves! That's not going to resolve anything," she had fumed.

"Uh . . ."

"She even causes trouble for Mr. Naofumi. If you don't help keep her in line, Mr. Naofumi may end up hating your precious Atla!" Raphtalia had warned.

"Him? Hate Atla? That's impossible! This is Atla we're talking about!"

"You think everyone loves Atla unconditionally, do you?"

"Brother, don't listen to her!" Even while she had cautioned Fohl, Atla had looked for openings in Raphtalia's defense.

"A-Atla is my precious sister who everyone loves!"

"And I'm asking if you think that's in the best interests of your sister!" At Raphtalia's outburst, Fohl had backed away in something close to terror.

"If you don't caution her about these tantrums, she's the one who's eventually going to suffer," Raphtalia had gone on.

"W-what? Atla? You think so?"

"Do you know the kind of person that Mr. Naofumi doesn't like? Women who use others, trample them, and enjoy their suffering!"

"You're right. When Atla trampled me, he did have a very unpleasant look on his face."

"Indeed. If you truly want the best for Atla, you need to take the reins and raise her into a respectable woman. Isn't that what a good brother should do?" Had Raphtalia been aware that she was saying something a bit odd? Did a brother have that authority? That said, though, Fohl was not only Atla's older brother, but also her parent-like figure. So maybe Raphtalia wasn't so far off the mark.

"Oh my. Don't get too carried away, little Raphtalia," Sadeena had cautioned.

"Hmmm? I'm exhausted. Isn't Master back yet?" Filo had whined.

Ignoring this background noise, Raphtalia had voiced her concerns directly at Fohl. As though snapping back to himself, Fohl had looked at Raphtalia.

"You're right. I've been so fixated on Atla I've not been thinking about her at all. I've come to accept him, a little, but I'm not going to let that guy take Atla, no matter what!" Fohl had spouted. He accepted me? If I'd been there, *that's* what I would have asked about.

With that, Fohl had swiftly turned and launched a technique at Atla. His sister barely saw it coming and just got out of the way.

"Brother, is this some kind of joke?" she had questioned.

"Atla, if you stray from the true path, I will stop you with everything I've got!"

"You're betraying me?"

"Betraying? I am, and always will be, your ally. I've realized that if you remain so selfish, the one you wish for may end up disliking you. As your brother, I will ensure that you grow into a fine, responsible woman!"

"Hah. So you're finally turning on me, brother? I won't hold back, even for you." And so Fohl and Atla's scuffle had begun, and as a result, tonight Fohl had been the winner.

This was all starting to make my head ache. I pressed my hand to my forehead and sighed.

"Maybe he's a little too muscle-brained?" I suggested.

"Well—I think maybe it's also my fault for beating the bushes a bit too hard," Raphtalia sighed.

"This isn't your fault, big sister!" Fohl blurted out.

"If we're getting into ages, I'm younger than you!"

"That doesn't matter!"

Hmmm. This might actually clear up the problems with Atla a bit. If I lectured her, she would be just happy to have me lecture her. It would definitely be better if Fohl could take over that role.

To be honest, she did need a bit more discipline.

Back when she was sick, Atla had appeared pretty disciplined. They do say love changes a person, but still.

"Everyone is tired, anyway, so I'm going to bed too," Raphtalia announced and turned to go.

"Yeah, goodnight. Fohl, you're watching Atla?" I asked.

"Yes. Not on your orders though."

"Sure, yeah, yeah. If you can curtail your sister's rampages, you won't get any complaints from me. I'll help out when I can."

"Help out? What does that mean, exactly?! You don't have designs on Atla—" he began, but I glared at Fohl so intently he promptly shut up.

"We've been together long enough now that you know what I meant. I'll chat with her every now and then, nothing more," I finished.

"O-okay." He didn't look especially happy, but Fohl left. Maybe he was going to check on where Atla was being held.

I was exhausted, anyway. Time to get some sleep.

So that's how my day ended.

The next day.

We headed toward the old city during the day,

reaching the point where tomorrow we'd be launching our attack. After finishing our meeting, we were in our lodgings. The houses were small here, so we were staying in the best lodgings in the town.

As a continuation of the day before, we were training prior to taking a bath.

I launched Air Strike Shield, experimenting with whether I could imbue magic into my skills. Then I looked closely at Air Strike Shield, seeing spots where the flow of magic was weak.

"Atla."

"Yes?"

"Try destroying the magic shield I just created."

"Of course." Following my orders, Atla—as I had expected—struck where the magic was weak. With a splitting crack, the shield crumbled easily.

I knew it.

In which case . . . I tried activating the skill while concentrating the magic and life force in my body.

"Air Strike Shield!" Then Atla struck the new shield and destroyed it. I checked, and once again she was striking at a point where the magic flows were weak.

That settled it. She knew the spot to strike at.

"It didn't change much," she said.

"Yeah. Another failure," I admitted. To be honest,

this method wasn't all that different from imbuing magic at the point of casting a spell.

"As the source of your power, the Shield Hero commands you. Read the truth once more and protect this soul! First Guard!" I focused my magic, and at the point of expenditure, I pushed in more prior to release. Hmmm, that took more magic than I expected. It had even decreased my SP.

That one looked like a success.

To be sure, I checked the effects using my own status. Yes, it was clearly more powerful than a normal First Guard.

I was right, then. I'd learnt from magical texts that adjusting the amount of magic when casting a spell could increase or decrease its strength. I'd always intended to be firing off the strongest possible spells, but it looked like there was a whole higher level.

Hmmm, I had the feeling this was going to be even harder than learning magic.

Combining the information from S'yne and Rishia, it seemed certain that life force was a different element from SP. But could it be something similar? If I could come to understand this feeling and imbue it into my magic, it felt like I'd further be able to enhance my skills. After all, simply defending enemy attacks using the defense value of my shield, as I had been until now, was eventually going to hit a limit. If there was some way to increase the strength of my magic, that was something to really be happy about.

"Like—" S'yne gave a practical example. What just happened? It looked like she was just gesturing with her hands, but the Keel doll pantomimed bumping into something.

"You mean like this?" Atla copied her and created something—something like a wall?—even more powerful than the one created by S'yne.

"This is like your power, Master Naofumi! I did it!" Atla beamed. At a glance, it could indeed be taken as a recreation of the Air Strike Shield.

"S'yne is pretty skilled, isn't she?" Atla admitted.

"I know." She looked like such a natural, so why didn't she pull some of this out when she fought us? Looking at the durability of the wall that she had created, maybe she would only make ones that weren't all that reliable.

"Rishia, when will I be able to learn this?" Itsuki asked, watching the unfolding events.

"Have a little more patience," Rishia replied.

"With this power, I might even surpass you and Raphtalia, brother."

"I won't allow that." Raphtalia's voice was hard.

"Me either! Stop me if you can! Atla!" Fohl and Raphtalia were both pushing hard at Atla. I didn't think it was such a bad thing, but maybe I should stop it.

"Rafu!" Raph-chan jumped down from Raphtalia's shoulder.

"That reminds me, S'yne, have you finished what I requested yet?"

"Right here—" With that, S'yne pulled out the item I ordered from her, a miko outfit for Raph-chan, and handed it over.

"Ah! Well done. Come on, Raph-chan. Put this on."

"Rafu?" I put the miko outfit on Raph-chan and checked her over. Yeah. Just as it suited Raphtalia, it really suited Raph-chan too. The only issue perhaps was that Raph-chan didn't normally wear clothing, so it looked a bit like cosplay.

"Rafu, rafu, rafu," Raph-chan was copying Raphtalia, posing with a wooden stick.

"Yeah, perfect! Raph-chan. I bet people will find you just as appealing as Raphtalia in her miko gear!" I said.

"Rafu!" Here in Q'ten Lo, with their deep faith toward the Heavenly Emperor, there might be many who understood the appeal of Raph-chan. I wasn't about to give up spreading the good word!

I gave Raph-chan a stroking that some might consider excessive. If I did that to the real Raphtalia in her miko outfit, she'd get real mad, that was for sure.

"Oh my." Sadeena looked at us and smiled to herself. What was so funny?

"Kwaaa!"

"I want to wear that too!" chimed in Filo.

"Gaelion, I've already equipped you with a festoon. Isn't that enough? Filo, well, I'm not sure it would suit you." Putting a miko outfit on the Western-looking beauty like Filo felt like a bit of a mismatch. It definitely wouldn't suit her as much as the one piece she was currently wearing. So I told her, "I don't think it would suit you in human form."

"What! Then I'll do what Raph-chan does and wear it as a filolial," pouted Filo. I considered that for a moment. Hmmm, it might suit her, but then I also considered what Filo would look like walking the streets of Q'ten Lo in her filolial form.

"In your filolial form, though, you wear that—what is it, bib-like thing, right?" Filo walked through the streets in her filolial form wearing a getup a bit like a Tosa dog. In that regard, she went well with Gaelion.

"But I still want to wear that."

"Okay, sure, sure. Later. If you want to wear

something different, maybe try a loincloth in your filo-lial form?" I thought that would go pretty well with her stocky form.

"That's what Keel wears, right? Wouldn't that be strange?"

"I reckon it would suit you more than a miko outfit." Although Melty would probably have something to say about it, it also sounded like a veiled way of calling Keel strange.

"You think so?"

"W-why is Raph-chan wearing a miko outfit!" Raphtalia raised her voice, finally noticing, but I decided to just ignore her.

Time passed, and the sun started to set.

We weren't doing the night parade today. We'd basically already done one during the daytime.

"Ah, Master Naofumi. Today, at least, I will spend some quality time with you," said Atla.

"We just trained together for ages," I grumbled.

"That's still not enough for me. I want to be with you forever and ever!"

"Even in the bath? That's a bit much. Fohl, you do see where this is going?"

"Y-yes!" Atla was still trying to resist her now more-controlling brother, but the situation wasn't great.

"I'm heading to the bath, anyway," I announced.

"I've heard there are hot springs effective at soothing curses in the vicinity of the old city. The bath here is hot spring water too." I nodded at this information from Raphtalia. Maybe there was a place like the hot springs on the Cal Mira islands?

Sounded good after all the curses we've suffered recently!

"I'd love to join you for some coed bathing." Atla's words made me a little uncomfortable.

"I won't allow that! Your nakedness will not be put on display!" So did her brother's. I'd bathed with Raphtalia and Filo before, of course. Although Raphtalia was really like my daughter so there was no need to worry about that.

"I'd like to bathe with little Naofumi too," chimed in Sadeena.

"Oh look, another pervert!"

"What? You don't want to get naked together?" Sadeena proceeded to hug me from behind.

"Sorry, not interested."

"Lots of the bathing in Q'ten Lo is coed," Sadeena went on. I had seen at least one public bath. It looked pretty Edo-ish too.

Raphtalia explained, "There were places like that in

Kizuna's world. L'Arc wanted to go, but Glass got angry about it."

"There was some talk about peeping with Motoyasu too, before he went wacky. What a pervert," I commented. Anyone in L'Arc's position could have all the women he wanted, although he seemed to prefer Therese the most.

Raphtalia continued. "He was good at compartmentalization, I'll give him that." Yeah, that sounded about right. I could almost see him starting to drool.

"Anyway, watch our own perverted ladies to make sure they don't bother me in the bath."

"Very well," she said. Women trying to get into the men's bath? That just didn't sound right, but I decided to leave that topic well enough alone for the time being.

So I went off to bathe in the hot springs.

"Ah, Master Naofumi! Brother, I won't forgive you for this!"

"You don't have to. If you're trying to crawl into a bath with some guy, I have to stop you! I'm not letting you be such a loose woman. I've hardened my heart in order to make you into a fine and upstanding young lady!"

"I'm already fine, thank you!" No, sorry, but he was right. There was something wrong if she wanted to charge into the men's bath.

In any case, they were as crazy—and noisy—as ever. Kizuna . . . things were more lively now. I didn't dislike it, just wished they'd keep it a little more under control.

Chapter Nine: The Miko Priestess of Carnage

"Phew."

I entered the bath area at our lodgings and let out a sigh. The room was full of steam. I'd just wash myself and then get into the bath.

"Oh my!" I certainly didn't like the sound of that voice. I looked in its direction, and for some inexplicable reason, Zodia was already there, in the bath, looking over at me.

She still had her clothes on, even! This was all a new one to me.

"Good evening, sweet Naofumi. What a coincidence, meeting you here."

"Coincidence? In the men's bath? And I told you, drop the 'sweet.'"

"The men's bath? I admit, I got totally lost and just ended up here." Amazing. I'd known she had a terrible sense of direction, but coming into the men's bath? By mistake?

Even more amazing, after what I saw yesterday, I could almost believe it was possible.

"This is hot water too. I thought it was cold."

"Are you still drunk?"

"No, I'm not."

"If you say so." Zodia came out of the bathtub and closed in with me.

"I could wash your back, if you like?"

"This is the men's bath. Out!"

"Oh dear. You don't like me? But I'm so clean!" What was she talking about now? If any of those others saw me like this, the uproar would be unprecedented. Just having wandered in here because of her sense of direction clearly wasn't going to cut it as an explanation.

I had to get Zodia out of here, right away.

"Not interested."

"You're so stiff! And not in a fun way. Can't you be a bit softer?"

"No."

"Come on. After a bath is a great time to play."

"You're talking about the promise from yesterday?" I said. Zodia nodded to my question. Maybe I should call in security and set a trap for her?

"If you lose, you have to strip," she stated.

"Keep your clothes on! It's a card game. Stop taking things in a weird direction!"

"Then we'll just play cards," she conceded. "But I want to play more types of games." She really had believed in my promise and come to play with me. If she was Sadeena's sister, this could end up getting pretty messy.

I really wanted to be wrong about this. If I wasn't, well, we'd just pile on and capture her alive.

"Anyway, just go and sit in a chair in the changing room."

"Sure thing!"

"Just to confirm, why did you come here today?"

"To take a look at the Heavenly Emperor."

"And you haven't seen her yet?" Just how bad was her sense of direction, seriously! If I wasn't reading this wrong, anyway, then after my bath I'd introduce her to Raphtalia and the others along with playing the game. As I considered all this, Zodia walked off toward the changing room. What a hassle . . . Then a breeze blew past me. She'd gone out, then?

Growing more concerned, I hurried through my bath.

"Phew. Here, I'm done. I'll play with you now—" Zodia wasn't there though. "Hey! Hello?" I called, but she didn't appear. Maybe she'd wandered off into the women's bath. We had the entire lodgings to ourselves, however, so I definitely would have heard a commotion if an unknown individual had been spotted wandering around.

"Ah, Master! You finished in the bath?" Filo chirped up.

"Rafu!" It was Filo and Raph-chan. I could still hear some background noise, suggesting the struggle with Atla was ongoing.

"Yeah, all done. One thing, Filo, Raph-chan, would you go and have a look in the women's bath for me? There might be a woman called Zodia in there."

"Really? Sure, okay."

"Rafu." The pair of them went to do as I asked and then came right back.

"No one there."

"Rafu?"

"Hmmm. So where's she gone?" That gust of wind wasn't her wandering off again, was it? She must be lost again. We'd have words, if we met again. Of course, combining her random comings and goings with her sense of direction, who knew when that might be. I didn't want her turning up in my bedroom.

"Master Naofumi!" Atla was yelling.

"They're still going at it? Can't they pipe down a little!" I shouted.

"She's using the things S'yne taught to her to play with big sis and her brother," Filo told me. Hmmm. Atla was definitely getting stronger. At least Raphtalia and Fohl were keeping up. "Sadeena is siding with Atla, saying that looks like more fuuuun. She wants to enjoy bathing with Masteeer toooo!"

"That drunkard, stirring up trouble again." The final battle was close. This wasn't what they should be wasting their time on. "I'd better go and stop them, anyway."

"Yeah. If they want to get in the bath with Master, they just have to jump over the fence," Filo chirped.

"Rafu." Filo hadn't done that this time, but she'd clearly been getting some ideas. I'd have to be careful going forward. With that, I headed back to Atla, and that calmed everything down.

"Today was fun too, little Naofumi," Sadeena remarked.

"That's easy for you to say." I looked over at Sadeena, who was fanning herself in the garden after her bath. Raphtalia and the others were tired and so they'd already gone to bed. Atla had been trussed up again and rolled out and was now sleeping under the watch of Fohl. She'd been on a real rampage recently. Hopefully this would help her cool off.

Sadeena had transitioned from bathing to drinking. With our forced march and all the training, Raphtalia and the rest of the gang were pretty worn out. It was strange, to be honest, that Sadeena still had any energy.

Me? I wasn't as exhausted as I thought.

Maybe it was because I'd got a good handle on using life force, and being focused on defense, I didn't have to move around too much. I should probably give out some nutritional supplements.

"So, little Naofumi, what do you need from me?" Sadeena went on.

"Well, there's some stuff going on."

"I'll strip down and standby, then."

"Where the hell did that come from!" Dammit. Why was I having so much trouble with people like this recently? I wasn't looking to settle down in this world!

"Thinking about it, I've heard a fair bit about Raphtalia's history, but there's lots of other stuff I don't know. I need to ask some additional questions, or problems may come up," I explained.

"Oh, that's all this is? Can't you just ask the other revolutionaries about it?"

"That's only going to get me fragments. Sadeena, this is about you too. There are too many holes in my knowledge of your past. Not to mention, it seems you have a sister now?"

"Little Naofumi. A woman needs to maintain some mystery if she is to allure men."

"Enough games. I launched this whole attack on Q'ten Lo in order to deal with Raphtalia's problems." At my demand, Sadeena took a drink, looked and me, and then slammed the cup down. Huh? There was a cup on the opposite side from me?

"Very well. Having come this far, it may be worth explaining things a little more." Her voice was different from her normal mocking tone. She sounded just like she had when she drank Raphtalia under the table prior to the Q'ten Lo attack. So she was finally ready to discuss this seriously. "What do you want to know first? You already know some details about Raphtalia's parents already, correct?" They were the bloodline of the Heavenly Emperor and left the nation due to the fighting over succession. I knew that much.

"I would like to hear that from you too, but first things first. I need to ask about you, Sadeena." Lots of people knew Sadeena, and she was often called by various names, including the water dragon's miko priestess and the miko priestess of carnage. I knew she'd worked in lots of different professions, but I had so much more that I needed to ask, especially in regard to how she never held back, even slightly, when fighting her own kind. We'd recently been able to capture them alive more often, but until entering Q'ten Lo, many of them had chosen to kill themselves rather than be captured.

I continued to inquire. "You're incredibly strong for one of your race, and I've never seen anyone use magic like you." We'd fought members of Sadeena's race numerous times, but I was yet to see anyone use the same lightning magic as Sadeena. I'd expected to face a horde of Sadeenas, but that hadn't happened. Not yet. Still, those battles hadn't been easy, with the nullification of our hero weapons forcing a reliance on pure technique.

"Oh my, you might be right. You've been doing so well, little Naofumi, so I guess I can share more of myself with you." With all her mocking stripped away, for once Sadeena actually started speaking honestly. "The village, settlement, whatever you want to call it, that I come from. We have some serious issues, even among our own race."

"Differences between your people, you mean?" I wondered. There were numerous different types of killer whale, after all. Quite different when compared to each other. A total of four types had been observed, if I recalled correctly, including resident fish eaters, transient marine mammal eaters, and offshores, or something like that. So they were a race like that, similar but not the same.

"You're careful with use of your demi-human and

therianthrope forms, aren't you? Any reasons for that?" I pondered.

"I stay in my therianthrope form as much as possible, it's true, in order to appear my most capable. I only use my demi-human form when I want to avoid attention, things like that. It was like that in Siltvelt, right?" I remembered Werner and those guys paying attention to that. The demi-human form was used as a way of showing no intent to attack. Sadeena likely created the impression of her therianthrope form being her normal state and then used the demi-human form for infiltration and the like.

"Although in Q'ten Lo the orca whales are probably treated as a related species and the same race," I ventured. This linked back to my previous discussion on killer whales. Those without the ability to turn into demi-humans were just called orcas. They were a closely related but different race and also treated differently from the "orcinus." Yes, this could all get confusing.

"Maybe my family was a little more involved with our bloodlines. Humans do that too, sometimes, don't they?" she contemplated.

"Yeah, sometimes. It was pretty clear in Melromarc, places like that." The queen, and Melty, probably had good families and were definitely invested in bloodlines.

The queen said something about the bloodline of the Shield Hero when Witch framed me.

"My family is the house that serves the water dragon and the house who carries out the punishments of the Heavenly Emperor. In other words, his executioners. The house that does all the dirty jobs, basically," she explained.

"Hold it there." Man, having a sister to replace Sadeena? A pretty twisted family.

"Yes?"

"So you serve the water dragon but act on behalf of Raphtalia's family? Isn't that a bit strange?"

"Well, like I said, it's our role to do the dirty jobs for those of noble standing, although it's treated as delivering the punishment of the gods," she went on. Hmmm. A complicated position, then.

"So you basically do the stuff the water dragon and Heavenly Emperor don't want to?"

"Oh my, well, if you put it like that, yes. The miko are positioned as the miko in service of the two gods."

"Okay, so moving on. Sadeena, you can use that lightning magic because of what? You've received some kind of special blessing?" I asked. Sadeena was a melee fighter and could use magic, and even cooperative magic, making her an incredibly versatile, all-round fighter.

Even if her innate abilities weren't considered, her specs were just too high.

"Oh, you're making me blush! All of these probing questions."

"Stop joking around." Sadeena had a talent for diverting the topic with those kinds of comments. I wasn't going to let her escape this time though.

"I was born with this lightning magic. It's rare too, so I'm told. There have been others with this power in my family, apparently, so maybe it's a family thing?"

"Hmmm. So you were born with it?"

"The orca whale and orca are generally based in water magic, but my family tends to have quite different properties."

"So it's an aspect of your family?"

"Maybe. But I'm an especially rare example. Just like how you don't get drunk, little Naofumi." How could I respond to that? Eating the rucolu fruit was considered disgusting. People even considered it sacrilegious. "By the time I was self-aware, I was aware of my lightning magic and could already use it." Being able to control lightning freely underwater, that had to be powerful. To be honest, the only time I'd even seen her close to being in trouble was when she fought us—and even then, I wasn't sure she was being serious during that battle.

So the fight with the Demon Dragon? Maybe that was the only time she really couldn't do anything.

"My house has long served the water dragon, you see. I started my work as the miko at a pretty young age and underwent rapid maturation since I was small." Demi-humans and therianthropes could be rapidly matured by leveling them up. Raphtalia had a big gap between her appearance and actual age too. Did this mean Sadeena had received a special education since she was small?

"After that, I started doing work for the village and nation. That's why I don't have many friends my own age," she said.

"It all makes sense now."

"Oh, little Naofumi, you're so mean!"

"Yeah, yeah. How did that environment turn you into this person, then?"

"Who knows? I'm not sure about that myself." Was this really just her natural personality?

"Also, I guess being able to train as much as I liked at the castle of the Heavenly Emperor in the old city is a part of it. I had the chance to learn whatever martial arts I wanted, from all sorts of people."

"You make it sound simple."

"You think it's okay for me to be a bit conceited here? Like, maybe I'm just an Atla-level combat genius?"

"Asking if it's okay to be conceited is a bit odd, you know," I quipped. It was true though. In all aspects, combat sense, everything, she was a bit of a high-spec monster. In fact, I almost felt like asking what she was bad at. In terms of being able to learn anything by watching it, just like Atla, Sadeena could indeed be said to have the same combat sensibilities.

"You do have an excellent sense for combat. I'll admit that," I maintained.

"You praised me! Yay!"

"This isn't a 'yay' situation!"

"My real reason was the drinking after the training, of course."

"I should have known. So you've been drinking since way back when?"

"Yeah, come to think of it. I guess I was avoiding reality. I had a lot of pressure from my family, stuff like that."

"I bet I could have had an honest conversation with you back then too." I said. Sadeena gave a wry smile at my comment.

"If I'd met you back then, little Naofumi, maybe I would have turned out like Atla." I didn't think they were so different even now, but I managed to hold that in. Still, if Sadeena came at us full strength, I didn't think

Raphtalia or Fohl would be able to stop her.

She continued. "We're getting off topic, anyway. I did three jobs. First, my work as the water dragon's miko priestess. This involved listening to the voice of the water dragon, receiving his blessings, and conducting divine ceremonies. Well, my parents did the ceremonies, so I really just listened to the voice of the water dragon." Sadeena was the miko priestess. A bit of a delinquent one, perhaps. I could easily picture her stealing holy wine and getting wasted on it. "I can still say all the prayers," she said.

"Okay."

"You're not interested in what I did as miko?"

"I just need an overview, not a play-by-play."

"You really don't cling to the past, do you, little Naofumi. I love that about you."

"I don't see why," I said. It didn't sound like much of a compliment.

"Next job, the miko for the Heavenly Emperor. Here there were also a variety of priestesses serving other things. And priests as well. If you must know, I was the representative of my species. When it came to the crunch, I had to fight a variety of foes as the symbol of authority."

"So more a general than a miko?"

"You're not wrong. These jobs are treated as priest-esses and priests because they serve a god. The old guy's master, the one who gives you so much trouble? Technically, he's also a priest." Man. That pickup artist, a priest?

Anyway, this meant it was like a noble rank, a title given to the best of the nation's generals and artisans. Hmmm. This really was quite a unique culture.

"Then, as an extension of that, the one responsible for handling the dark side of the country was the representative of the orca whale race, the water dragon's miko priestess," she continued to explain.

"You were an executioner? One who puts criminals to death?"

"That's right. My role was that of executioner. That's why I was called the priestess of carnage."

"I see." From what I was learning of the nation when Sadeena was here, it was clear she had occupied a pretty twisted position. It seemed there was still a lot I wasn't being told too.

"I had to perform all sorts of different executions. Shocking with lightning magic, chopping off heads with a katana, running them through with a harpoon. All sorts."

"Whew."

"There are all sorts of detailed stipulations about how to conduct the execution, depending on the crime. We might be a small country, but you'd be surprised. It also fed back into the issues we were having as a nation." In regard to executions, my limited experience was just violent comics and games and materials from long ago that I'd seen online. So I was completely unable to imagine the suffering of Raphtalia and the others, those who had undergone real torture.

"At my own discretion, I also sometimes fought the condemned. Like, if they could beat me, they could go free. That made it easier for them to accept their fate. A fight to the death rather than just being put to it." Sadeena had been forced to perform executions, just because it was her job. So she'd alleviated her guilt by giving the other side the illusion of a chance. I wasn't affirming her decision, necessarily, but someone had needed to do it. The dirty jobs, in the right way.

To put it one way, Sadeena was somehow broken as a human. But with an awareness of that, she'd also managed to overcome it. Somehow, even though she was older than me, I felt a weakness in Sadeena I hadn't seen before.

"I see." It would be easy to provide some cheap sympathy and pretend to understand, but that wasn't going to console Sadeena. That said, about the only thing I could do was sit at her side and silently listen to what she had to say.

So silence it was.

Sadeena gave her wine bottle a shake, gave me a cup, and then poured. She didn't want sympathy. Just listening was enough.

I took the cup, which brimmed with wine, and drank it down.

Sadeena laughed, and it didn't look like bravado to me; she really was enjoying this moment. Even if Sadeena suffered everything that I'd personally been through, the same litany of pain, she might still be sitting there laughing.

In fact, I was starting to feel a bit stupid, dragging so much baggage along with me. Just thinking that, though, certainly wasn't enough for me to be able to cut it all free.

"Sounds like a workplace with a lot of problems."

"Do you think so?"

"Yeah."

"My only real concern was not being an oracle."

"Ah, that suspicious power again," I said. That comment got Sadeena laughing. It didn't feel like she was drunk, but something else. Something a bit different.

"I was a terrible actor back then, so my worries were pretty obvious," she lamented. She never showed anything of her true self nowadays! "The blessings of the Heavenly Emperor would have allowed me to do some incredible things, so I was told. They must have been talking about the sakura stones of destiny. They weren't strewn about like they are today back when I lived here." Did this mean that only being blessed a little by the Heavenly Emperor had formed something of a complex for Sadeena? "My parents were pretty hard on me because of that. Always expecting so much. They weren't much like real parents to me at all."

"They just threw you into the work, from the sound of it."

"Yes. As early as I can remember, I was likely a match for them in raw strength."

"And I'm guessing your parents weren't weak. You were just too strong. The only reason you aren't an oracle is because you can handle your drink, meaning you didn't lose yourself and spout spiritual nonsense like those other lightweights."

"Oh my." Sadeena laughed at that too. "You might be right. I never made any serious mistakes, and if only I'd also been an oracle, it was said I would have been the greatest miko in history."

"Hey. Don't downplay the one power I've got—not getting drunk!"

"I know. It all seems very silly now. It was just a bunch of people getting drunk and proclaiming that their ancestors were visiting them and other impossible stuff," she lamented. What a crazy situation. These were the kind of abnormalities that only came into view with a wider perspective. I was almost starting to feel sorry for them.

My own parents, too, had been pretty hands-off. All parties had already been aware of that fact. Reaching my age, and coming to know something of the world at large, I understood now that there was such a thing as compatibility between parents and children. It wasn't that either side was at fault, but I did believe I had some experience with a case of incompatibility.

All of that said, Sadeena's family was really twisted.

Sadeena had been forced into becoming an adult without knowing the joy of being a child. I started to wonder if maybe I'd been doing the same thing to Raphtalia. Maybe she needed more time to blow off steam and act her age a little?

"The Heavenly Emperor at that time was Raphtalia's grandfather. He was sick all the time. He and Makina would abuse me all the time, saying I was a corrupted miko without any oracle powers," Sadeena continued.

"I hate them both already."

"Can't be helped. In either case, just as I was coming to feel these days would continue until I died, I met Raphtalia's father." Sadeena looked up at the sky as though enjoying the memory.

"The next Heavenly Emperor?" I said.

"Yeah. He had a real sense of responsibility, such credibility, and always had people around him." Even as she said it, Sadeena looked at me.

"Yes?"

"When you were looking after the kids in the village, little Naofumi, you reminded me of him. Maybe a bit softer. That kindness was the same."

"I'm not sure what to say to that." I mean, I was acting like a parent to Raphtalia, so I could maybe see some overlap there, but I wasn't kind. I was a dictator.

"After all the punishment I'd taken, he consoled me and asked me if there was anything wrong. Then we talked about all sorts of things," she went on. A key meeting in her life, huh. Hard to imagine a time when the robustly competent Sadeena had struggled with anything. "He could also hold his liquor. Boy, the man could drink. He could even hold his own against me, pretty much." She was obviously enjoying reminiscing and gave me a smile. "He was the greatest person I'd ever met, until you."

"So you liked him because he could drink? Or as, you know, a man?" I asked.

"Hmmm. We didn't really have that kind of relationship. Of course, I felt love for him, but he never looked at me like that. I mean, I wasn't exactly going around proclaiming my feelings," she explained. She wasn't? Then something had changed, because she was always trying it with me. She never did that with Raphtalia's father? She continued. "Among all the children of the Heavenly Emperor, he was the closest in the line of succession. But he had some younger half-siblings, I think." There had been some assassinations or something, right? Raluva had mentioned them.

"Carry on. Just what you remember," I said.

"Raphtalia's father also showed me around the old city. Took me to lots of interesting places."

"Sounds promising."

"He was a considerate person, but—perhaps due to that—it also felt like he'd experienced his fair share of bad stuff. He started talking to me because he wanted to know what kind of things an executioner really did."

"Curiosity killed the cat. He sounds like the type to get caught up in all sorts of trouble."

"You might be right, but I also have that to thank him for his saving me. Back then, I really was having a very hard time of it." She had been very unlucky with the life she was born into. That was a fact. It probably couldn't be helped if her personality was a little twisted as a result. She went on. "It really made an impression on me when, after hearing about my work, he apologized for asking so casually about such a painful topic."

"That was the first time anyone had said something like that to you?" I inquired. Sadeena looked up at the sky without any of her normal joking around. "You really did love him, didn't you?"

"Hmmm. Not in the way you are thinking, perhaps. Not after meeting you, little Naofumi, and comparing the two experiences," she reckoned. Seriously! But still, she knew her own mind. "And anyway, he already had someone he liked."

"Raphtalia's mother?" I ventured. Sadeena gave a quiet nod. Was there something there too? She divulged more. "She was a raccoon type, I believe, far from the Heavenly Emperor by blood. Of course, that didn't make any difference to Raphtalia's father. He chose her anyway."

"How did the two of them meet?"

"She was a maid in the castle. A great cook, and she

could handle other housework too. Smart, and kind. A real homemaker mom, you know? Raphtalia's father was totally smitten, and she made him work to win her over." From Sadeena's response, the whole chain of events sounded quite pleasant to behold. "Time passed like that, anyway, with the health of the Heavenly Emperor gradually getting worse, and so the discussion turned to who would take the position next. That was when the attacks started on Raphtalia's father, who was next in line. They called him unworthy to hold the post due to his general demeanor." Yeah, I heard about things like this in Japan's history. In the Edo period, all that infighting among the harem. I hated those bitter power struggles among women—or perhaps more accurately, those who infested a world that was finally at peace after a long period of conflict.

In any case, I could see why Raphtalia's father would run away from that power.

She went on. "He'd never done anything publicly wrong, but the rumors stuck. The condition of the Heavenly Emperor only worsened after he met with Raphtalia's father too." That definitely sounded like some kind of plot. "He told me that if things carried on like this, the struggle to become the next Heavenly Emperor was going to get him killed. If the only other choice was to get embroiled in an unwanted conflict, he decided to flee and asked me to join them."

"He dragged you into something nasty."

"Not really. Raphtalia's parents were the only ones who were nice to me, and I was completely out in the cold when it came to the struggle to become emperor." Without that suspicious oracle ability, it seemed her standing had been pretty low.

Hah! Imagine believing that Sadeena had no natural abilities. Did they even have eyes?

"He was looking for people to aid him. I talked with the water dragon about what I should do, and he told me that I should go along to protect them."

"So you chose to leave."

"Yes. From the water dragon, some other collaborators, and Raluva and the current resistance, I was given the ostensible punishment of having my level reset, and then I was assigned to protect Raphtalia's parents." So she had played the role of protector back then too. She continued. "During our time on the road, Raphtalia's parents became like my own and taught me all sorts of things. Gave me a taste of what a normal household was like. From my point of view, they are like my real parents. Those memories are more precious to me than anything." That explained why Sadeena treasured

Raphtalia's parents, and Raphtalia, so much. "After that, we drifted through many countries, just letting the flow take us, until we ended up in Melromarc, with their exclusion of demi-humans. And that was when we met the governor who wanted consolidation with the demi-human nations."

"It sounds like a difficult time. The way Raphtalia talks to you, though, it seems she keeps her distance a bit," I wondered. They didn't feel like sisters who had been raised together. Sadeena was more like an older girl from the same neighborhood.

"That's because once little Raphtalia's mother got pregnant I kept a little more distance, of course. Raphtalia's father didn't seem to mind, but I didn't want their daughter turning out like me!"

"I don't think they could have made that happen, even if they'd wanted to."

"Oh my!"

So these two people so precious to her had died in the first wave. Of course she would care for Raphtalia. Receiving no love from her own parents, Raphtalia's parents had instead provided so much love and caring.

Thinking of it like that, Sadeena really was like Raphtalia's big sister.

"That's given me some background on your origins,

Sadeena, and about Raphtalia's parents. Finally, I need to hear about the bloodline of the current Heavenly Emperor," I declared.

"In regard to that, I don't know any more than the reports."

"I guess not." The information provided by Raluva was that the battle for succession had seen many assassinations and other skullduggery, and now there was only one person left in Q'ten Lo who was the bloodline of the Heavenly Emperor.

Furthermore, that person was a child.

A child who loved filolials, had given the order to protect life, and placed sakura stone of destiny blessings on his underlings like he was giving out candy.

The real power lay behind the throne, then, with the Heavenly Emperor simply acting as a figurehead. Makina was the real one pulling the strings.

Then she stated, "Still, I never believed I'd be back here in Q'ten Lo, trying to take the nation. Never even dreamed it." With that, Sadeena took a drink. There was a cup across from her, even if no one was there. Maybe she was making an offering to Raphtalia's parents.

"Like we have a choice. If you've got a complaint, share it with the people here who let this mess happen," I sneered.

"I'm not complaining. It does feel strange, though, once having been so fixated on a pointless position."

"Hmmm." In a rare moment for me, I moved close to the eloquent Sadeena, gave her a hug, and patted her on the back.

"I think Raphtalia's parents would be proud of you too. Maybe they'd tell you that you're pushing yourself too hard. That you need to relax a little," I consoled. She was always so bubbly but was already clearly trying so hard. The reason she was stirring up trouble with Atla was surely because she wanted to confirm Raphtalia's real strength.

"But I've failed to protect so many people. Those in the village, and even Raphtalia's parents themselves," she lamented.

"I know this isn't going to be much help, coming from me. But I'm still going to say it. What do you think you are, an all-powerful god? It would have been incredible if you could have saved them, of course, but unfortunately, none of us are gods." At least when I had Raph-chan on my head, I hadn't seen any ghosts in the village. Raphtalia also seemed to have been suffering from nightmares, but she'd gotten over it. "I'm only capable of making irresponsible comments, perhaps, but if anyone said things like 'Sadeena, you should have saved us! You liar!' I'd say we just cut them loose. If there's someone who relies on others that much, we don't need them." Wasn't that the case? Wasn't that relying completely on someone else? I was the Shield Hero. How many times had I been left wondering why I had to defend those so reliant on me?

Of course, defending people was my only way forward. So I defended them.

I asked her, "Would Raphtalia's parents have said something like that?"

"No, never. They were more the type to run ahead and try to distract the enemy, if it meant saving their allies."

"Exactly. Sadeena, you searched for the Lurolona slaves in Zeltoble in order to save Raphtalia. I think that's more than enough." Even if the slave hunters had been tracked, it would have been difficult for Sadeena, a demi-human therianthrope, to rescue Raphtalia and the others from the village if they reached thoroughly corrupt Melromarc. So she had saved them indirectly in Zeltoble. She'd done everything possible for them.

Indeed, her only piece of bad luck was that I had purchased Raphtalia. It could be that I was the one Raphtalia didn't need.

I consoled, "Anyway, now I'm the one acting as a

parent for Raphtalia. I'll be careful to do my best without applying too much pressure so that you don't have to worry." I stopped hugging Sadeena and looked at her.

"So I should be aiming to become your wife and Raphtalia's step-mom, then?" she probed. I could only sigh in exasperation. There was no reasoning with Sadeena on this point. She then announced, "Well then, little Naofumi. I'm going to do my best too." Sadeena tried to stand up as though she was ready to jump right on me. I kept her down with gentle pressure on her shoulders and stood up first.

I had to get out of here. She was ready to pounce.

"No need to try too hard! Don't lose yourself in drink. Try getting some sleep instead!" I asserted.

"Oh, little Naofumi! Don't you dare run from me!"

"What's all this noise—Sadeena! What are you doing?" Raphtalia turned up, coming to see what all the noise was about, and that only exasperated the situation. Business as usual, then.

In the end, there wasn't time to talk about Zodia or whether she was actually Sadeena's sister.

Chapter Ten: Shield Power-Up Method

The following morning, we held our final war council and marched on the old city.

"Today we need to capture this so-called old city. Do you think they'll come at us full strength?" I inquired of a nearby officer.

"According to our scouts, they have deployed their forces in front of the old city and are ready to engage us at any time," the officer reported. So our enemy, too, was really going to get serious this time.

"They're not going to be annoying by holing up behind fortifications, are they?" I groaned.

"Do they stand a chance against us though?" Sadeena questioned. If they had a sakura stone of destiny barrier, maybe—but if I was the enemy, I wouldn't fancy my chances.

Heroes were useful at a time like this. Especially me. With my sakura stone of destiny shield, it made it tough to take us down, and Raphtalia and Itsuki were especially high-powered. It would be difficult without some skilled officers capable of taking each of us down.

Then there was the policy that Raphtalia was

marching under: to abandon the order restricting the harming of animals. She had much support from the people, meaning keeping them under control was definitely going to be demanding resources.

Another officer ran up and shouted, "Reporting! Information is coming in that those under the Heavenly Emperor are raiding the settlements we have taken!"

There it was, then. That was their play. Attack the exposed locations and slow down our progress. We were fighting to defeat the false Heavenly Emperor, perpetrator of the forbidden, and so we needed to gather a certain amount of support from the people. If we ignored the attacks on these towns and villages, the people might end up thinking that nothing was going to change other than who it was standing over them.

What choice did I have? I'd send out a selection of the most annoying among my retinue.

Atla and Gaelion. Fohl could go too.

"What is it, Master Naofumi?" Atla snapped to attention.

"Kwaa?"

"Yes?" Fohl chimed in too.

I could have also asked Itsuki to go, but—nah, they should be fine.

"Go capture the brigands causing trouble in the

towns and villages we've occupied. It doesn't matter how many days it takes; maintain the peace until I call for you. You'll need to work in tandem with the Silt-velt troops following from behind." Atla was well-liked in Siltvelt. They had sent considerable numbers to the revolutionary cause too.

"Very well!"

"Kwaa!"

"Why do I have to follow your orders again?" Fohl was as rebellious as ever. Then Raphtalia stepped in.

"Fohl. Will you please do this for me? Atla is excited to do this for Mr. Naofumi, and you're the one best suited to stop her from going too far. I think it would be safer for her to get away from the front lines too."

"Ah, if you think so, big sister. Very well."

"Kwaaa!" With that, Gaelion turned from baby into father mode. Atla and Fohl climbed aboard.

"We will execute your orders to the letter, Master Naofumi!" Atla dutifully replied.

"Kwaaa!"

"We've got this," Fohl too conceded. With that, Atla and her party flew away on Gaelion.

"Right, that should handle some of the issues behind us. In either case, we've got an excellently located base of operations right in front of us. Let's go."

As we approached, a large castle and city came into view, with forces arrayed in front of them, standing ready to fight at any moment. They were seeking to control the field, making us come to them. When we also formed up into easy-to-fight formations and started to close in, one of the enemy units raised a flag indicating they had no hostile intent and started to move toward us.

One of our officers came running up and announced, "It's a messenger unit. Rather than spill meaningless blood in an all-out conflict, they are inquiring as to whether this could all be settled by having two representatives from each side fight. For their side, the water dragon's miko priestess will be fighting."

"Oh my!" Sadeena exclaimed.

"They have the gall to attack the towns and villages behind us, and then this? Send them packing!" I barked. Upon receiving my response, the distant enemies showed surprise on their faces, and then they retreated. It was starting to look like their command structure wasn't in the healthiest position.

A short while later, they started to abandon the defense of the old city and withdraw completely.

Again, an officer appeared and stated, "Another message has been received. Due to an oversight on their part, the water dragon's miko priestess declared that they will simply hand the old city over to us and then depart." It looked like she had control of her forces, at least. A strong sense of duty, perhaps. I'd really wanted to see her—if only to make sure she really wasn't Zodia.

We could have chased after them, put the boot in a little, but doing so against an enemy who was leaving of its own accord would paint us as the bad guys here. Best not to do that.

With that, then, our resounding—resoundingly easy—victory in taking the old city was complete.

Entering the old city, we found ourselves warmly welcomed.

The people were practically begging us to take over, and even some of the enemy soldiers stayed behind to join the revolution. Honestly, the real reason for being so well received was clearly because of the idiocy of the current Heavenly Emperor.

With that, anyway, we headed swiftly toward the castle in the old city.

This should have been a major base of enemy operations, but we were arriving after the enemy leaders posted here had already fled to the east. I really hoped I wasn't underestimating the stupidity of these guys.

"We salute the true Heavenly Emperor!" chanted

men who flipped to our side. With the capture of the old city, skilled generals who had been demoted to posts out in the sticks were now siding with our forces, increasing the size of our lands at an incredible pace. Our forces were expanding at an almost unnatural rate.

Just how much stupidity could the forces of the opposing Heavenly Emperor pull off? It was like they were going for some kind of record.

After that, Raphtalia was shown to a place called the Sanctuary in order to perform the rite of appointing her as Heavenly Emperor. We left the castle, passed through a forest of tall, verdant, beautifully mossy trees, and came to a spot within it that had a yin-yang seal depicted there.

A small, well-maintained river was running between the trees. It really was all quite picturesque.

"Here we shall perform the ritual of appointment for the Heavenly Emperor. Lady Raphtalia, please, step this way," an important-looking official announced. Raluva, Sadeena, and other key figures in the revolution all formed a circle around her, and the showy ceremony got underway. Raphtalia herself looked as though she was being consumed by the very air here, withering away before my eyes.

The miko outfit looked great on her though.

When the enchantment-like blessing finished, the light from the massive trees—ah, they were sakura lumina, of course—started to twinkle down onto Raphtalia.

"Ah. What's going on? I feel something very strange," she murmured as the light bathed her. Wow, it was like her tail was glowing! What was this, a beast transformation? Was she going to turn into Raph-chan?

"Mr. Naofumi, please don't make that look. I dislike the sparkle in your eyes."

"Concentrate on the ritual, please, Raphtalia," I told her. She sighed at my tone.

"I know, and I am. I'm starting to see something in my field of vision, actually. Is this—the blessing—the ability to activate sakura stones of destiny?" Raphtalia said, beckoning me over.

"What is it?"

"I'm not sure. Mr. Naofumi, give me your hand—" As she asked, I put my hand out. Then Raphtalia took it with both of her own hands, raising them all up as though praying and then touching them to her forehead. Then some text appeared.

Pacifier's Blessing received!
Spirit Binding Limited Release 2: seal resistance (medium) acquired!

"Hmmm. I tried to apply more than that, but they were repelled," she stated.

"An affinity problem, most likely. So? Can you activate the sakura stone of destiny barriers now?" I asked.

"Yes, it looks like it."

"Oh my!"

"I should start by applying them to everyone here. They are definitely going to need it in the future."

"Yeah, good idea." And so everyone received the blessings of the Heavenly Emperor, through Raphtalia. That should provide us with some means to resist the interference of our enemies. If they put up a barrier, our barrier would apparently nullify it.

"There is something that concerns me. What's that back there?" As I asked, I pointed to a place farther inside where the ritual was being performed, beneath a large tree. "Isn't that a dragon hourglass?"

"I was wondering the same thing," Raphtalia said. It definitely looked like a dragon hourglass, buried in the roots of the tree—although it also looked to have a slightly different design. Was it functioning, then?

"I think that's what it is. This is where they used it on me, back when I was here," Sadeena mentioned.

"So it is, huh?" I remarked.

Sadeena explained more. "Yes. I received the protection of the Water Dragon and had a special class-up.

I never would have returned to that level of strength without the help of you and the others, little Naofumi." Thinking about it now, Sadeena had past experience with both class-ups and resets, then.

I see. So this was where it happened.

"Seriously, if you knew there was a dragon hourglass here, you could have said something," I grumbled. With this we could use Raphtalia's Return Dragon Vein to go straight back to Melromarc. "We've been away from the village for a while. I've been getting a bit concerned."

Raphtalia concurred. "Indeed. We've captured a lot of Q'ten Lo too, so I'd like to just take a quick trip back and check things out."

"Excuse me, Lady Raphtalia, but what exactly are you talking about?" Raluva ventured. He and the other revolutionary leaders clearly had some questions.

"Of course. That dragon hourglass is used to implement class-ups, right? Well, Raphtalia can also use them to instantly travel to distant lands," I told them.

"S-she can? But we really cannot afford to have Lady Raphtalia, the very pillar of our revolution, go off traveling at this point in time," he went on. I gave Raluva and the others a bit of a glare, eyes narrowed. Raphtalia was also applying a bit of silent pressure. It wasn't like we were doing this for the sake of the nation, and the revolutionaries were definitely aware of that. Having them come out with this now didn't sit right with me.

"We'll come right back. In either case, we need to spend a few days here, appealing to the new order we've created, correct?" I told them. It would be difficult to clash with the Heavenly Emperor's forces right away. We'd been forced to send Atla and the others out to deal with their silly makeshift attack strategy too. It would be a few days before we were whole again. Taking that time to bolster our strength didn't seem like a bad idea.

"What's this? I see three stone tablets of some kind," I reported.

"What could they be? Maybe we can learn some kind of special magic from them?" Raphtalia replied.

"I wonder." I approached and took a better look at the text on the tablets surrounding the dragon hourglass.

"It's the Hero language," she asserted.

"Yeah. It's got some magic text on it too, meaning only certain people can read it. This is heavy stuff," I remarked, and as I touched the tablet, text floated into my field of vision. It was the exact same text as back in the Orochi's stone chamber. I read it out.

"Holy Shield power-up methods, number one: share the power-up methods from other holy weapons *and* vassal weapons," I read aloud.

"Oh my. We've seen that before," Sadeena said.

"Is that—" S'yne began.

"She is asking if that's true about the vassal weapons," S'yne's doll finished. As S'yne traced the text with her finger, she went on. "Apparently, she cannot read it."

"Looks like only the Shield Hero can," I announced and punched the tablet—a bit rashly, perhaps. "Get off my back! Just how many of the same thing do they need to leave lying around?"

"Mr. Naofumi, calm yourself," Raphtalia soothed.

"Itsuki!" He was also with us, so I called him over. I didn't get a chance after the ruins collapsed last time, but I really needed to see if it said the same thing for Itsuki.

"Can you read this?" I asked him.

"Let me see." With that, Itsuki read the tablet. He'd been studying a bit of magic, so he should be able to handle this by now. Rishia had been training him pretty hard.

"Bow Hero power-up methods, number one: increase the capabilities and rarity of the weapon itself and find powerful rare weapons." This was what Itsuki had explained to us before, wasn't it? Just more information we already knew.

"Looks like this is a power-up method that you have already used," I stated.

"Seems likely. Still, Naofumi, this is the first time we've found a clear explanation of sharing power-up methods," he replied. Yeah, that was a good point. It felt like stumbling over an instruction booklet.

"Let's take a look at the other two," I said. Itsuki and I both read the next one.

"Holy Shield power-up methods, number two: trusting and being trusted leads to an increase in abilities." The crystal on my shield glowed.

Itsuki's, meanwhile, was an explanation of ore enhancement.

"This is a power-up method too?" I wondered.

"Mr. Naofumi, does that ring any bells?" Raphtalia asked.

"Huh?" At Raphtalia's question, I took a moment to think back. Had I experienced anything like this? Trust? I believed in Raphtalia and the others, but was that boosting my abilities?

Raphtalia began, "When we were in Melromarc, fighting the high priest of the Church of the Three Heroes, or when fighting the Spirit Tortoise, you were pretty tough, Mr. Naofumi. But then, in Kizuna's world, you complained about not improving as much as before."

"Yeah, you're right. I did." So at the times I was improving better than I expected, maybe that bonus had unknowingly been in effect?

"I felt far more powerful during that time too. Perhaps being trusted by Mr. Naofumi was providing a bonus to my abilities," she went on. Yeah. That sounded likely. Back then, Raphtalia had quickly got stronger and stronger. Of course, she was far stronger now.

"This might also explain why Ren and I were weaker," Itsuki flatly stated, his voice still lacking all emotion. Those two had started to be hated by their countries and people, after all. Branded as being weaker than expected.

That said, if you didn't believe in the sharing of power-up methods, maybe they didn't work at all? Hmmm. Convoluted.

"Let's look at the next one." I also had a feeling that actual understanding would lead to an enhanced modifier. The sharing of power-up methods was definitely a thing. My abilities had enhanced since checking the text in the Orochi's stone chamber.

Giving consideration to all of this, I looked at the third tablet.

"Holy Shield power-up methods, number three: energy boost." When I read the explanation text, the item EP was quietly added to status magic. I continued. "The heroes have an energy that they draw out automatically as power from the weapons, and this is always active.

Assigning this energy to skills will allow more powerful skills to be used. Anyway, that's what it says." Which meant what? We had auto Muso Activation? It sounded like simple possession of a legendary weapon provided a permanent, complete state of Muso Activation. "Energy Boost" was also there now, under Help. So if Muso Activation was already active, it shouldn't be possible to activate another one and have two running.

"Energy Boost?" Itsuki followed something with his eyes and then manifested a burst of life force.

"Feeeeeh! How is Master Itsuki suddenly able to use life force?" Rishia suddenly blurted out. I checked, and the flow of life force from Itsuki had definitely increased—and from me too—although they had a slightly different quality. Everything seemed to click into place when I considered Hengen Muso Style as the artificial recreation of this power.

"EP have now appeared, which we can mix into skills, magic, and even attacks. They seem to work in combination with SP and magic, but just being aware of them consumes them too. This is going to require some practice," Rishia explained. Acquiring this so easily? So what had all that hard work been for? Man, this world could be a real pain.

Still, it all came down to how it was used. Get that

wrong and it would simply chew through the points with no effect. So maybe we'd now achieved easy use of life force, but it still didn't mean we understood it. That seemed the way to think of it.

"Raphtalia has a vassal weapon from another world, so they can't be shared," I said.

"That's right. It would be convenient if we could do that, but I can already use life force, so it isn't so vital," she replied. She couldn't use Muso Activation though. She'd been able to imbue it into skills for a while, having learned it from Glass, if I remember correctly.

It looked like S'yne could do it too. To be honest, it was a bit annoying that they could do all this stuff as though taking it for granted.

I didn't really feel like I'd got much stronger.

"Still, why do you think the shield power-up methods are written here?" she asked.

"You think maybe it has something to do with that stuff Glass talked about? The fusing of the worlds due to the waves? Siltvelt and Q'ten Lo are both nations of demi-humans, right?" I replied. That made them the territory of the Shield Hero.

Indeed, looking at a world map, there were many demi-human territories. Taken in that light, it perhaps wasn't so odd that the power-up method for the shield would be hidden in Q'ten Lo—although here they had the odd name of "spirit implements."

"Well, if we bring Ren and have him read these tablets, we might understand more," I surmised. All sorts of reasons came to mind, such as the order in which the worlds were fusing. We were still at the stage of collecting materials, prior to being able to make a judgment.

"Yes, good idea. Shall we take a quick trip to Melromarc, then?" Raphtalia suggested.

"Sounds good." Ren was currently the only hero there, and that, among other things, had definitely been weighing on my mind. This would all be pointless if the village was taken out while we took Q'ten Lo.

With that, then, we used the dragon hourglass found in Q'ten Lo and transferred back to Melromarc.

Chapter Eleven: A Brief Return Trip

We traveled to the village using Portal Shield.

"We're back!"

"Rafu!" Filo and Raph-chan gave cheerful shouts.

"It looks like there haven't been any problems here," Raphtalia stated.

"Ah, they're back! Yay!" Keel spotted us and rushed over. "Welcome home! Have you defeated those bad guys trying to kill Raphtalia?" The last time we'd talked to them it had been the morning before leaving Silt-velt by ship, so a fair while ago. Hearing Keel, Ren also showed up.

"Naofumi, how's it going?" he said.

"We just found a dragon hourglass during our trip, actually, so we came to check in at the village," I explained.

"I see."

"We've made good progress though! What about you?"

"No more attacks have come at all. I'm thinking it's since they worked out you're striking at Q'ten Lo," he answered. Hmmm. So they didn't have the leeway to strike here anymore. They'd had issues with things like language already. And bringing in more manpower over such a distance wasn't going to be easy. Not to mention, with the homeland under attack, they'd need everyone they could gather back at home.

"One thing, Naofumi. What did you say to Eclair prior to your departure?" he questioned.

"What do you mean?"

"Eclair has been complaining about something you said to her. About not having any capacity as a governor? Something like that?"

Uwah. Yeah, in order to keep Melty happy, I might have told Eclair to back down. I'd only told the truth though, so it couldn't be helped. It was a fact that Eclair had spent far more time training than she had dealing with paperwork.

Best to just ignore this topic and carry on.

"If the village isn't going to be attacked, Ren, I'm adding you to the invasion party. You're with us now. No ships involved anymore, so you'll be fine."

"Phew, good thing." Ren nodded, looking relieved. He really didn't like swimming, did he? "I admit, it was a bit worrying, watching this place in your absence. Everyone in the village has been quite worried, with S'yne gone as well." For that reason, having S'yne here had been quite convenient. Even though she wasn't supposed to go, she went anyway.

"They have anti-hero techniques and other unique stuff, but honestly, the enemy is so stupid it's actually getting a bit ridiculous," I quipped.

"It's sad, almost, that I can't deny that statement at all," Raphtalia muttered, sounding almost lost for words.

We proceeded to give Ren a simple breakdown of everything that had happened in Q'ten Lo. Of course, that included having discovered the weapon power-up methods.

"So this will help make us stronger?" he asked.

"I want to see Raphtalia's homeland for myself!" Keel's eyes were shining, tail wagging, as he asked. "Take me with you! Please, take all of us with you!"

"Even so, we still don't know when the village might be attacked. I'm worried about leaving this place too undefended," I said.

"So why not take everyone from the village?" Ah. Take everyone here to Q'ten Lo? I looked at Raphtalia, and she was making quite a face.

"That's too many people, surely. We'll take you for a visit once everything there is taken care of. Just hold on until then."

"I thought it was a pretty good idea," Ren said.

"If we all go into battle, leaving the village empty, what happens if thieves show up?" I cautioned. We had gold and other valuables here, in no small number.

"We could leave Melty in charge. How about that?" Hmmm. That was an option.

"Mr. Naofumi." Raphtalia still wasn't convinced.

"Look at it this way, Keel. We're in Q'ten Lo, essentially fighting a war. I'm not raising you all to fight on the battlefield, so just have a little more patience," I explained. We couldn't afford to get distracted from our true goal—to rebuild and prepare for the waves.

"I see. Too bad," he groaned.

"Once all the problems there are cleared up, I'll take you." It was a good place for a bit of sightseeing. I'd definitely give it some thought.

"Maaaster! Can I go and see Mel-chan?" Filo was clearly glad to be visiting.

"Yeah, off you go. Just stay in the village and we'll get you later, so have some fun."

"Yaaay! Mel-chan!" Filo was gone in the blink of an eye.

"One other thing. They have hot springs over there that are effective on curses. Seeing as we didn't get a portal to the Cal Mira islands sorted out, maybe we can use them to heal ourselves," I surmised. We were suffering from a number of cursed heroes, including myself, and it was about time we took care of that. We were definitely at a disadvantage in battle due to the weakening they caused.

"Rafu." Raph-chan went to greet the monsters in the village. We should probably go about recovering Rat and Wyndia from Siltvelt too.

"I have to say it again, this teleportation is really convenient," I commented. A distance it would take weeks to cover on Filo or Gaelion, traveled in an instant. "Normally it should be available at all times, but there are too many regions we can't use it now. It's a real pain."

"Yeah," Ren mumbled.

"So? Ren, have you learned to swim?"

"Bubba Sword can now swim about fifteen meters! I taught him!"

"Hmmm." I looked at Ren, and he looked away. All of this time, various techniques, and he could only swim fifteen meters?

"Don't be too hard on him, Mr. Naofumi," Raphtalia reprimanded.

And that was how we ended up taking Ren to Q'ten Lo.

Rat and Wyndia had made good progress with their

ecology research in Siltvelt. It was a perfect jumping-off point to bring them with us. When I showed a branch of sakura lumina to Rat, her eyes had sparkled as she investigated it. Her curiosity in Q'ten Lo was definitely increasing.

"Oh! That looks like an interesting ecosystem! Count us in!" she exclaimed.

"Where's Gaelion?" Wyndia asked.

"On a separate operation, providing transport to Atla and her group. We'll meet up again with them soon."

"Okay."

"Right, we're going to go and check out the vicinity."

"Go ahead. There might still be enemies around here, so be careful."

"I know the drill." With that, the two of them headed out. They were going to be joining the rear support but bringing them with us looked to definitely advance their research.

After that, I also checked in with Imiya's uncle, who was running the weapon shop.

"Master and Erhard are here?" he asked.

Seeing as he wouldn't be gone for long, I had him close up shop and led him to Motoyasu II's workshop in Q'ten Lo.

"Yeah. They should have arrived at the workshop by now. Let's go and see them. Come with me."

"Sure." Imiya's uncle, if I remembered correctly, had his training as a blacksmith interrupted by family issues. He'd filled in a few gaps by helping the old guy out, but this was a good opportunity for him to get some proper experience.

As another plus, it wouldn't hurt to have another pair of eyes on Motoyasu II.

All of those factors in play, I took Imiya's uncle to the old guy and his master.

"Oh? It's Tolly! Kid, what's going on here?" the old guy asked. We'd arrived at Motoyasu II's workshop to find an incredibly large forge. Everything was well tended to, and it even included an ironworks. The furnace was always lit, and the smokestack on the roof always belched smoke. It even had magical facilities. Just from that perspective, the old guy's store couldn't hold a candle to all this. Of particular note was a device that looked to have some real magical properties, an oven that looked like it might bake bread connected to some kind of handle.

"There was a dragon hourglass in the old city. Knowing you've still got a lot of work to do, I had him close the shop at home and brought him here," I told the old guy.

"That makes me worry a little about Melromarc, but

that's definitely a big help," he said.

"Geh! Now Tolly too?" Motoyasu II looked first at Imiya's uncle and then glared at me. "You fiend! How much pressure are you putting on me?"

"Just shut up and keep working. You can have your fun once you've taught the old guy and Imiya's uncle all of your techniques!"

"Shut it! I had a splitting headache that lasted three days, thanks to you!" he bellowed.

"Don't look at me. You ordered those drinks," I snapped. I only made the, shall we say, *adjustments*.

"It's been tough watching master and making sure he doesn't run off," the old guy commented, crossing his arms. "With Tolly here that should get easier."

"Well, okay. I'll do my best," Imiya's uncle said, looking like the responsibility was maybe a bit much for him—a reaction very much like his niece would have given in the same situation.

"Oh, and those Spirit Tortoise materials you were asking about, old guy? I made the arrangements, so just say the word."

"Great! That's a big help. If my master and I work on them together, I'm sure we'll be able to make some great new gear!"

"Damn your eyes, all of you! Very well, Tolly! I'm

going to hammer you into shape, so I expect a cut of your profits later!" he growled. What crazy conditions. He was training two students, so he expected to see a return? Well, bad luck, pervert. Any profits created by Imiya's uncle would be coming to me. Nothing for you, old goat!

"Ah, something else. I brought Ren along too, the Sword Hero," I announced.

"Huh? Is this the moment you introduce me?" Ren spoke up, having quietly listened to us until that point.

"Yes. We've got a sword that looks pretty good. I was thinking of having you copy it, Ren," I told him.

"It's still being purified. I've no idea what will happen if you lay your grubby fingers on it," Motoyasu II growled and pointed to the weapon hanging on the wall in a corner of the room. "Even with the facilities here, this is going to take a bit more time."

"A sword? Interesting. It does have an incredible energy. Like, I feel the sword . . . throbbing, I might say." As he spoke, Ren placed his hand on the hilt of his own sword.

"Ah? Interested in weapon-making, are you?" Motoyasu II spat.

"Ah, well. A little. I do like to collect fine weapons."

"Hmmm. You've got a woman-repelling aura about

you, much preferable to that Shield moron. I think we're going to get on. Very well. Maybe I'll teach you a few things, if you'll help me escape later," he went on. Seriously, he had some stones. Saying stuff like that right in front of my face!

"S-sure, that sounds good. My name is Ren Amaki." What the hell was Ren smiling for? He'd been roundly mocked! "Woman-repelling" was not a compliment!

"Enough of this, anyway. Ren, you just keep an eye on that old perv," I commanded.

"Very well." He nodded. With that, I left Ren at the workshop.

"My sword! Noooo!" Motoyasu II's cries rang out the moment after we left.

"I'm s-sorry! I completely forgot. My curse makes things I touch degrade!" The damage was one sakura stone of destiny sword. It wasn't going to be easy to get Ren to copy any weapons. I promptly ordered him to head to the hot springs as soon as possible in order to fully recover from the curse.

Chapter Twelve: Past and Present

A few days had passed since the occupation of the old city.

In order to expose Raphtalia's appeal to as many as possible, we were showing her off around the city, dressed in her miko outfit. Having already captured two-thirds of Q'ten Lo, the country now basically belonged to us. And in the eastern city representatives of each race from across the nation were turning against the Heavenly Emperor and choosing to join our forces.

Atla and her party had been stamping out fires too, extinguishing much of the drama caused by the Heavenly Emperor's forces. While it seemed that the opposing water dragon's miko priestess had apparently given orders to end the terrorist-style attacks, many of those on her side were not paying much attention.

The main suspects, of course, were the underlings of the poisonous power behind the throne. She had to be quite the imbecile herself to believe that was all it would take to defeat us.

Honestly, I'd started hoping that the water dragon's miko priestess would quickly switch to our side and just end this. The standing Heavenly Emperor was getting quite the reputation for trickery and deceit, and the more damage those tactics did, the more people turned to Raphtalia.

On the other battlefields after taking the old city, Ren and Itsuki had taken an advance force and marched on the eastern capital—but all the village and towns along their route had capitulated without bloodshed.

The water dragon's miko priestess, who had fled in the face of the enemy, had been taken back to the city in the east. The sakura destiny spheres deployed by any who did resist were, as we had expected, canceled out by the sakura destiny spheres placed by Raphtalia, who now could do that since she underwent the rite of succession.

With that shift in the balance of power, the Heavenly Emperor's forces couldn't touch Ren, Itsuki, or Sadeena. Atla and her party were continuing to put down any resistance that occurred behind us. Atla was working well with the forces coming in from Siltvelt, and the suppression was apparently proceeding apace. Ren had been quite complimentary about the techniques possessed by this nation, but now it was possible to just muscle through on the basis of our superior stats. Sorry, did you say civil war? What civil war? *That* was basically the point we were reaching.

In all honesty, it almost looked like we could just end the Q'ten Lo invasion and return home, but I was yet to achieve my goal of punishing those who had started all this.

"Mr. Naofumi."

"Hmmm?" Raphtalia appeared during a moment of downtime in planning our operations. Sadeena and most anyone else who could fight were away on the front lines. I was going to join them tomorrow. S'yne was posted in front of my room as I took a break. She'd completely become my bodyguard. Tomorrow we were going to take Filo, who was waiting on standby. With her speed, so long as we didn't meet any enemies, we'd reach the eastern capital in a single day.

We were getting pretty close.

"What direction is the operation going to take?" she asked.

"For a start, we need to secure the opposing Heavenly Emperor. He needs to be punished, of course, and if we don't completely extract the festering pus at the heart of this nation, we're just going to end up repeating all of this again," I said. According to our incoming information, the current Heavenly Emperor was simply being used. He'd been raised up without even realizing it, and the real ones pulling the strings were those around him.

"If we're doing this, we're doing it right."

"Exactly. That said, I think learning about your origins, Raphtalia, has been one good thing about all this."

"I'm not really bothered about all that. I'm happy to learn about my father and mother, but I'm still just myself. Raphtalia from Lurolona, that's all I need to be." I looked at Raphtalia's face. She clearly had complex feelings about this whole queen business. Once we saved the world, and once I'd gone home, which path would Raphtalia choose? By some measure, it looked like the results were already in.

"Sure, Raphtalia, but still. It's a fact that the political situation in Q'ten Lo is unstable. If you choose to hide yourself away, a large number of people are going to lose their guiding light."

"I know."

"I understand you don't want to accept this burden. Until you can step aside, then, it's about how much we can settle things down here, or who we can leave it all to."

"Yes—you're right." Not exactly convinced but having no choice anyway—that was the kind of nod Raphtalia gave. We did have options though, all sorts of them. We could open the borders and merge with Silt-velt, even! I was sure that side of things would work out.

"Rafu."

"Master, is the meeting finished?" Raph-chan and Filo said as they poked their heads into the room.

"Not yet. Working the details out between all these races isn't easy. Everyone is so concerned about saving face. Seriously, I wish we could just cut these guys loose!" It was all such a pain, the politics so corrupt, I wanted to toss it all over to Siltvelt, seriously. It was no better than Melromarc. Talk about power corrupting completely.

That said, there were also some promising individuals—but spotting them wasn't easy either. I also had to keep an eye on those who had flipped to our side. Just in case.

Still, in either case, we couldn't count out the pressure from Siltvelt. They knew how to pile it on. The authority of the Shield Hero was pretty easy to use. A big factor was also using Raphtalia's Return Dragon Vein to use the dragon hourglass to bring in some of Siltvelt's best. Rumors were spreading of the returned Heavenly Emperor calling forth an infinite army of warriors, just like a real god.

With this rapid accumulation of forces on our side, it really didn't take that long for us to march on the eastern capital.

Around the time the eastern capital came into view. A messenger was sent forth, exactly like at the old city.

"We've got another request for a battle between representatives," a reporting officer announced.

"Is there any need to give them the time of day?" I retorted. We had them on the ropes, surely. There were a settlement and large town to the north of the eastern capital; maybe they planned on running away up there?

That said, the opposing water dragon's miko priestess seemed to have quite a keen sense of duty, so I was almost thinking of taking her up on the offer.

"If the Heavenly Emperor's forces should win, then so long as we retreat, they promise not to press the attack. That note is included, swearing to stand by these promises as a general—and as a miko priestess of Q'ten Lo," the officer reported. There was indeed a note, written with some kind of letters and symbols. Hmmm, had I seen that writing before somewhere?

"Oh my, they look serious this time. Are they planning on buying some time, perhaps?" Sadeena commented.

"Looks that way," Raluva agreed.

"What do you mean?" I asked.

"That symbol there is like a promise, made as the representative of the race, the defender of the town. If you break it, it means throwing mud on the deepest trust. It's not just one's house, or one's clan, but on the level of not being able to live in Q'ten Lo at all." So a promise that absolutely could not be broken. It sounded as serious as a slave seal.

That said, this was the idiotic Heavenly Emperor's forces who had been breaking the seals on monsters sealed away since ancient times, so wasn't it just the teensiest bit hard to trust them?

"They have also designated our representative, however. The previous water dragon's miko priestess. What shall you say?" the officer finished. We all looked at Sadeena.

"Oh my. Me?" Sadeena exclaimed.

"Yes. It seems the present water dragon's miko priestess really wants to fight you. If we agree to this fight, she is even willing to wait a few more days," he explained.

"So what? We've no obligation to accept this. I don't see any reason to take part in an operation that will just let the enemy general run," I snorted.

"Then we reject the proposal and attack?"

"Not sure about that either." Unable to make a choice, I was deep in thought—

"Huh!?" Filo looked up at the sky. A sudden wind was blowing up, causing a tornado that passed right in front of our forces. It was a pretty dense little twister.

"That's some powerful magic. The raw power is making my skin tingle."

"It's the ritual magic Great Tornado. Being able to perform magic of this quality, they've got someone with real skill leading them. We won't be able to take them with a rapidly formed force."

"I still think we can break through their lines." So what was this? Some kind of warning? Hmmm. Honestly speaking, we had no obligation to listen to them. I could only make the decision based on the rumors we had heard so far—and that tornado pushed my impression in a pretty negative direction.

Still, it could be considered a better proposal than pointless bloodshed.

"What happens if we win?" I asked.

"The water dragon's miko priestess will surrender without resistance."

"And the Heavenly Emperor? Are they going to sur-render too?" The reporting officer shook his head in reply. Of course not. So this was hardly a discussion—and yet she had proven good to her word once already. This was starting to feel like a general simply suffering under a stupid ruler. Taking her up on the offer might not be a bad idea.

"Little Naofumi, I'm happy to do this," Sadeena offered.

"She's your kid sister, right? You sure?"

"She's also an opponent I clearly have to overcome, and as the previous miko I have a responsibility to show the present miko exactly how strong I am."

"I see." It looked like Sadeena wanted the fight, so why not accept?

"Very well. Spectators can at least attend, I presume?"

"Yes. However—" The reporting officer turned his gaze to Raphtalia. Yeah, good point. It might be safer if Raphtalia didn't go.

"Mr. Naofumi—" Raphtalia really looked like she wanted to go along. Honestly, she was safer at my side anyway. If I deployed Shooting Star Shield, we could deal with any sudden assassination attempts too.

"It'll be fine. I, as Shield Hero, will be there to protect her."

"Thank you!" Raphtalia was very happy to hear she got to go. Honestly, I would be more scared to have her away from me.

"Rafu."

"I'm coming tooooo!" Filo sounded a bit too cheerful.

"Nhh—" S'yne had her hand up too. She didn't want to leave my side. We were well beyond a second, third, or fourth by now. A full crowd was going along.

"Very well, all of you. Just stay alert."

With that, then, we set out to where the present water dragon's miko priestess was waiting to engage her sister in battle.

Maybe battlefields during Japan's warring states period were like this? Just an idle thought as we proceeded as the representatives of the revolutionaries. It looked like the miko and others from the idiot Heavenly Emperor's side were coming toward us.

In the middle of the territory between the two forces, there were people—well, a number of soldiers—and then a killer whale therianthrope holding a katana and waiting.

So she was a katana user.

Perhaps matching her opponent's style, Sadeena also went therianthrope and closed in. I turned my attention to the opposing miko.

She was a little shorter than Sadeena and looked well-rounded in places. When I compared them, they had different colors too. Of course, their clothing was totally different. Sadeena favored a waistcoat and loincloth-like fold while her counterpart had a heavy vest, holder, and baggy pants. How was I telling the difference between a waistcoat and vest? Just the atmosphere. Considering the newcomer the second-player color . . . was too video-gamey a way to look at it.

Also, she had some kind of pattern of red tattoos across her body. She looked a bit more like a shaman than Sadeena, perhaps. There was a different atmosphere about her compared to Zodia too, but I still couldn't tell for sure if it was her or not.

I was about to say something, and then Sadeena took a step forward. If she didn't notice me at this distance, anyway, she was surely someone else. Such a string of ridiculous coincidences couldn't continue forever.

"You are my sister?" Sadeena asked. No reply. The killer whale therianthrope representative gave a wordless nod, then took a bottle from her vest pocket and drank it down. What was she doing, some kind of doping?

After finishing the bottle, she took out another and threw it to Sadeena, who took off the lid and sniffed the liquid.

"Oh, I know that aroma. A local brew!" she said. Okay, this wasn't just a gift of wine, right?

"Now our conditions are the same, Sadeena! I'm going to prove myself superior to you, once and for all!" the opponent shouted.

"If you're an oracle, I'd say that makes you superior."

"You are joking! Do you have any idea the extent to which I've been compared to you?" Her animosity was like a palpable wave.

"No idea at all. It isn't like I was rated that highly myself."

"You have no idea how this nation suffered without you, do you?! Don't you understand how feared you were? What a monster you were considered?" So Sadeena's departure had negatively impacted stability in the region. I took a look at the troops arrayed behind her opponent, and it backed up this story. They weren't taking any chances against Sadeena. It was quite the number of troops.

"You shouldn't believe all the rumors," Sadeena quipped.

"But there were so many of them! Now just imagine being forced to follow in the footsteps of the one who created them all!" Wow, she was really holding a grudge. I guess this was one possible family scenario. In my case, my younger brother was the golden child, so things were a bit different.

"I did feel bad about that. Even after I found out, I didn't expect those two to try this hard to make a replacement for me," Sadeena explained.

"I have—I have seen hell! How hard do you think it's been for me, trying to become an equal to you?"

"Isn't it just crazy, trying to create someone to fit into the hole I left behind? Someone who can do exactly the same things that I could?" she said. Seeing as Sadeena was so exceptional, had they thought a younger sister would just be the same? These were some really twisted parents.

It also looked like they really had evaluated Sadeena highly. Mocking her for not being an oracle had clearly just been harping on her single weak point.

"I can see why the water dragon would abandon you, doing all this even after you could talk with him. I'm going to have to go and have some words with those two, as well," Sadeena offered with no condemnation but also no sympathy. She sparked with electricity. "You stipulated me for this battle, and as one who was the water dragon's miko priestess, I'm going to have to take this fight seriously, aren't I?"

"After all this, you're the one the water dragon turned to! I will never accept that!" Spilling over with intent to kill, the present water dragon's miko priestess pointed her katana. Sadeena already had her harpoon raised, ready to fight at any moment. She was clearly in a better place, mentally, and starting out, that looked to give her an advantage.

Huh? What now? Her opponent was starting to be wreathed in wind?

"Sadeena. I hear you've received the blessing of a spirit implement. You'll need to fight me at full strength!" the opponent roared.

"Oh my. I'm far stronger now than I was when I left this place behind. Are you sure you want me to use everything?"

"Of course. I'll reply with all of the powers that the Heavenly Emperor has bestowed upon me. You'll also get a taste of my own powers! The powers of an oracle!" The other miko took more wine from her pocket and drank it down again. Huh? It looked like the patterns on her skin were starting to glow.

"It would be rude not to share my name with you, of course. I am Shildina, the current water dragon's miko priestess and the priestess of carnage. That's also the name of the one who has surpassed you, Sadeena! I am most proficient with wind magic. Now you'll learn to fear the power of the oracle!" Her voice had changed from a voice filled with anger to a tone more like the one Sadeena normally used.

"Oh my! You actually are an oracle?" Sadeena exclaimed.

"Let me show you the power of the voices of the

heroes and our ancestors!" With that, Shildina took a rectangular card-like object from the holder at her waist and threw it into the sky. It fell back to the ground, depicting a beautiful arc—almost as though the moment it landed was the signal for the fighting to start.

"Haaaaaaaaaaaaah!" she screamed, and the instant it landed, Shildina dropped her body low and charged in, swinging her katana in a wide arc. Sadeena lightly deflected that attack with her harpoon while at the same time using that energy to spin on the spot and attempt a pound with the harpoon's handle.

"You swing that katana like a broom! Try to be more elegant!" Sadeena prodded. For a moment, it looked like the handle of Sadeena's weapon was going to land on Shildina's back.

"You'll need to do better than that!" Shildina replied. The wind that Shildina had deployed behind her absorbed Sadeena's attack and blew up into a massive gale.

"That's a clever little trick. I've got a few of those myself." Sadeena caused lightning to flicker across her entire body in an attempt to forcefully push back the wind.

"Hah!" Seizing the opening, Shildina thrust her hands in front of her and pressed what looked like a ball of wind into Sadeena's stomach.

"Getting too fixated will only slow you down!" Skillfully exploiting the opening in the incoming attack, Sadeena used her tail to strike Shildina on her waist, and then she followed up with a kick for good measure.

"Uwah." Sadeena won the first attack, then. Shildina swiftly swung her own tail, however, as though repelling those attacks, and struck hard at Sadeena's thigh.

"Oh, so you hit me too!"

"You mock me, sister. Ancient magic can also be used like this! As the source of your power, I order you! Read the truth once more—"

"Do you really think that will work on me?" Sadeena sneered. She could use the Way of the Dragon Vein. There was a possibility she could even stop Zweite-class magic using that.

Sadeena too began to chant. "Oh Dragon Vein, oh power of the earth—oh my, impressive! You have some resistance to enchanting impediments too. Well done." It looked like even Sadeena's powers of disruption weren't enough. Then it all came down to the skills of the user, meaning Shildina and Sadeena were likely around the same skill level.

I tried reading the spell too, just to see if I could cancel it.

What the hell was it?

The magic being cast by Shildina could be called both magic and Way of the Dragon. It was bordering on cooperative magic!

"Wind God, become the power to defend me and blow away my enemies! Drifa Wind God Armor!" Shildina completely took her hands off her katana and crashed into Sadeena with her entire body. Of course, with wind also wrapped around her.

It looked a lot like Filo's Spiral Strike. No, perhaps more like Sadeena's Water Dragon Destruction?

"Cheeky!" Sadeena skillfully twisted her harpoon to leap into the air, avoiding the attack. "Here I go!" One instant Sadeena was attempting to use the opening to attack, striking at her opponent's back. The next moment she canceled the attack and back-stepped away.

Why didn't she attack?

"Maaaster, that girl is incredibly skilled with wind magic. If Sadeena had finished that attack, she would have only got cut herself!" Filo explained. So she was fighting someone with command of invisible blades? I narrowed my eyes and looked more closely.

Yeah. Using both Way of the Dragon Vein and life force, I was able to perform an analysis. Didn't help me work out what was going on though! It could be called magic, maybe. But what was it—some kind of attack that continuously emitted wind?

"Oh my, you've got some interesting moves," Shildina quipped, continued to be wreathed in blowing wind. It was almost like armor swirling around her. Then she used her magic to make the katana she had previously discarded rise up into the air. It was like Float.

That reminded me. Ren had Float skills unlocked, but he didn't like to use them. He said that moving the sword used too much of his concentration. Did Raphtalia also have similar skills? If so, they might be useful, I thought idly, spinning my Float Shield.

"Mr. Naofumi, are you thinking about something else?" Damn, Raphtalia had noticed me. I needed to concentrate on the battle.

"That's not enough! Not enough to stop me!" Sadeena spun her harpoon, causing a rain of sparks. She was clearly being assaulted by multiple wind blades. Into that was mixed Shildina herself and the floating katana.

Sadeena jeered, "Oh my. Such an interesting line of attack! I think this might be fun after all." It was frankly a little scary that Sadeena could keep up with the pace of her opponent. "After all those attacks from Raphtalia and Atla, this is nothing." She was incredible.

Personally, of course, I would just throw out Shooting

Star Shield and block them all. It wasn't easy to visualize wind magic, but there were still ways to handle it.

"Hmmm. Wooooow! I wanna try it tooooo!" Filo chirped.

"I bet you could, Filo, if you put your mind to it."

"I don't know how to speak with two voices like that though." That did raise an interesting point about Shildina's spellcasting. She only had one mouth, but it was like she was speaking using two voices, each saying different things.

Was that magic-casting using her oracle powers?

"Now then, after the little show you've put on for me, time I gave you a performance of my own." With that, Sadeena quickly incanted some first-class magic.

"First Lightning Bolt! First Chain Lightning!" Lightning sparked around Sadeena.

"That won't work on me! I can simply blow magic of that caliber out of the air!" With that confident response from Shildina, wind sliced across Sadeena's magic and knocked it away. "In fact, I'll even use that lightning for myself!" Shildina's wind gathered Sadeena's lightning together and then unleashed it back at her, mixed with her own katana and the blades of wind.

The conducted lightning, the slashing katakana and wind, and then Shildina's own body tackle all closed in on Sadeena.

"Well now! Did you think that's the only level of magic I can use? Next try this!" Sadeena looked up at the sky. "If you think wind magic is exclusive to you, that'd be a big mistake." Sadeena drew in power from the clouds and the air.

"I, Sadeena, draw on the power of the air and beg that you fulfill my request. Dragon Vein, defend me and repel my enemies! Wind Seal!" With an audible crunch, magic with wind resistance appeared in front of Sadeena.

"I'll shred those defenses in an instant!"

"Oh, did you think I prepared all this just to stop your attacks? Magic can also be used like this!" In the same moment that Sadeena stopped Shildina's attack, she also used the wind defenses to stop the impact of her opponent's wind.

It was little more than water thrown onto a hot stone, however, and her defenses were shredded in an instant. Of course, for just that moment, the density of Shildina's wind armor also looked to drop considerably. That was all though. Nowhere near close to actually stopping it.

"That's it? Really? Talk about a disappointment!" With a confident smile, Shildina unleashed an attack of wind and lightning at Sadeena.

"Oh, I'll meet your expectations yet, sister! The very

idea of using lightning against me was a foolish one!"

"What!"

Sadeena snapped her fingers and the lightning Shildina had been using increased in output and bounced back from her. "I unleashed it knowing you would make use of it with your wind, so of course I also expected this!"

"And so what if you did?!"

"Oh my. Can't you tell? Can't you see what's happening around you right now?" At Sadeena's words, Shildina took a startled look around.

Static electricity was crackling in the air, and the ground was starting to spark as though—yes, as though lightning was about to fall. Right where she was standing.

When using the Way of the Dragon Vein, too, and perhaps on purpose, clouds had gathered and formed.

Indeed, the sky had quietly been filling with thunderclouds.

"I'll just summon up a gale and scatter those clouds!" Shildina spouted.

"No, you won't. There's too much of my lightning spread through the wind," came the reply. With a mocking tone, Sadeena swung her harpoon down at the ground. "It wasn't easy to set this up without you interrupting it. So I'll cast it quickly. Let's see which of us can endure the most. Drifa . . . Thunder Bolt!"

Shildina tried to get some distance, but Sadeena skillfully drew her in with the harpoon and then dropped the lightning on both of them together. Amid a brilliant, sparking flash, a thick bolt of lightning dropped from the clouds above and struck the two of them.

Shildina was the one who let out a cry, her wind armor being forcibly stripped from her by the lightning, gradually being peeled away and turning into mist. The wind blades were already gone, and then the katana became a lightning rod and sucked the lightning into the ground. Shildina was left breathing heavily.

"Oh my, you did well to withstand that. However, I'm not going to stop attacking you now," Sadeena bellowed. They had been bathed in a massive amount of magic, and yet neither had suffered any substantial damage. Shildina at least had the decency to be breathing heavily.

Sadeena continued. "Drifa Lightning Speed and Thunder Guard! Come on, you're not done entertaining me yet! I'm going to start incanting even faster!" Once imbued with lightning, Sadeena had the ability to drop attack magic onto herself and make use of it. Certainly not someone I wanted to fight. She pressed her attack with precise, tight movements.

I still ached, sometimes, from the Zeltoble coliseum.

"Don't get too full of yourself!" Shildina reformed her wind armor, narrowed her eyes, and pointing her katana at Sadeena. "We're just getting started! I've got plenty more power than this!"

"So go ahead. I'm not stopping you from using it!" Sadeena shouted, and she and Shildina had both dropped back a little and glared across the intervening gap. The lightning and wind from each were still clashing around them, but this wasn't magic they had unleashed on purpose. Just a secondary effect of their preparations for their next attack.

"T-this is quite incredible," Rishia muttered as she observed the fight. She wasn't wrong. Had sibling rivalry ever been taken to quite this level before? Not to mention it was all being unleashed by two killer whale therianthropes. Seriously, there was no telling how deep Sadeena's well of power went.

Still, watching this battle, with Sadeena using lightning and Shildina wind, it looked like a battle between the gods of those respective elements. I probably felt like that due to Descent of the Thunder God, which I had used before as cooperative magic with Sadeena. They also probably both had water magic, acquired from the Way of the Dragon Vein.

Lightning that seemed alive struck at Shildina, who dodged an attack from the harpoon while diverting the lightning with a stream of water mixed with wind.

"This is quite odd. This entire battle is starting to, well, look quite beautiful," Raphtalia remarked.

"I was thinking the same thing," I noted.

Both sides had no choice but to watch the unfolding struggle, captivated by this clash of incredible techniques.

"Think you can handle this? Lightning Strike Harpoon!" Sadeena threw her lightning-charged harpoon at Shildina, who repelled it using her katana enwrapped in wind. Sadeena raised her hands and the harpoon made a circle in midair and flew back to her.

She even had control of magnetic forces? Lightning was pretty versatile.

"Want to push this harder?" Sadeena entreated. The harpoon took on more lightning with a further crackle, growing three massive prongs. Sadeena herself also took a moment to top up again, more lightning striking her.

"Hmmm. I need to refill my magic a little," Sadeena mentioned as she took a bottle of alcohol out and started to drink. Even now, she seemed totally at ease. Shildina, however, did exactly the same, knocking back her own drink with a satisfied sound. "Oh, you like to drink? We can settle this with alcohol, if you'd prefer," Sadeena remarked.

"I won't lose to you at that either! I'll show you, hic, the true power of an oracle!" Hah, was she starting to get drunk?

"Sis, please. I've had my suspicions for a while now, but don't tell me, you're already drunk?" Sadeena asked, somewhat in surprise. For her part, she always acted like she was drunk even when she was sober.

"I'm not drunk. I've got this," Shildina turned to look at her own troops behind her, and a single harpoon was thrown at her feet. A rusty harpoon?

"Oh my! That's quite the blast from the past. My old harpoon!" Sadeena gasped.

"That's right. The harpoon that you left here in Q'ten Lo," Shildina explained while gripping it tightly in her hands.

"Rafu?" Raph-chan started to look intently.

"What's going on?" I asked her.

"Rafu, rafu!" I couldn't tell if she was trying to explain something or just upset. I turned to Filo.

"Right, she said something moved from that harpoon and went into the little sister," Filo translated. Was this another oracle thing, then?

"It's not often I'm forced to do this. Very well! Allow

me to show you the true power of the water dragon's miko priestess!" With that, Shildina tossed the harpoon aside again and gave Sadeena an unsettling smile. What was going on? The very air surrounding Shildina seemed to have changed in quality.

"Drifa Lightning Speed, Thunder Guard!" Hold on! Shildina activated the same lightning support magic as Sadeena! "Of course, I'll be using this too." She also reapplied her wind armor, looking very pleased with herself as she was enveloped in both lightning and wind.

"Oh my! You can even use lightning magic? That's odd though. Your magic felt the same as mine, right there," Sadeena remarked.

"This is the power of an oracle! You, the miko without any oracle powers, will now be defeated by the very ideals that you cast aside!" That sounded like the crux of her resentment, but what ideals? "After one extraction, I can then seal them in a card like this!" I saw it for myself this time. She took out a white card and sealed some kind of magical power inside it. That caused a pattern to appear there—an illustration of lightning and a killer whale?

It looked suspiciously like the card that Zodia gave me.

"I see. So this is what it really means to be an oracle.

You can transfer the intent imbued in objects and other things into cards, carry them around, and then replicate them for yourself when needed. That's quite incredible!" So the reason she was reaching the realms of cooperative magic was perhaps due to some application of this oracle power.

Shildina used wind magic. That made it possible to perform simulated incantations using the vibrations of the air. So she used the oracle power for the awareness and her magic for the incantations. Maybe that would allow one person to use cooperative magic?

Hey, and maybe Filo could copy that to perform cooperative magic alone too.

"You can use wind magic too, right, Filo?" I asked. "Think you could use it to create incantations and cast two spells at once?"

"Huh? Hmmmm—" Filo crossed her arms and thought, then tilted her head as she tried to cast the magic. "I tried to make two spells from a single spell, but I couldn't do it. The magic all just spins around," she concluded. Yeah, while Filo's explanation was inept and difficult to understand, it was clear that this was an extremely high-level technique. It wasn't something that could be copied easily.

Still, to be able to collect the emotions remaining

in the harpoon that Sadeena had left in Q'ten Lo and turn them to her own advantage . . . Could she do that? So all she needed was relics from other great heroes to get stronger and stronger? If that was the truth of this "oracle" ability, no wonder it was given such importance.

"You might be impressed now, but that's soon going to change to terror," Shildina promised. It looked like Shildina's personality was also being affected, however. She was starting to sound more and more like Sadeena.

Shildina continued to proclaim, "If I combine my own powers with those of the miko still called the strongest of recent times, there's no opponent I cannot defeat. But just to make sure—" A katana flowing with twisted power suddenly burst up from the ground, and Shildina grabbed it. Wow. That thing was clearly a seriously cursed item. Should she really be handling something like that?

"Guwah! Now! Bring it on!" she shouted. The life force around Shildina was starting to change color. It clearly didn't look like she was up to any good.

Maybe it was time for us to help out? Even as I had that thought, Sadeena glanced over at us and played the situation down. "Impressive. Being able to capture the awareness held in anything is not something you can do just by getting drunk," Sadeena commented, voice still casual. "Well then. I'm going to show you the biggest attack I've picked up recently." A deep rumbling sound started to reverberate from around Sadeena.

"You barely deserve this, but I'll finish you in a single attack!" a voice that didn't even sound female rang out.

"Uwah!"

"Rafu!" Filo and Raph-chan were looking at Shildina in terror.

"I think you'd better stop her quickly," Filo offered. "It's so sad, looking at her."

"Rafu."

"Sad?" I wondered. So this was what might have happened to Sadeena if she'd remained here and grown up in such a twisted environment. It really was feeling like we needed to step in—

Sadeena and Shildina were ready to launch their special attacks. Shildina got there first. Her two black katanas, wreathed in lightning and wind, swept down toward Sadeena. That was all it took to send two dragons roaring toward her.

"Eat this! I am the ultimate priestess of carnage!" Shildina yelled. Then she transformed—no, created out of magic—a black and white killer whale, sweeping both of her swords down again to send it chomping toward Sadeena.

The two dragons and killer whale-patterned wave attack headed straight for Sadeena. The target of these attacks, however, just placed her harpoon in front of her and concentrated, repeatedly chanting more magic.

Then the attacks landed.

"Try this! Thunder God!" A rain of lightning flashes descended from the heavens, scattering the dragons and the killer whale.

Hold on! Thunder God? That was magic that had totally looked exclusive to beast transformation support, but now she could use it even without my aid? Or maybe she only had to do it once and then she could do it all the time?

Raphtalia asked, "Can Sadeena use that magic even without your help, Mr. Naofumi?" Lightning continued to crackle around her, like some crazy battle manga.

"Guwaaaaaah!" Shildina got a bottle-nose full of high-density lightning and was sent flying away.

"Those attacks looked strong, but you've got a density issue. To put it simply, you diluted them too much, letting me just shrug them off," Sadeena scoffed.

"Kh-kuwah—"

"Fohl didn't use any particular special attacks when he was transformed. Maybe she just pulled it off on instinct?" I guessed.

"I wonder," Raphtalia responded. I looked at Sadeena and she had the audacity to wink. Hilarious!

Still, depending on how we used it, beast transformation support showed the potential for realizing great growth. Shildina stuck her swords into the ground and climbed back to her feet.

Was she just tough, or was this also due to the blessing from the Heavenly Emperor? It didn't look like she was using Astral Enchant. I narrowed my eyes to check, but—as I expected—I couldn't tell what was going on. It was support magic with some kind of special criteria, making it impossible to judge using my eyes.

"There's something else too. You may have recreated my feelings from the past, but surely it goes without saying that the me from right now is stronger than the me from the past. Right? Don't you understand that?" Sadeena pleaded.

Yeah, I mean, good point.

Maybe she could trace the awareness of Sadeena from the past using an item that she once used, but trying to use that against the current Sadeena clearly wasn't going to work; that past copy couldn't match the experience of the current one. As well as the cursed sword, she was also likely doping with other stuff as well, but that only prevented any kind of unification.

She continued. "You're like one of those people who have multiple elements all patched together. You need to learn to use them more effectively."

Thinking about it now, Rishia was someone who had multiple elements. Elemental—the all-round element that combined the elements of fire, water, wind, and earth. It was both difficult to control and there were few who could use it, due to issues with its basic nature.

It was magic that suited Rishia's general "jack-of-all-trades" persona, anyway.

Sadeena continued to lecture her. "I do sense incredible skills and hard work, that's true. But—indeed, because of that—the more you borrow abilities from other people, the bigger the openings you leave."

"Borrow from others? You're joking! This power is mine, plain and simple!"

Sadeena shook her head, sadly responding, "If that's the power of an oracle, then I'm glad I never had access to it. But it's placed you in a better position than me, right? So just be happy with that."

"I won't—won't accept that! I have to prove, beyond any doubt, that I'm the true miko!"

Sadeena did not let up. "Not to mention, magic is seriously influenced by your emotions. You won't defeat me fighting in such a deranged state! You need to find a little more leeway. Get a little more comfortable."

Shildina plucked another card from her holder and held it up. Her wounds immediately started to heal. So that let her use healing magic too? Pretty convenient. Like an all-around warrior who could handle almost any situation alone.

Sadeena had monster-grade strength, that was true, but her opponent was no slouch either. Shildina took out something that looked a lot like a rucolu fruit, crushed it in her hand, and licked the remains.

"Oh my," Sadeena exclaimed, looking on enviously. Shildina hiccupped but stayed standing. Oh? She could handle it? So there was someone else capable of eating it—other than me.

"This is no time to be howding bwack, but I really didn't want to have to use this," she babbled. She had started to slur her speech. Shildina took out a card and struck a pose. The card showed a hammer and a ying-yang symbol.

"Raful!" It definitely got Raph-chan excited about something. Though vague, there was something cherry-pink colored emitting from the card. What was it?

"Hmmm. What do you think that is? It looks different from the blessing," Raphtalia wondered.

"You can see it too, Raphtalia?" I said.

"Yes."

"Dis my fwinal twump card!" She was almost unintelligible now. "Just you wapch dis!" Appearing to have received some kind of power from the card, Shildina's pattern started to glow. At the same time, growing—faintly—what looked to be a tail made of magic, Shildina turned into her demi-human form. But due to her far faster movements than before, for a moment I couldn't even track her with my eyes. Wreathed in highly concentrated wind, I could barely make out more than a vague human shape.

Staggering steps quickly changed to fast ones. She was definitely moving better than she had done up until now. Then, multiple Shildina-like shadows appeared, surrounding Sadeena and attacking her. That tail—it reminded me of someone.

I slowly turned to look at Raphtalia.

She and Raph-chan were following one of the shadows with their eyes.

"Oh my! Illusions? You think that's going to be enough to confuse me?" With that, Sadeena skewered one of the Shildina clones with her harpoon. That wasn't the shadow Raphtalia was watching though.

"You poor fool. So you're using sound waves to detect them. Fine, but you can't even tell that I want you to see through them, eh? You need to be more careful, eh!"

Eh? Her mannerisms had changed again. Was this her trump card?

Shildina grabbed the harpoon sticking into her, turning it into a ball of wind, and sent the weapon flying away. In the same moment the other copies all jumped at Sadeena.

"Oh my. You've improved your density already. This is pretty tricky magic too. Almost like—" Sadeena began. Of course, Sadeena avoided the incoming attacks with her lightning magic and physical prowess, but it was starting to look like she could actually be in trouble.

"Sadeena!"

"Rafu!"

Raphtalia and Raph-chan both shouted just in the moment that the demi-human Shildina smashed down with her sword, now transformed into what looked like a giant hammer wreathed in a whole storm of wind.

However, even that was just another wind clone. A ying-yang pattern unleashed by Shildina bounced onto Sadeena and turned into geometrical lettering, binding her.

"Oh my, that's quite a unique spell. I can sense it slowly scattering my own magic," Sadeena said, still sparkling with charged lightning. She clearly couldn't keep up.

Then Shildina, still wreathed in her wind, looked over the battlefield. Spotting Raphtalia and me, she let out a murmur.

"Hmmm—"

With a snap, Sadeena broke free of the bonds and charged at Shildina, of course, in combination with a lightning-charged harpoon attack. Shildina dropped her wind-wreathed hammer to her waist and then stepped in, quick but dangerously deep.

"Five Practices Destiny Split!" A ying-yang appeared on the head of the hammer and then crashed into the charging Sadeena.

Of course, Sadeena avoided that while thrusting with her harpoon—

"O-oh my?" The power of the ying-yang hammered into Sadeena as though guided by an unseen hand, scattered her lightning. A magic trigram appeared, and five balls started to circle around Sadeena.

"Earth Defeats Water, eh!" In the same moment Shildina murmured that, Sadeena collapsed.

"W-what's going on here? You're moving—much better than before," she murmured.

Shildina responded, "Impressive. Being able to take that attack and still speak? That's a passing grade. Still not sure if I can defeat you, eh!" Sadeena was resisting, but it was like something was binding her down, preventing her from even standing up. "You've got some moves, I'll give you that. Previous miko, in actuality, this victory belongs to you. I'm cheating to win, eh!"

What was this, then? Some kind of transformation with a time limit? It had to be oracle-related. An attack involving possession by a god, perhaps, and having it fight in her stead? So rather than things like Sadeena's residual thoughts from the past, now she was possessed by far a more powerful awareness.

But then, for some reason, Shildina pointed out from among her wind at Raphtalia.

"Defeating those currently in power could be fun too. I'm not going to let this chance slip by, eh," she went on. With that, the wind scattered and the demi-human form of Shildina was revealed.

"Huh?" I checked out Shildina again. Yeah, so I'd been right. Coincidence can be a frightening thing.

"I knew it. It *was* Zodia." In the moment I said that, Shildina—no, Zodia—looked at me and opened her eyes wide in surprise.

"Nuh! I'm becoming unstable, eh—" Shildina said and her unnatural tail suddenly vanished. She really was messing with some bizarre and dangerous powers. Although the direction was likely different, it felt close to a hero using the Curse Series.

"Oh my," Sadeena exclaimed, and her therianthrope also ended. Trying to stand, she collapsed again. She continued to try to stand but didn't appear able to do so. That was a pretty powerful binding spell. However, Shildina was looking only at me, as though the battle with Sadeena meant nothing at all anymore.

"Sweet Naofumi. What are you doing here?"

"Because I'm the Shield Hero, of course. Didn't you notice me standing right next to Sadeena and Raphtalia?" Maybe not. She'd certainly been concentrating hard. Thinking about it now, the name "Zodia" was also close to the ring name that Sadeena had used in Zeltoble, "Nadia." That wasn't the only thing about them that was similar. The noises she made as she got drunk—indeed, just the fact that she loved to drink—and her response when I ate the rucolu fruit, all were exactly the same too.

"You're kidding." Zodia was looking at me, sobering up and looking pretty sleepy.

"Do you two know each other?"

"Yeah, this is the girl with no sense of direction who I went drinking with, accompanied by Motoyasu II. She wanted to play with me—and I mean that completely innocently," I noted.

"Becoming friends with an enemy, without each side realizing? That old chestnut again. Just like when we fought Sadeena," Raphtalia sighed. Ah, now even Raphtalia was spotting the tropes.

"Please, give me some credit. I'm not *that* dense. I had plenty of suspicions."

"Say, Naofumi, if you've got a moment—"

"What? If you want to fight, bring it on! I take it Shildina is your real name?" I sneered. If she had the strength to contain Sadeena, she had to be quite a monster. This battle wasn't settled yet, but she definitely had some nasty attacks at her command.

"You're lying, aren't you? You can't be the spirit implement user who accompanies the revolutionary Heavenly Emperor. You just can't!"

"Yes, I can. Can't you see this cursed shield?" It was insane, having to point all this out.

"So you're Sadeena's boyfriend?"

"No! Where did that come from?"

"Oh my! What's going on, exactly?" Sadeena was also puzzled about this interruption to the battle.

"Oh dear."

"Don't tell me, Shildina, you've taken a shine to Naofumi? Then why don't we all play together?!" Sadeena shouted.

"What are you talking about?" Tension turned to exasperation. "I thought this was a serious battle!"

"I think we've moved a bit beyond that now, haven't we?" I wasn't happy about it, but I actually agreed with Sadeena. Shildina was acting really odd.

"Does sweet Naofumi already belong to you, Sadeena?"

"What are you talking about? You must be kidding!" My reply made Shildina's expression visibly brighten.

"So—" she began, but the next moment her patterns started glowing on her body. Then Shildina gave a cry and wrapped her arms around her chest.

"Guwaaah!"

"What now!"

"Rafu!" Raph-chan pointed at the holder at Shildina's waist. That was pointless, though, because we couldn't see anything. Shildina was still breathing heavily.

"Are you okay?" I drew Shildina to me and checked her over. It was instantly clear that those markings were the problem.

"Rafu, rafu, rafu!"

"Let's seeeee. According to Raph-chan, she has a hole in her soul, which is a really weird shape. She was fighting by putting some kind of power or something into that hole in her soul," Filo translated for Raph-chan. Raph-chan could see ghosts, after all.

So this was the truth of the oracle power? A technique to create a gap in your soul and then be possessed by spirits of your ancestors?

"And?"

"Rafu, rafu!"

"She had something incredible in her soul back there, but now something nasty has entered from those patterns and is trying to take her over," Filo went on. Some kind of soul interference?

"Very well. Get back," Raphtalia said and turned her sword into a spirit blade and adopted a slashing stance. "I'm going to cut the flow now. That should sort this out."

"Rafu." Raph-chan jumped onto Raphtalia's head and pointed. It looked like she knew the spot to cut.

"What are you doing to the water dragon's miko priestess? You men! Take the life of the imposter Heavenly Emperor!" an enemy soldier shouted. Agitated by our actions, some of them were preparing to fight. It didn't look like they had any intention of keeping their promise not to get involved. There was only a small group of them, however, with most of the enemy Heavenly Emperor's forces looking worried and confused.

In any case, the soldiers attacked us with arrows, spears, swords, katanas, magic, everything they had.

"Sakura Destiny Sphere, Shooting Star Shield, Air Strike Shield! You guys! Put anyone who strikes first back in their place!" At my orders the revolutionary forces gave a shout, piling into the enemy charging toward us.

"Right there!" With a downward slash, Raphtalia chopped around Shildina's shoulder. With a snap, part of the text came off her body. The pattern had started to flash less, but it continued to flash nonetheless.

"Guwaaah! S-stop it! Uwaah!"

"Rafu."

"We've suppressed the encroachment, to some degree, but seriously! Just what is this pattern?" Raphtalia asked.

"It looks like slave markings, but the color is a bit different. Perhaps—yes, like this!" Sadeena said and drank some wine, then touched the pattern while imbuing it with magic. The flashing slowed down even more, but it still didn't stop.

"Release me!" Shildina knocked Sadeena and me back, unsteady on her feet, and glared at us. Something was really disrupting her calm, but what?

"No one wants me, do they?! I'm not wanted— uuuh—I only have one who accepts me! This is the proof of that! Don't get in my way!" Shildina shouted and stood up, as though protecting her patterns.

"Someone accepts you? Who?" Sadeena furrowed her brow.

"But Lady Makina's orders are absolute! I must kill

Sadeena and then take the life of the false Heavenly Emperor! Guwah! Stop it—get away from me!" Shildina raged, striking herself as she went. More of the patterns flaked away.

"Rafu?"

"Hmmm."

"Oh my!"

"What now?"

"Well—the flow of evil-looking power that I saw with Raph-chan's help has scattered, and a large light went into Shildina," Raphtalia explained.

"You saw beautiful power flowing in from the surrounding Dragon Veins, right?" Sadeena inquired. Shildina stood, watching us, her arms hanging down.

"Hmmm. Not bad for emergency measures, eh? Pretty good, eh?" Shildina started again. This sounded like the personality Sadeena had previously contained. She looked over at me and nodded a few times.

"Holder of a spirit implement, justice is with you, eh! I have a job to do myself."

"Huh?"

"Stop fighting at once, eh! Our forces are surrendering to the revolutionary army! Consider those who will not comply to be our enemies! Join the revolutionary forces in capturing them! Those are my orders, eh!"

"What the hell?" I think everyone around me may have said it at the same time. The confused defenders proceeded to attack those fighting us from behind and capture them. The command structure seemed pretty solid.

"Right, I'm off to finish this quick, eh," she said, and with that Shildina wreathed herself in wind and vanished.

"Huh? What was that?" Raphtalia and Raph-chan were looking into the sky. What now?

"She vanished using magic and then used wind magic to fly through the air to the castle in the city."

"Wind magic can do all that?" I asked.

"She can fly? I want to try!" Filo was shouting.

"I'm not sure. I've never seen magic like that." We were talking about someone capable of incanting co-operative magic alone, so it probably wasn't something anyone could copy easily.

"What happened to my fight? Can I go and let off a bit of steam?" Sadeena appealed. I guess her fun had been interrupted. Looking around, I noticed that a serious fight was starting. Everything was moving a bit quickly, even for me. The defenders of the city had started fighting among themselves too.

Just what was going on?

"Rafu?"

"Hmmm?" Filo and Raph-chan were both looking at me for some reason.

"What's up?"

"Well, Raph-chan says that your pocket has started glowing, Master."

"My pocket?" I looked down at the pocket Rafu-chan was pointing at and then took out the card that Shildina had given me.

What exactly were they? Shildina had definitely used them to trigger some kind of ability. They weren't the same as the talismans from Kizuna's world. They looked more like playing cards.

"Rafu."

"What? Well, apparently, she can hear a voice from there asking for help—that part of her soul is there inside."

"I see." I wasn't sure why she gave it to me after we only just met, but it seemed pretty important. When I thought back, she'd really had a great time drinking and playing cards. The expression on her face had been totally different from when she was in battle.

"I'd like to help. Should we go after her?" Raphtalia inquired.

"Yeah, okay." We turned toward the eastern capital.

It was small when compared to, say, Edo but still large enough to be a town, with a castle and everything. "If we get in there and capture the Heavenly Emperor, their commander, then we've won. She's the one who ran off in the face of the enemy. She can't complain if we go after her." Smoke had started to rise from the castle in multiple places. What was Shildina doing? I was starting to think we could just leave her to it and everything would get wrapped up, but we really did have to go ourselves.

Ren and Itsuki came over.

"We can't let this chance slip away. We're going in."

"Okay!"

"Off we go!"

"Rafu!" With that, as energetic as ever, we mobilized our forces and struck out into the eastern capital.

Chapter Thirteen: The Past Heavenly Emperor

"What now?"

We'd invaded the town to find smoke filling the air as we approached the castle. Leaving the chaos in the town to our forces, we headed on toward the castle. The gates were open. It looked like we were free to come and go. There was more smoke too. Was the place on fire?

"Those who can use water magic, put out the fires. No need to hold back if anyone is looking for a fight!" After giving these orders, I deployed Shooting Star Shield and advanced in the lead. I'd taken a look at the layout beforehand.

Our goal was to capture the opposing Heavenly Emperor. Once we took out their leader, everything else would surely fall into place. That said, with all of this going on, it seemed unlikely our target would be sitting like a moron in the main keep.

I knew I wouldn't be. I'd have been right out of there. You can't do anything if you're dead. Escape, live, and make more plans. It seemed highly likely to me that he just wasn't here.

Considering these things while searching the castle,

we came across the bodies of soldiers, along with some other well-dressed corpses. There was another noble nearby too, still alive and very frightened.

"S-save me!" He bowed his head while begging for his life. So pathetic I could barely shake my head in disgust. However, this was also the kind of guy who'd spill his guts at the drop of a hat.

"What happened here?" I asked him.

"I don't want to die! N-no, please! I can't face the terror again!"

"Stop whining and share what you know. Or do you want me to kill you?"

"—suddenly appeared in the c-castle, using terrible power! Defeating everyone, one after the other! If we don't get out of here right away, we're all dead! So please—haaaaaaah!" With a look of sheer terror on his face, the noble looked up at Raphtalia and then collapsed on the spot.

"W-what does that mean? He fainted after looking at my face?" she said. He'd been trying to surrender to us and then fainted upon seeing Raphtalia?

"Were you making a scary face again? Like when I said I wanted S'yne to make some Raph-chan merchandise?" I chided.

"Mr. Naofumi, just what do you think about me?"

"You're like a daughter—"

"That's enough. I don't want to hear it." Huh? Raphtalia's mood seemed to have only got worse. So she really didn't like me playing parent to her? She was at a difficult age, I guess.

I decided to check out the corpses.

"Some of them have had their necks slashed by something sharp. These others—man, what is this?" I questioned. The soldiers had been cut down by something sharp, like a sword, with clean cuts. The well-dressed ones were gorier, as though their upper bodies had been smashed into mush by something big and heavy. It was likely Shildina's work, but how had she done this?

"A blunt weapon?" Raphtalia wondered.

"Hmmm?" Filo took her morning star out from under her wings and started swinging it around. Stop that! That wasn't it. Something bigger than that.

"It's definitely bigger than the morning star Filo is holding. Look at the way they've been crushed. I'd say maybe it was a hammer?" Ren muttered as he carefully checked the bodies.

"Sounds right."

"In either case, we need to proceed with caution."

"Understood." And so, we proceeded with caution.

Following the trail of dead bodies, we came out in the garden at the rear of the castle.

This looked like a training area, lined with scarecrows equipped with all sorts of weapons, including shields, sword, and bows.

There were even scarecrows dressed up to look like Raphtalia. These were definitely training dummies. It looked like there was a well here too.

"This the end, eeeeeeeeeh!" we heard someone shout, and then the ground shook. A hole radiating with cracks appeared in the center of the training area, and then blood exploded out in a circle.

"Seriously, how foolish, eh. As one standing above others—she was the vanguard. She was no good, even as a person, eh," announced a girl standing there, dressed in a miko outfit and carrying a massive hammer.

She looked a lot like Raphtalia—a shining, full tail, long hair, and beautiful features. If someone told me she was Raphtalia's sister, I would have believed them.

"I was surprised at Sadeena having a sister, but now Raphtalia too? Does she have a sibling as well?" I wondered.

"I don't think so. Maybe she's the Heavenly Emperor that we're here to kill?" That was Sadeena's take on things, but Motoyasu II had called him a bratty kid, and Raluva and the others had talked about the opposing Heavenly Emperor as though he were a young boy. So this didn't match the information we'd received so far.

"Don't tell me he's a cross-dresser! One of those otoko no ko, 'male daughters?'"

"Just that coming out of your mouth, Naofumi . . . you really are an otaku," Raphtalia reprimanded.

"You, shut it," I said as I glared at Ren. Of course, I was an otaku. A big one.

"No, I don't think she's the Heavenly Emperor," Raphtalia replied, hand on the hilt of her sword and ready to draw at any moment.

"You're right, eh. The me you see before you, I am no longer the Heavenly Emperor." The girl in front of us, the girl who looked like Raphtalia, lightly lifted her hammer and placed it on her shoulder. The way she was speaking, I'd heard that before.

"You're Shildina, surely. Why do you look like this?" I asked her. Yeah, she sounded exactly like Shildina had before she flew away.

"I have defeated the pus festering at the heart of this land—defeated Makina. Of course, the owner of this body put up a bit of a fight. The holder of a spirit implement and the descendant should understand that, eh."

"Understand?"

"You don't? Don't understand even that?" she said. As we tilted our heads in puzzlement, the speaker nodded as though looking right through us.

"R-rafu!" Raph-chan chose that moment to make a surprised noise. What now? What was she surprised about? As I wondered, Raph-chan smoothly jumped onto me, climbed onto my head, and pointed at the girl. With Raph-chan's support, I saw that it was definitely Shildina. She was possessed, the power of the oracle over her, like a ghost covering her body. So the girl we had been seeing, who looked like Raphtalia, was an illusion covering the actual body of Shildina.

"Rafu! Rafu, rafu, rafu!" Raph-chan was going crazy, as though to say I was looking in the wrong place. I narrowed my eyes further and behind Shildina—a blurry image rising from a smashed carcass on the ground—I saw another ghost-like figure appearing, something twisted and dark, like a Soul Eater or like Kyo.

It looked like—a woman? I couldn't quite put my finger on it, but her face unsettled me somehow. What was she? Her presence was so dark it almost put Kyo to shame. My cursed parts were jabbing me with pain.

This evil-looking creature leapt and struck at Shildina.

"W-watch—!" Faster than I could warn her, the

patterns on Shildina's body started to glow.

"Gah! You're stubborn, eh! I already defeated the caster!" Shildina struggled as she spoke, thrashing at the ghost clinging to her back. The creature was relentlessly reaching toward her chest.

"Guh! There are still some—patterns left, eh," she groaned.

The evil-looking woman said, "I never thought you would resist the patterns and try to kill me. But if you think that's enough to stop me, you're making a big mistake. I prepared you, my spare body, for this exact eventuality." Spare body? Hold on a moment!

"You are twisted indeed, hag! One moment you disparage Shildina. The next you try to take over her body!" the hammer girl said.

"Look at you! Like you're one to talk," Sadeena commented. Considering the situation we'd walked into, it seemed the poisonous Makina was the one Shildina—or should I say this hammer girl—had just smashed to a bloody pulp. Now it seemed she had turned into a ghost and was trying to possess Shildina.

The ghost explained, "You talk about being an oracle, giving it all a mystic spin, but really you've just got a super-convenient body that can easily accept souls or remnant thoughts. I'm finally getting too old, unable to maintain my youthful beauty, and you're also good friends with that piss-stinking little brat, all of which makes you an excellent body to take over. That's why I performed the ritual on you, ahead of time, just in case. The right decision, clearly."

"Gah! I won't let you take Shildina's body, eh!" the hammer girl said.

"If you got a little feisty, I did think that I'd just kill you. But very well, that body belongs to me! Give it back!" Just how vile was this woman? She'd clearly had her eye on Shildina's body from the start. All this talk of being easy to transfer to and taking over other people, the very ideas made me think of Kyo and his homunculi. It really pissed me off. Seriously, none of these bad guys had a single original idea among them.

Taking over the body of someone else just because you were old and your beauty had faded? You had to be kidding.

"Give it back? Eat shit! That body was never yours to begin with!" The vindictive ghost almost made it sound like Shildina had been born solely to give up her body. Maybe she hadn't been created specifically for that purpose, but I could still easily imagine the life that Shildina had been forced to lead.

Born to replace Sadeena, forced to do a job she had

no interest in. She had looked so happy, had so much fun when she was playing with me. For just a few brief hours, that was all.

"What are you so mad about?" Ren, who had been silently watching the unfolding events, asked me.

"One of those people who had been killed has turned into a ghost and is trying to take over Shildina's body," I replied.

"What! Is that a thing now?" he asked.

"Yeah, and even worse, she reminds me of that one very special bitch. I want to help, but I don't have any means of attack, do I!" I said. It would be perfect if I could attack with the Soul Eater Shield, but seeing as I could only aim for a counter, it wasn't very efficient for me. Not to mention, if the enemy figured out that fact, then I really was rendered powerless. My bringing up Witch had definitely made Ren uncomfortable though.

Itsuki as well, from the look of it.

"This is bad! I want to help too, but what can we do?" Sadeena asked.

"Got any attacks that will hit a ghost?"

"I wonder if holy water might work?"

"Mr. Naofumi, I've got this! This is the attack to handle ghosts!" Raphtalia said and changed to her Soul Eater katana, which was used for fighting spectral bodies.

Ren and Itsuki matched her.

"Save her, Raphtalia! Everyone!" I shouted.

"We're on it. Somewhere behind her, right?"

"Yeah, that's right!"

"No problem!" Raphtalia dashed in, Ren behind her, and Itsuki fired an arrow. However, Raphtalia and the others couldn't see ghosts for themselves. They headed toward the point Raph-chan and I were both pointing at, each swinging their weapons through the empty air with almost comedic conviction.

"Hahaha! You'd be better off staying out of this!" Makina deployed a suspicious-looking defensive web, avoiding the attacks from Raphtalia and the others before extending black tendrils to envelop them all.

"Guwah! Why is my body so heavy? A status effect from a ghost-type enemy? If only I could see her! If I could see her, I could defeat her!" Ren was groaning. She should be a ghost, but being unable to see her suggested maybe she was classified as a spirit. We managed to see Kyo partway through the battle when we fought him though. She was strong too, even though she wasn't corporeal. She was clearly a vengeful ghost now, so why couldn't we see her?

"Futile, you fools. Futile! You seriously think such pathetic attacks can touch me? Hahaha!" Her laugh sounded so much like Witch it only exacerbated my irritation. Was there no way to finish her off?

"Rafu!"

"Yeah, Raph-chan! Get in there!" I said. Raph-chan ran forward to support Raphtalia and the others. A foe who couldn't be seen was a tricky thing. It looked like she had control of maybe half of Shildina's body too, because she was using wind magic to blow Raphtalia and the others away.

"Rafu!" Perhaps realizing that Raph-chan was providing support, she started to focus her attacks on Raph-chan.

"That's not—enough, is it. Draw out more—more power from the spirit implement. The weapon with the power to hunt souls, eh!" the girl who *looked* like Raphtalia and was possessing Shildina offered this advice.

Draw out the capabilities of the weapon that hunts souls? I changed to the Soul Eater Shield and narrowed my eyes. It did have a special equip effect called "Soul Eat," so maybe that was the key here?

I focused my awareness into the shield, allowing me to vaguely see the shape of this vengeful spirit.

"Raphtalia! Ren, Itsuki! Imbue your Soul Eater weapons with power! It'll let you see her!" It seemed that the Soul Eater weapons had the hidden ability to let you see spirits.

"Draw out . . . the weapon's power—I see her!" Raphtalia shouted.

"Yes! Right there!" Ren too.

"I can hit her!" Itsuki yelled.

Raphtalia and Ren repelled Makina's binding, and then both of them unleashed attacks toward the ghost. Raphtalia took the lead, then Ren, while an arrow Itsuki fired struck right in her forehead.

"That's where she is? Then let me have a go too!" Sadeena took out some holy water and incanted some Way of the Dragon Vein magic, targeting the spot Itsuki's arrow had struck.

"I, Sadeena, draw out the power of this holy water and state my ardent wish! Dragon Vein, strike down my foes! Saint Aqua Blast!"

"Gyaaaaaah! Curse yooooooooou!"

The shot of holy water Sadeena created landed right on target, and the raging Makina turned into a demon and attacked. However, she was no match for us anymore.

"Selfish creatures like you have no right to exist!" she spat. I stood in front of Raphtalia and the rest of the party and took her attacks on my shield. My Soul Eater Shield's countereffect was triggered and stole away Makina's strength.

"Well done! Eh!" Freed from her captivity by our attacks, the hammer girl swung her hammer to the side and smashed it into the ghost of Makina. Then it looked like she cast some kind of spell.

"Guwaah! You'll pay for this!" But the evil ghost wasn't giving up yet. "I'll make you regret getting in my way with some serious pain!"

"There's no way left for you to survive in this world, eh!" The hammer girl stamped down hard with her foot, the sparkling of her hammer increasing in intensity, and a shockwave flew out.

"Guwaaaaaah!" Makina vanished without a trace, scattering red and black debris in the air. It didn't look like she was coming back from that.

With a flash, the pattern that had been covering Shildina was completely removed.

"That's the end of her?" I asked. So this would be our only meeting with the venomous viper Makina. I was still disgusted by the idea of taking over someone else's body, especially after death.

There had likely been an execution in her future, anyway, so maybe we should just consider this the short-cut to her inevitable fate.

"Killing her was the only way to save Q'ten Lo. I've finally done it, eh," the hammer girl said, sounding very satisfied with the outcome, anyway.

She went on. "Well then. Once this little trip ends, I'm not sure when I'll get to come out again, eh." That wasn't her first comment like this. If she just stayed inside Shildina, that would make her no better than Makina.

"You want a fight? Do you really think you can beat all of us?" I couldn't be sure, but from our exchanges so far, it seemed like she wasn't adversarial.

"You're not a number I couldn't handle, if I push myself a little, eh. Your spirit implements don't sound like they're in the best of shape either. But still . . ." the hammer girl looked at Raphtalia and then thrust a finger at me. "Holder of a spirit implement, you have a card that Shildina gave you, correct?"

"Y-yeah, you mean this?" I said and took out the odd-looking card. Then, for some reason, Shildina pointed at Raphtalia.

"I stipulate the Heavenly Emperor who serves the holder of a spirit implement. If you agree to duel me, one on one, I will free Shildina, eh. Of course, you must also supply aid to the weakened Shildina afterward."

"What!" I shouted.

"Holder of the shield spirit implement. That is a crystal taken from Shildina's heart." It sounded like I'd been given something pretty important without even re-alizing it. Shildina hadn't held back with her gifts—this was some heavy stuff! Something was definitely control-ling her too.

If it came down to a choice between Makina and this mysterious individual who looked like Raphtalia. I wondered which one we should prefer.

"She's a strange one, giving something so important to someone she hardly knows. I struggle to understand why she'd do such a thing—I guess maybe, thinking she no longer needed it, she wanted the first person of the opposite sex she ever really liked to have that important part of her, eh?" the hammer girl wondered.

"Oh my—" Sadeena exclaimed.

"Former water dragon's miko priestess! Stop right there. You may think you see an opening, but I assure you, attacking me will bring only pain," she shouted at Sadeena. She stopped Sadeena in her tracks, before she even had a chance to move. There were no openings to strike at her.

"What if we refuse?" I said.

"Then Shildina dies, eh." Gah! A part of me wanted to ask if we really cared? She wasn't a *complete* stranger though. She was Sadeena's sister too, and I couldn't bring myself to hate her. It was easy to imagine the suffering she had been through, and I also wanted to grill her—maybe just a little—about why she'd give something so important to me.

"You're starting to sound a lot like Makina," I said.

"Say whatever you like. This is payback for ever having listened to her venomous tongue, eh."

"Mr. Naofumi." Raphtalia looked straight at me. "Let me do this."

"Hold on—" This was almost like she was trying to kill Raphtalia by holding Shildina hostage. We couldn't just swallow these ridiculous demands. So what if it might appear cowardly? There was no need for Raphtalia to fight—

"Please. This is all because I was unable to break the curse binding Shildina," Raphtalia pleaded.

"But still—that curse—" As far as I could see, the patterns had been destroyed.

"Not to mention, if we run for it now, then I'm sure more damage will occur." Raphtalia continued to make her case.

"You said it. If you were the kind of Heavenly Emperor who'd made a run for it, then as a pacifier I would have to end you here," the hammer girl announced. Pacifier? That was the name of the weapons the Q'ten Lo lot owned.

"Just who are you?" I inquired. The person, whoever it was, possessing Shildina's body looked at me and answered.

"You need to understand the meaning of being an oracle to understand who I am. You may consider me a residual thought. Enough talking, anyway. Will you accept or not? That's the only question here," she barked.

"Mr. Naofumi," Raphtalia said, looking at me. If we didn't accept, both Raphtalia and Shildina could be killed. I wasn't keen on letting Raphtalia fight alone—but there was no more time to debate this.

"Very well," I said. If it looked like Raphtalia was about to lose, we'd jump in and save her. I'm pretty despicable, all things considered, so if this person possessing Shildina looked to be getting worn down in the fight with Raphtalia, I'd put an end to things by blindsiding her if I had to.

With my approval, Raphtalia gave a bow.

"Thank you very much," she said. Meanwhile, the person possessing Shildina pointed at the card.

"If you can place that against my chest, the hole in my heart will be filled and the binding broken. If you see an opening, go ahead, try for it, eh," she jeered. Indeed, that sounded like it would be effective. It was a fragment of her soul, right? Maybe it would even heal her weakened, unstable emotions?

"Raful!" Raph-chan nodded multiple times. So that sounded like the truth?

I gave the card to Raphtalia.

"I'm counting on you," I told her.

"Fear not. I'll win, I promise. For the sake of everyone who has brought me this far! Especially you, Mr. Naofumi!" Raphtalia gripped her sword tightly and tucked the card into her top, a position from which she could easily grab it if an opening presented itself.

"That's an odd wavelength your weapon has. A spirit implement's vassal weapon? No, even stranger. The vassal weapon of a spirit implement from a different world, eh?" the hammer girl observed. Pretty impressive, being able to accurately account for Raphtalia's katana like that.

"Here I come," Raphtalia stated.

"Whenever you're ready, eh." Looking at the two of them, hammer girl and Raphtalia, they both felt pretty similar to me.

"Have you worked out who is taking over my sister, Naofumi?" Sadeena asked.

"I think so," I replied. She'd talked about residual thoughts, and Shildina clearly had the ability to place something into her soul and perform complex magic that she couldn't execute alone. And it surely didn't have to be a soul. Then there was the tail formed from magic and big changes to her appearance. Seeing as Raphtalia could see her true form, they had to be some kind of illusion. If the residual thoughts were being gathered and forming a personality, there was a high possibility that those currently controlling Shildina belonged to a past Heavenly Emperor. That was why her transformed state looked like Raphtalia.

The person possessing Shildina—the past Heavenly Emperor—looked at me.

"I'm fine with a handicap, holder of the shield spirit implement. Go ahead and cast all the support magic you like, eh," she told me.

"You mock us, surely," I stated. Just how much leeway did she have? If it would give us an advantage, anyway, there was no reason to turn her down.

"Sadeena," I shouted.

"I'm right here, little Naofumi." We were getting pretty smooth at cooperative magic now, but I wasn't especially pleased about that, perhaps.

"Descent of the Thunder God!" We cast Descent of the Thunder God on Raphtalia.

"And this is okay with you?" Raphtalia asked.

"It's fine, eh. I'll just use my own Heavenly Emperor powers," she announced and smacked down on the ground with the handle of her hammer. That was all it took to make sakura lumina immediately start to grow in the vicinity, forming sakura stones of destiny and then creating a barrier.

So we'd just have to also use the sakura stone of destiny ourselves to create a barrier and nullify it—

"Ah, you just thought that using spirit implement fixed magic would be pointless, didn't you? Regrettably, while I did make some settings, I'm not nullifying that, so no need to worry," she told us.

"As if we'd believe that," I snorted.

"What a suspicious holder of a spirit implement you are! In either case, your little Heavenly Emperor wouldn't be able to cancel out a full-on barrier from me," she replied. Raphtalia nodded, sweat glistening on her cheeks.

"I'm sure you're right. But it's still a fact that I don't like being made to dance on the palm of your hand," Raphtalia said.

"You think I'll change the settings if it looks like I'm going to lose? That's quite an insult directed at a pacifier responsible for the fate of this nation. If that was my only alternative, I would simply choose defeat, eh," she said.

"Perhaps not to the extent of Mr. Naofumi, but if

you are lying I will teach you a painful lesson," Raphtalia told her. Not sure what I had to do with that, but very well. Point made.

"Well then. Let the fight begin!" The past Heavenly Emperor moved in an instant right up into Raphtalia's face and swung her massive hammer horizontally.

"Haaaaah!" Rather than block the hammer, Raphtalia leapt forward and—went through it? W-what just happened? Was there something wrong with my eyes?

I looked at the others to see that everyone else also seemed to be questioning their vision.

"Take this!"

"No, you take this!"

The past Heavenly Emperor swung her hammer, and fire, ice, and—my God—meteorites started to fly, not to mention that the Heavenly Emperor herself started multiplying into multiple copies of herself. At the same moment, Raphtalia also did the same thing, intercepting all the incoming attacks.

What was this? Some kind of illusion battle?

These incorporeal illusions started to trick the spectators. This was bad! I really wanted to follow the action, really needed to, but I was starting to have no idea what was actually going on.

"Naofumi, try looking not with your eyes, but your

other senses," Sadeena offered. I narrowed my eyes to view the life force and tried again.

By doing so, I finally saw both Raphtalia and the past Heavenly Emperor striking away at each other.

"Impressive! Keeping up with these tricky illusions. Good, good!"

"You won't fool me with magic tricks!" Raphtalia drew her katana from its scabbard, entered into her pseudo-accelerated state, and slashed. Her strike missed, so she followed through with the swing and unleased a skill as well.

"Stardust Blade!" Stars scattered from Raphtalia's blade and slashed into her opponent. This attack not only increased the attack power of her sword itself, but also offered an attack that could hit across a wide area. It also left the user pretty safe, a good all-round skill with effects much like the Shooting Star Sword, the skill Ren really loved. The stars flew toward the past Heavenly Emperor and struck her multiple times. Good! That one was her real body!

"Found you! Brave Blade! Crossing Mists!" Raphtalia drew her other sword and slashed at the past Heavenly Emperor. She was looking to weaken her first, then finish her with the card.

I clenched my fists in support, thinking Raphtalia almost had her—

"I'm not finished yet, eh!" The past Heavenly Emperor that we had both clearly thought was the real one dispersed like a puff of smoke, and then the actual real one appeared behind Raphtalia and attacked with her hammer.

"Guwah!" Raphtalia barely avoided the attack by jumping, landed, and her opponent immediately followed up. She barely got out of the way in time.

"You've got some resistance to illusions, eh. But you can't let a little trick like that catch you. You need to feel out a trap with a trap of your own before actually attacking."

"I can't believe I couldn't see through that," Raphtalia said.

"You are inexperienced with illusions, that's for sure. You have some resistance, and some knowledge, but you lack technique, eh," the past Heavenly Emperor told her. Yeah. That was probably my fault.

There was a time when I had Raphtalia learning magic.

Back then, I'd thought it best that I do as much as I possibly could for her, and so Raphtalia was responsible for raid attacks on the enemy, using magic to conceal herself and then striking at them from behind. However, from around the time we gained the ability to go to

Kizuna's world, she had started to rely more heavily on just the power of the katana vessel weapon, which had led to her magic ability to get left behind. Then they'd said it would be hard for her to learn the Way of the Dragon Vein due to the katana vassal weapon too.

That said, I didn't consider it a mistake.

Using someone with a tool as powerful as a vassal weapon just for raids was, especially in light of our past battles, simply not the best strategy, although it might have been a failure that I'd let her magic suffer a bit as a result. That was an issue for the future, anyway.

"Oh, I'm not done yet!" Raphtalia's tail swelled up, and she incanted some magic. "Hide Mirage!" Vanishing in a blink, Raphtalia moved through the illusion-filled surroundings, coming around behind the past Heavenly Emperor and swinging her katana—but the attack was intercepted on the haft of the hammer.

"Just vanishing isn't enough. If you can confuse your real position and then close in, that's the way to trick your opponent, eh." The past Heavenly Emperor continued to school Raphtalia.

"Gah!" It had only been a short battle, and already the strength of her opponent was becoming all too apparent. Just how many monster-level trump cards did hammer girl have?

"If this is going to be a clash of weapons, let me have a turn too," she said and the tip of her hammer started to glow, and then the past Heavenly Emperor swung it toward Raphtalia.

"Mighty Quake!"

"Ah!" Raphtalia barely avoided that too, and then the hammer crashed into the ground. Earth and dust were immediately thrown up, along with a shockwave from the ground, sending Raphtalia flying away.

"Just how strong is she?!" Raphtalia muttered, landing and falling back a little, shoulders heaving as she breathed heavily.

"You can't underestimate others just because you have spirit implements and vassal weapons." The past Heavenly Emperor was taunting in good form, bouncing her hammer on her shoulder as she offered this pearl of wisdom. That hammer—it looked like quite the piece of work.

I couldn't be sure, but I saw something that looked like a vassal weapon gemstone. Was she also using illusions to display the weapon that she used during her lifetime?

"I can't even land a single blow," Raphtalia gasped.

"You show potential though." This visitor from the past was still completely at ease. Indeed, she was toying with Raphtalia—who, by now, had become pretty strong—like she was nothing more than a baby.

Could Raphtalia really hope to win this fight?

"Hah!" With quick footwork she closed in with the past Heavenly Emperor and then sliced down into a space with no one in it.

"Powder Snow!"

"Aha! You did well to see through that one, eh!" the past Heavenly Emperor complimented. Sparks grated out into the air, and the past Heavenly Emperor appeared from a spot that had appeared to be completely empty.

Huh? She'd used our chat as an opening to trick us again? She could even fool my eyes when watching the life force? What kind of high-level trickery was this?! I was willing to bet that only Raphtalia and Raph-chan were truly keeping up with what was going on.

"Oh? That's a nasty skill, eh," she stated. Power scattered like snow from where she had taken the blow, and then it looked like the past Heavenly Emperor placed her hand on the damaged area and healed it.

So that attack had been effective?

"Well then. I think I'm pretty warmed up now. Time for me to show you what the Heavenly Emperor can really do, eh," she announced. With that, the past Heavenly

Emperor swung her sword downward while at the same time her tail swelled up.

The next instant she appeared in front of Raphtalia. Raphtalia tried to dodge the attack, but the past Heavenly Emperor used light footwork to switch to a horizontal strike.

Just the swing alone created a buffeting wind.

"Five Practices Destiny Split!"

"Uwah!" She scarcely avoided the attack—no, it actually hit her, barely—but then Raphtalia unleashed a skill.

"Kagura Dance of the Sakura! First Formation! Blossom!"

"You naïve little girl!" Five types of sphere started to float around her. That was the same attack that took Sadeena down! Just the barest hit was enough to activate it?

"Fire Defeats Metal!" The miko outfit worn by Raphtalia was ripped open, and a red line appeared on her katana.

"A status effect?" I wondered.

"You temporarily can't use that weapon, eh," she jeered. Just how versatile were her attacks? Then Raphtalia turned her katana into a different shape, one made with Demon Dragon materials.

"That skill you just used. It looks like you can perform a pseudo-recreation of Heavenly Emperor techniques. But if you don't hone them further, ready them for use in actual battle, then you'll find they just get repelled, eh," the past Heavenly Emperor continued to inform Raphtalia.

Raphtalia returned her katana to its scabbard and prepared for a draw slice.

"That stance! That focusing of power!" Rishia immediately responded. She was doing the whole exposition thing again. I remembered her doing that with Ren too.

"I know!" Now Ren himself was getting in on the explaining action. "It's a technique adapting the Hengen Muso Style, Moon Ripple!" Raphtalia unleashed a swift horizontal cut, and a crescent moon–shaped slash flew toward her opponent.

"Oh my! An attack technique that isn't a skill? However—" The past Heavenly Emperor began and took the crescent moon slash on her hammer. "—eh?" Raphtalia allowed herself a slight smile. She was probably sure the attack had landed.

However—

"Hengen Muso Style. I'm quite surprised you've learned such techniques, eh," the past Heavenly Emperor admitted. With just a slight swing of her hammer, she canceled out whatever it was Raphtalia had placed into her attack. "I'll give you credit for the idea. Let me have a go too, eh." She smashed the hammer onto the ground with a heavy thud, and with that, countless balls comprised of life force flew toward Raphtalia.

What the hell was that? Was each and every one of those was an attack with life force—a defense rating attack, which I could personally barely manage to draw out of myself?

Just how many techniques did she have access to?

"I can't let those hit me—" Raphtalia shouted and leapt into the air, just to find the past Heavenly Emperor standing where she came down, already swinging her hammer.

Watch out!

Even as I thought that, even as I took a step forward, Raphtalia turned into smoke and vanished. I narrowed my eyes and finally saw that Raphtalia had actually avoided it by jumping in the opposite direction.

"You did well to avoid that, this time. I'm wondering if maybe I should just kill you, eh," the past Heavenly Emperor bragged. She was getting some dangerous ideas. This wasn't just about training or testing Raphtalia. That said, if Hengen Muso Style wasn't going to work, how could she fight this opponent? I just couldn't see a path to a finishing strike.

"I'm not out of tricks yet. Not yet—" With that Raphtalia raised her katana in front of her and adopted the stance for the Eight Trigrams Blade of Destiny. In the moment she started to focus her attention—

"You're completely exposed!" the past Heavenly Emperor announced, and as she closed in, Raphtalia was forced to drop the stance. As I'd feared, that was an attack she couldn't unleash without some allies pinning down the enemy. That also meant she couldn't use the Supreme Ultimate Slash of Destiny. That could only be unleashed quickly with the Sakura Sphere of Influence and blossom blaze protection.

In either case, attacks that didn't rely on skills just took too much time. I really couldn't think of an approach here.

Was the only option to deploy a new weapon and rely on a new skill, then? Was that it?

Even as I considered that, the past Heavenly Emperor—looking like she'd had enough now—poured power into her hammer and swung it down at Raphtalia.

"Could you have failed my expectations any more completely? How the bloodline of the Heavenly Emperor has fallen," the past Heavenly Emperor contemplated.

"Kuwah! Haaah!" Raphtalia desperately parried and avoided the attacks, but it was really starting to look like little more than a child trying to fight an adult.

Shit! My only choice was to step in and protect Raphtalia. Just as I was about to take a step forward, Raphtalia—who was closely watching the past Heavenly Emperor—realized that her tail was full and fluffy.

For just an instant, she appeared to sparkle right to her hair.

"Haaah!"

"Woah!" Raphtalia's counterattack forced the past Heavenly Emperor to take a big step back.

"Keep showing me the same attack and I'll eventually learn to beat it!" Raphtalia pointed out. Then she placed her hand on her katana blade and adopted a stance. It looked like the sword had started glowing with something other than life force, magic, or SP.

Not to be outdone, the past Heavenly Emperor struck at Raphtalia with her hammer.

"Five Practices Destiny Split!"

"Five Practices Destiny Thrust!"

Raphtalia's katana and the past Heavenly Emperor's hammer clashed, and then again, over and over. Perhaps due to the clashing magic, petals of magical power scattered around them, causing all sorts of illusions to form.

"Fire Defeats Metal," shouted the past Heavenly Emperor. Raphtalia quickly responded.

"Metal Quells Fire!" As a result, this time she repelled the weapon-destroying attack. So she'd found a way to nullify it?

"Ah, your true Heavenly Emperor powers provided the answer, eh?" the past Heavenly Emperor commented with a whistle. "Try this then, eh! Water Defeats Fire!"

"Fire Quells—" Raphtalia couldn't complete the cancellation in time, bouncing from the clash of weapons and blowing away the magic from the blade itself. Was that nullifying the imbued effects or life force or whatever?

"I can't change!" Raphtalia lamented. No! Interference with weapon changing! I'd suffered it myself numerous times, but I hadn't expected to encounter this technique here! "No! Tree Grows Fire!" Raphtalia's katana bloomed into fire, and the blade started shining.

"Hmmm, a little rough, but well done. Yet all you've really done is left yourself open!" the past Heavenly Emperor shouted and flickered out of existence, then appeared a little distance away, charging a massive amount of power! What was with the quickening of this power?

"Now observe! This is the technique of the Heavenly Emperor!" she boomed. Countless clones all flew together toward Raphtalia, whose only choice was to narrow her eyes and try to spot the real one.

"There!" With both swords back in their scabbards, she gave that shout while adopting a draw slash stance. "I can't focus my strength as quickly, as potently, as you. This is the best I can do—try it out!" Raphtalia stamped down heavily on the ground, causing a large ying-yang mark to appear there. "Kagura Dance of the Sakura! Second Formation! Beginning Blossom!" Readying a deep swing, the past Heavenly Emperor smashed her hammer down toward Raphtalia.

"Ying-Yang Eight Trigrams Split of Destiny!" The clash of strength on strength caused a wave of oppressive pressure to spill into the surroundings. The very air crackled, throbbing with the ferocity of the conflict.

"Five Practices Destiny—" Raphtalia and the past Heavenly Emperor continued to beat at each other. Five balls started to float around the past Heavenly Emperor, and it started to look like they were defending her during her attacks. As though competing with her, five balls were also floating around Raphtalia.

That wasn't all though.

The sakura lumina growing close to the city all started to glow, and even though it was still daylight, they started to shine into the sky like spotlights.

"Spring Blossom Tree!"

"Kagura Dance of the Sakura! Third Formation! Third Blossom!" The two attacks clashed, scattering light and darkness in the vicinity, which then scattered like petals.

It felt like the first time I truly understood the meaning of the magical nature, both light and darkness, possessed by Raphtalia. The light was for more than just refraction, and the darkness for more than concealment. Her basic nature comprised both light and darkness, like the ying-yang, allowing her to make use of seemingly opposing attributes.

Clashing, the two weapons bouncing off each other sounded as though they were going to ring into infinity.

"Wood Defeats Earth! Earth Defeats Water! Water Defeats Fire! Fire Defeats Metal! Metal Defeats Wood!"

"Kagura Dance of the Sakura! Fourth Formation! Fifth Blossom! Sixth—Blossom—ugh!" It looked like maybe Raphtalia was losing ground. But no, the past Heavenly Emperor was also starting to crack.

"You've done well to keep up this far. Those strings of attacks are likely increasing in attack power with each skill you unleash, but they also burn through your strength in a short period of time, eh," the past Heavenly Emperor observed.

"You think I don't know that! I'm still not giving up!

Haaaah!" Raphtalia responded.

"Have a taste of my own special attack! Divine Clash of the Five Practices!" Countless clusters of five balls each gathered together and vanished into the hammer, preparing an attack imbued with incredible power that then swung straight for Raphtalia. The magic symbols running across the floor formed a five-pointed star and now appeared to be exerting pressure on Raphtalia.

Responding, Raphtalia caught it on her sword and scattered the pressure from the area around her, but then another pattern appeared on the ground. Without backing down, Raphtalia unleashed all of the power of her sword. The balls around her started to rotate at high speed.

"Finally, I can do it! I'll use the yang to oppose the controlling power of ying and cancel them out!" Raphtalia declared.

"I saw you honing that ability even as we fought, eh. Now this all comes down to a single moment! If you don't want to die, come at me, eh!" the past Heavenly Emperor dared.

"Haaaaah! Divine Birth of the Five Practices!" With a cracking sound, the magic symbols deployed around the pair of combatants shattered. In the moment the past Heavenly Emperor realized her attacks had been neutralized, she tried to get some distance, but Raphtalia immediately closed in and swung her sword.

"I'm not finished yet! Hazy Moon!" Seizing the smallest of openings, Raphtalia's attack splintered the haft of the past Heavenly Emperor's hammer and bit into her shoulder.

"I just need a little more! Just a moment more! Haaaah!" she roared and drew the other katana from its scabbard. The accessory with the special effect pseudo-haikuikku wouldn't work in this world. What Raphtalia was currently using was something that slightly increased her current speed. Still, that slight increase could be enough to make all the difference.

"I'm still right here, eh!" The past Heavenly Emperor wasn't giving up yet, swatting at Raphtalia one-handed with the shortened hammer. But just before it landed, Raphtalia vanished.

"Huh? Remarkable. Vanished in an instant." The past Heavenly Emperor almost sounded impressed.

"Illusion Blade!" That was the first technique she had learned and was now her final attack, carrying all of her remaining strength—all of the magic and SP and life force she had. Raphtalia popped back into existence behind the past Heavenly Emperor and slashed down with all her might. "This is the end!" Raphtalia screamed and took the card out from her top, which looked like it gave the Heavenly Emperor room for a counterattack. But the past Heavenly Emperor did nothing and just accepted what was coming.

"Gah. I guess that's a passing grade, eh," she conceded. The card hit her chest, and with a flash of light it vanished inside her. "You're lacking in many ways, but you've also got real vigor. I think I may well make an exception and leave things in your hands rather than eradicating you here, eh." After ruffling Raphtalia's hair, the past Heavenly Emperor gave her a round of applause. Raphtalia kept her sword up and watched, suspicious.

"Hold on a moment. You weren't fighting seriously?" Raphtalia gasped.

"I wouldn't say that. I fought you with the maximum power I could place in this body. If you can't surpass me, you have no right to be a pacifier, especially if you are in collusion with the holder of a spirit implement."

"A pacifier? Aren't they the ones meant to stop the heroes?" Raphtalia wondered.

"If you failed to display the power to overcome me, then you would be unable to give the fools that will surely appear what they deserve. I pray that you will continue the bloodline of the Q'ten Lo Heavenly Emperor, free from the claws of pride," she concluded. That was the

past Heavenly Emperor's murmured response to Raphtalia, and she placed her hand on her chest. The general
atmosphere wasn't really conducive to anyone else butt-
ing in. "You've caused quite a lot of turmoil across this
nation, but you showed me something interesting here
at the end, eh. Do your best not to lose to them! Now
then, the ghost from the past . . . will return there, eh."
With that, the hammer held by the past Heavenly Emperor cracked, shattered with a splitting sound, and her
glowing tail also turned into mist—the transformation
ended, revealing Shildina, who promptly collapsed.

"Got you!" Raphtalia caught hold of her.

"Looks like you won," Shildina whispered. The rest
of us dashed forward and checked Shildina out. She was
breathing raggedly, and her vitality was low. We needed
to take certain steps or her life would be in danger. We
still didn't know if she would respond to us, but she was
Sadeena's sister, and I did have a lot of sympathy for her
situation.

We needed to care for her as best we could.

"I'm going to treat her. Those with healing magic
and knowledge of healing herbs, help me out. Everyone
else, prioritize taking the castle! You must be exhausted,
Raphtalia, so you stay with me. Sadeena, you help with
the healing too!"

"Y-yes!"

"As you say!" With that, we paid witness to the battle between the Heavenly Emperors and then started taking care of the aftermath.

Chapter Fourteen:
The True Terror of Monsters

We treated Shildina as best we could and then sent her away before heading to the main keep ourselves. According to those left alive in the castle, the current Heavenly Emperor was still there, all alone.

"He's just a young boy, correct? Knowing he was cornered, maybe he's sent everyone else away and is just waiting alone?" I asked of Raluva when he came to report to me. The kid had given all sorts of stupid orders thus far, but maybe at the end he was finally acting a bit like a real ruler.

"Actually, it seems Makina told him this would all be over quickly and left him alone in the keep," Raluva reported.

"While Makina herself actually tried to escape using a secret passage. We saw what happened to her after that," I said. Raluva nodded. That just made me hate her even more. She'd caused untold damage to this nation and yet taken no responsibility. Just as when she tried to take over Shildina as a ghost, I was reminded horribly of Witch. If it wasn't for the queen, Melromarc might have ended up exactly like this place. She'd really got under my skin, making me think like that.

"Rafu." Huh? Raph-chan was clinging to something that looked like a ball. What was it? I did want to check it out, but we carried on, reaching the main keep and proceeding to the Heavenly Emperor's room behind the audience chamber.

We opened the sliding door.

"W-who's there!" The speaker was a boy, maybe around eight years old, dressed a bit like a priest. He was looking in our direction with fear in his eyes, clutching onto a stuffed toy clearly modeled after a filolial chick.

He was even younger than Raphtalia when I first met her. So this was the moron who had been acting as Q'ten Lo's emperor?

His room was packed with filolial merchandise. It started with pictures and included stuffed toys and even wooden carvings and bronze statues. I took a moment to look for ones made of gold and gemstones—yep, there we go—although on closer inspection it was just gold leaf. The gemstones were cheap ones too.

It also looked like there were lots of books, but about what? A quick look at the covers revealed more images of filolials. All of those depicted were white with cherry pink coloring. Exactly the same as Filo. Just why was that coloring so popular?

"W-where is Makina? Someone! Anyone! Shildina! Help me!" he shouted. It looked like he didn't have a full understanding of the situation and had just been left—abandoned—here. What to do, then?

It was really starting to look like he'd just been used and had no real understanding of good and evil for himself. That said, his frivolous application of the protection of the Heavenly Emperor was definitely a lingering problem.

"Ah! That outfit! I'm the only one important enough to wear that!" the kid yelled, pointing petulantly at Raphtalia. It looked like the first order of business was to make sure he understood exactly the position he was in. Just capturing him without any explanation and putting him to death was a situation I definitely wanted to avoid, but it didn't change the fact he was going to come off his high horse, down from all that power, with a bump.

"Sorry, kid, but anyone who might have sided with you is either dead or captured. You're not important. You're not *anything* anymore. You must understand that much at least, right?" At my question, the kid hung his head and gave a nod.

"I thought that was the case," I stated. Oh? Looked like maybe he had a better grip on things than I first thought.

He began to speak. "Makina said she would be right back, but after all this time she still hasn't returned, and sometimes when I was hiding I heard people saying things about me that weren't all that nice. But still . . ." The kid—no, he was too smart for that, at least worthy of being called a "boy"—went on. "I still wanted to believe in them. That they would end this chaos and come back to me."

"Sorry that didn't work out for you," I scoffed. The boy remained silent in the face of, let's be honest, my pretty dickish comment. Hey, I wasn't his babysitter.

"Please, Mr. Naofumi," Raphtalia pleaded. Of course, she had picked up on it. "Can't you be a little bit nicer to him?"

"I know, he's just a boy. But this is still the one who sent all of those after your life, Raphtalia. That's a big problem, even if we cut him some slack," I stated. The very fact this boy was such an ineffectual leader had led to Raphtalia being targeted. If he'd actually been in control, assassins might never have been sent out just because she put on a stupid outfit.

Wringing what bravery he could from his trembling body, the boy looked at us and spoke strongly. "So what will do you with us? We are defeated, correct? Then take us where you will and execute us if you must. But those who followed us are without blame in all of this. Will you please see right by them?" he begged. He had it all the wrong way, of course. Those who "followed" him were the true criminals here, making this boy far closer to blameless than they were. Honestly, from my perspective, they were the ones I wanted to execute.

Still, his tone was now markedly different, and was that the royal "we"? He'd had some training in his post, a least. Hmmm, when I took into account his attitude as a whole, with a proper education, he might have turned out okay, I thought. He was still related to Raphtalia, after all, even if he was just a distant cousin or something.

"We'll see. I'm not inclined to take it easy on you, but we're definitely starting by taking away your title of Heavenly Emperor. What happens after that, we'll decide later." At my words, the boy quietly closed his eyes and quelled his trembling. Our intel suggested his parents had been killed while he was still a babe, and he'd clearly come through his own share of hardships.

With our capturing of the eastern capital, anyway, the state of play in Q'ten Lo would dramatically change, with almost no one left who could oppose our forces. The old city would be restored and would be called the "Royal Capital," and peaceful rule could be expected to be restored as well.

We'd done a pretty good job extracting the puss, from the look of it.

Of course, by the customs of this world, if we were announcing the birth of our new authority to the people, then we should hold a public execution of the captured Heavenly Emperor. But I wasn't so sure about that.

In either case, those who had set all of this up would definitely get what was coming to them. Not to mention, at this point, my own purpose here had pretty much been fulfilled.

"Maybe we'll give him a slave mark and see how he holds up under torture?" I'd suggested in order to see what his reaction was to that, and think about his future based on it.

"I-if that is to be our punishment, we shall accept it!" he stuttered. Oh? He was pretty forthright about it. He had some awareness of his responsibilities as the Heavenly Emperor, then. Even if his awareness of the concept of "torture" wasn't especially fleshed out, he had to know it would be painful and scary.

Yeah. I was having a hard time really hating the boy. Considering the information we had already collected, he was definitely only being used.

That's what it seemed like, anyway. But I wanted to make sure. See his true self.

"Hmmm. Just give me a moment," I said and ordered Raphtalia and the others to stay there to watch the kid. Then I took the human-form Filo with me out of the room by basically pushing her out.

"Maaaaster, whaaat's—?"

"Filo, I want you to turn into your filolial queen form, stay silent—that bit is important!—and follow me back inside, then stare at that boy. When I give the signal, I need you to grab his collar with your beak and lift him into the air. If you do everything I say, to the letter, I'll make you a special meal later," I explained to Filo.

"Really!" Filo looked really happy, then turned into her filolial queen form and followed me back inside, practically skipping.

"Oh? Mr. Naofumi, just what—why is Filo in that form?" Raphtalia began.

"Oh my?" Sadeena exclaimed.

"What do you think Naofumi is planning?" Ren inquired.

"Don't ask me!" Itsuki said.

"Feeeh?" Rishia mumbled.

This was how my other companions in the room all reacted to this turn of events. It was pretty easy to imagine what their reactions would be to what was going to happen next.

"Ah, a filolial!" The boy's eyes lit up and he moved over to her. Yes, that's right. This was the idiot Heavenly Emperor who made the proclamation about not harming living things because of his love for filolials. So this was the best way to really see his true nature.

The boy rushed over to Filo and started to stroke her plumage. Filo looked to be enjoying it and turned her gaze on the boy. I'd told her to keep quiet, in no uncertain terms. If she'd spoken, even a few words, she and the boy might have quickly become friends. Filo had that way about her. But she stood true to my instructions and said nothing, just continued to look at the boy.

It didn't take long for his smile to fade into fear.

Just as I thought. From all this merchandise he had collected, I'd been pretty sure that he didn't really understand much about real filolials. To frame it in terms from home, he was like a super otaku. I could place the sentiment because of my own otaku tendencies—the type who loved the heroine of their favorite show rather than a real woman.

In other words, he didn't know a thing about real filolials.

"Eh? A-aaaah!" Heh. Ah, Filo. She'd completely forgotten how everyone in the village had first been so scared of her. "Waaah!" She was in a great mood, her appetite stimulated by my promise of food, even as she continued to just stare at him.

Indeed, stare and salivate. She was looking at the boy like a bird of prey staring down its next meal.

The boy's face completed its descent into terror, and his legs almost gave out. Truly, if she had spoken, the entire scene would have played out quite differently. At the moment, his reaction was quite a bit like Melty's had been.

That said, Melty had still done her best to make friends, even with a starving filolial. Just as I'd surmised, this boy had a liking for filolials, but he wasn't all that familiar with them.

I gave Filo the hand signal.

With that, she started to move slowly toward the boy. She made a slurping noise, looking exactly like a predator closing in on prey.

"W-wah! S-stay back! Please, save me before I'm eaten!" he screamed in terror. Filo stopped and looked at me, clearly uncomfortable. Maybe she realized that I'd set her up. But she immediately started moving again.

She wanted to eat my cooking that badly?

When I asked her about it later, she said she'd thought it was a punishment for causing so much trouble for Raphtalia and the people of the country.

"Oh my," Sadeena said again. I felt a crowd of cold looks collecting on me.

"Ah—can I ask, just what are you doing?" Raphtalia took the initiative to ask for everyone.

"First things first, he needs to be punished," I announced, making sure he could hear me, of course. But I also spoke in such a way that hopefully the others would cotton on. "If he loves filolials so much, I think he deserves to die by being eaten by one. Eaten alive, no less!"

"N-no! Please, spare me that!" he begged. Ah ha! Finally, we were reaching his true nature. No matter the regal front he tried to put on, he was still just a child at heart. And even if he had been used by those around him, he needed to be punished for making the proclamation against hurting living creatures and placing blessings on the sealed monsters.

Experiencing this terror for himself seemed about right. Have him feel for himself the damage done to the people of his nation by monsters.

"W-waaaaaah!" The terror of being attacked by a filolial, in exactly the form and colors that he loved so much, was surely going to be burned into the child's brain.

As I thought that, I noticed one of the leaders of the revolution using a video crystal to record the proceedings. What were they planning now? That item had been imported from Siltvelt, if I recalled correctly.

At the point that Filo lifted the child up by his collar, they stopped shooting the video. That was it, then. Spreading this footage across the land as the execution of the Heavenly Emperor would put the people at ease.

"Gyaaaaaaaaah!" he screamed. Of course, he wasn't actually eaten by Filo.

Still holding the boy in her beak, Filo came over to me. After screaming for a while, the kid pissed himself and then continued to beg to be saved between gasping for breath. Upon finally realizing that no one was going to help him, he just struggled harder, but to no avail; when he finally gave up and slumped still, I ordered that he be released.

"Uh—" He gasped for air. Realizing that he was free, the boy tried to scramble away from the source of his terror. Raphtalia and the others looked on, not especially approvingly.

"I think maybe he's had enough now?"

"There's so much more I'd like to knock into him, but I guess this is a good first step." Now, at least, he had an understanding of how terrifying monsters were.

"Master, that was mean!" Filo scolded.

"Shut it. How would things have gone if the kid was Melty?" ·

"Huh? Well, she would have given me food and stroked me where I liked it and made me all fluffy and happy!" Exactly. Even if Melty was facing execution in this manner, she'd surely be able to overcome it.

That was the big difference between Melty and this boy.

"I-it's speaking! It's saying something!" Ren announced.

Filo had spoken to me in the language of Melromarc. She could also speak the languages from Siltvelt and Q'ten Lo too. Her experience of being put on show in another world had left her with the lesson of quickly wanting to learn new languages. For this boy, though, even a talking filolial was now a source of fear. He was curled up in terror in the corner.

"Boy. I'm going to tell you something very important," I began.

"W-what?"

"Filolials may have always just looked cute and fluffy to you, but they are vicious, violent creatures. You've experienced that for yourself now, haven't you?" I said.

"Boo to you!" Filo didn't like that characterization.

"Why are you being so antagonistic toward filolials now?" I ignored Raphtalia's sharp comment too.

"I'm guessing those you've touched in the past have

been trained not to get violent or been restrained," I continued. The boy nodded. He understood the difference now. "Wild monsters are not the same. In fact, you went around putting the blessings of the Heavenly Emperor onto horrible monsters that could have really harmed your nation. Do you understand what that means?" The boy lowered his head at my words, and Raphtalia held her tongue as well. It looked like everyone finally understood my intent with all this.

"Boo!" Well, everyone other than Filo and her puffed-up, indignant cheeks. In this moment, though, she was just helping to make my point.

"That terror wouldn't be the end of it either. You should have been chewed up, shredded by claws, covered in poison, died painfully—and that is what has been happening to your people. That's what you did, even if you didn't know it."

"We see. We understand now. In which case, we're truly not fit to be Heavenly Emperor. Everyone called her an imposter, but it is as you say. For one who serves the revolutionary Heavenly Emperor, we will give the throne to her," he stated. Wow! He was still a kid in many ways, but he knew what was going on. He wasn't some moron thinking just about money and luxury, so this would probably serve as punishment enough.

"I can't really speak to what's going to happen next, but it might be good for you to leave this country and see more of the world," I said.

"If we were to be given that opportunity—" he began. It was also worth noting that the idiocy of the Q'ten Lo we'd fought against had honestly helped us out, allowing us to take the nation so quickly. Banishment was likely more fitting than execution. If he really had just been used, it would be good for him to see the world and learn more about real life.

He was related to Raphtalia too.

Publicly, of course, we would tell people he had been executed. We could even take him to the village and privately call him Raphtalia's cousin or the former prince.

"Anyway, we'll decide exactly what to do with you later," I said. The boy looked scared by my words, but also receptive. Right, then. Seemed like a good chance to share some other important information with him. "Let me share something else important with you. Here's a monster that's much cuter, smarter, and more useful than any filolial," I said and picked up Raph-chan with both hands and presented her to the boy.

"Tali?" Rafu chirped. What! A new sound? What new evolution was this! Raph-chan cutely raised a hand to the boy.

"What are you playing at now?" Raphtalia snapped. She had clearly reached the limits of holding her tongue. But I carried on. The boy said, "I've n-never seen a monster like this before. Never even in a book!" With that, the boy reached toward Raph-chan. She purred with rafu sounds, enjoying being stroked by the child. Starting from the head, the boy stroked her on the cheeks, belly, hands, feet, and tail, and she even stroked the child's hand in return.

"Oh wow!" His eyes sparkled, and he clearly wanting one of his own.

"This little cutie is a monster made from the hair of your relative. Cuter than a filolial, isn't she?" I asked.

"Boo!" Filo continued her booing.

"Please, Mr. Naofumi. Stop this." Raphtalia didn't look pleased either. The others were just shaking their heads.

"That girl you see over there, she's called Raphtalia. The revolutionary Heavenly Emperor, and your relative."

"Okay."

"Those around you may have said the bloodline of the Heavenly Emperor was best if it was only you and that others were imposters and should be killed, but wouldn't it be better for your family to get along?" I inquired.

"Yes. Just why did everyone say she was my enemy when we're related?"

"Why do you think? Because, for the "everyone" you're talking about, Raphtalia being alive was a problem. An inconvenience. That's why they gave the orders to kill her."

"I see." Even though he was a child, he seemed to have some understanding of political affairs. It had been a quagmire of corruption, after all.

"Anyway, if you're going to be friendly with us, I'll let you pet Raph-chan a little longer." The boy looked from Raph-chan to Raphtalia and then nodded. "So rather than filolial merch, how about making some Raph-chan—" Raphtalia grabbed my shoulders tightly.

"Mr. Naofumi, I'm not sure what you are planning, but don't take things too far," she scolded. Gah. Enough for now. I could bring him into the light of Raph-chan worship later.

"Anyway. We're not going to treat you badly, and we can be a bit flexible, so you just need to learn more about the world."

"Very well. If you will give us—me—the opportunity, I'll do what I can to make up for all the trouble I've caused." Phew. Things seemed to have worked out pretty nicely. We took the boy into our protection and left the castle behind.

"You think this is okay?" I asked Sadeena abruptly.

"I think so. You've really risen to the occasion, little Naofumi, which I've loved to see, and I couldn't be prouder of Raphtalia."

"Although, this was all the fault of that miko outfit. If I'd never put that on, we wouldn't have got caught up in this conflict," Raphtalia sighed. No need to bring that up again.

"Tali, rafu."

"Why is she starting to say the rest of my name now?" Raphtalia asked, turning her complaining to Raph-chan now. She had lots of energy even though she'd just been in a major battle.

Amid this chatter, we quietly sneaked the boy out, and our invasion of Q'ten Lo finally came to an end. To be honest, I was amazed at the incredible speed we took the nation. They'd clearly been on their last legs, but "sloppy" hardly covered the way they had waged war.

Atla and the others who arrived late to the battle, of course, were upset at missing the action. But as Raphtalia had been the one doing the fighting, everyone else had only watched anyway.

Epilogue: Dusk

Two days after we completed our occupation of the eastern capital—

I went to visit Shildina, who was now a patient at the eastern hospital. She'd just recovered consciousness. I was accompanied by Sadeena, bravely coming to visit her sister, and the boy, disguised to hide his face and tail. The video crystal footage starring Filo from the other day had been spread far and wide, and the people believed the Heavenly Emperor had been put to a grisly death. Honestly, hatred for him had built up so much that it seemed like the only way to appease the people's anger.

Raphtalia, meanwhile, was busy with her new duties after the transition of power, and Atla was leading a party in mopping up the last of our enemies. Filo had gone off to play, saying she'd made friends with the children of the city. Ren and Itsuki were training with Rishia.

Shildina slowly opened her eyes with a groan and moved her face to look around.

"So you finally came to?" I said.

Shildina noticed Sadeena and me in the room and

tried to sit up, but she wasn't fully recovered and collapsed back onto the bed.

"Shildina!" When the boy cried out, Shildina looked for a moment between him and me and tilted her head.

"Seriously. You've only just regained consciousness, and you thought, what? You'd get right back to fighting us?" I shook my head, half in amazement, as I asked Shildina this. She just turned her face away, as though she didn't want to talk.

"You really did give something absolutely, insanely important to a person you'd only met once, didn't you?" I prodded. Someone who she'd shared drinks with, just once, she gave a piece of her soul. Just what was she thinking? I hadn't even been able to help her, in the end, either. Raphtalia had been the one to save her.

"Not really. You were the first man I'd ever met who I thought was really nice, so I gave you a card with a piece of my soul sealed inside it. It was something I'd thought I may never be able to give up," she admitted.

"You thought I was nice—I'm taking it, from your love of drinking, that's because I ate the rucolu fruit?" I asked. Shildina nodded.

"I love people who can hold their drink."

"Dammit! Both of you sisters, reacting in almost the same way!" I shouted. A real pair of drunkards.

"Oh my," Shildina offered.

"Stop that too. You look just like the sister you claim to hate so much," I said. That shut her up. Seriously, I knew from the way she talked that she hated her, but why did they act the same? Was their blood connection that strong?

"I thought you were nice. Is that wrong? It felt like, well, first love."

"And of all people, it had to be the god of Siltvelt, the one behind the revolutionary Heavenly Emperor. That's too much," I barked. Was it odd for me to be the one saying that?

"But in the end, you're Sadeena's man. That simply sucks."

"Hold on. How many times must I tell you, I'm not Sadeena's man!"

"Oh my." Sadeena, of course, took that moment to take my arm.

"Sorry, but that's not how things are between us." I pushed her off as I answered.

"Come on, have some fun with me!"

"Stop making this more difficult!" Seriously, this sister of hers was raised with an incredible complex about her. I wish she'd stop playing into that!

However, Sadeena was looking at Shildina with a

gentle smile on her face, as though to prove she was only joking that we weren't together.

"If you're my sister, you can't give up so easily. If you like Naofumi, then you need to get more aggressive!" she said.

"Enough joking around!"

"Stick with it, little sis. You can at least become his lover. You may not be able to defeat Raphtalia or Atla, but I reckon you could take up position, say, in front of Filo," Sadeena suggested.

"What are you talking about now?!" I bellowed. Atla was one thing, but Raphtalia was like my daughter. Lusting after my daughter would make me a pervert. Not that I was lusting after Atla either.

In any case, I had no plans to fall in love or have a family in this world!

Filo? Filo had Melty, although there had been those issues with a spear-wielding stalker recently.

"If you have any feelings for little Naofumi, anyway, you'll need to put up a good fight against me! Or are you just going to run away?" At Sadeena's words, Shildina narrowed her eyebrows and gave an unpleasant glare. She seemed to have a wide range of negative emotions, that was for sure. Her mental state was a lot like the people in the village who had been abused. Considering her age, I did want to help her if I could. "It's no fun, if you're just giving up."

"Please, don't tease her too much." I couldn't hold in a sigh. Sadeena was a pretty considerate person, generally, but it looked like she was having difficulty finding the right distance from her sister.

"You looked like you were having such fun in the bar that night. All we were doing was playing a game," I said. Rather than respond, Shildina turned her face to the side, as though she didn't want to talk to me at all. I guess I wasn't going to be able to persuade her after all. Freeing her from her twisted family really wasn't going to be easy. Yet I still sympathized with her.

I continued. "You have a terrible sense of direction, but if you want to play with me again, then come find me. Would that be okay?" She seemed to like card games, so that seemed like the best approach. S'yne was standing guard outside the room, and she showed me some spread-out cards.

She liked games too.

She overlapped with Raphtalia a little for me, being placed in such a terrible situation; was it just my ego that made me want to help her? Maybe I wouldn't be able to. Yet I still wanted to try, if I could.

"There's something else I ought to tell you. Shildina,

you have been relieved from your position as the priest-ess of carnage. If you want it, you can just stay the water dragon's miko priestess. I should mention that Sadeena has no intention of returning to the post of water drag-on's miko priestess," I explained.

"Indeed. I have some connection to the Water Dragon, but I don't want that position again," Sadeena concurred. Hearing this, Shildina looked at me in sheer surprise.

"The priestess of carnage is an important position too, but there's no need to have someone who hates it so much carry it out. Executioners can be hired, if one is needed," I stated. That whole system needed some extensive changes. Someone doing the dirty work to maintain the power of the Heavenly Emperor was a hateful idea. If it was needed, it should be someone who could compartmentalize it as just a job. "Or do you want to keep on doing it? If so, I won't stop you—but are you okay with that?"

"I'm on the defeated side, and yet you aren't going to execute me? You aren't planning on having Sadeena kill me?" Shildina wondered. Ah, so that was what she'd been thinking.

"Certainly not, nothing of the sort. Anyway, Shildi-na, would you tell me more about those two—about our parents? I can't hold it in any longer, I'm afraid," Sadeena said. She was clearly agitated, sparking with static electricity as she questioned Shildina. "Would you like to come with me, perhaps? I'm planning on heading home and spreading a little, you know, absolute terror around. I need to scare those two into making sure they never make another Shildina." Reports indicated that, as a member of the defeated forces, they were already desperately making changes. Part of me did want to see the faces of these morons whom even the Water Dragon had abandoned. But if I did go along, Sadeena would likely destroy the village *and then* introduce me to her parents, so I had no plans to join her.

"If you don't want to stay here, come with us. Just like the boy here, we won't treat you badly," I told her.

"We can have a lot of fun together, I'm sure! Although, first I need to go and make those two pay for trying so hard," Sadeena said, still going on about it, indicating just how angry she was. From looking at Shildina's condition, it was clear they'd been doing some pretty twisted stuff.

"But—after all I've done—" Shildina looked at the boy, so apologetic, and then looked down.

"Shildina," the boy said softly.

"So what's the relationship between you two, anyway?"

"Sh-she was someone who protected me, like a big sister. Someone different from those trying to use me. A friend," he squeezed out, looking at me.

"That's nice. A friend, he says," I said. It didn't look like she had much respect for him, so there was a high possibility the friend stuff was being carried in by the boy. Shildina looked at him, eyes wide in surprise.

"My lord Heavenly Emperor. I not only failed to control the past god but turned on Lady Makina and the others so close to you, defeating them with my own hands. I'm not worthy of such words from you."

"Hmmm, about that. How much do you remember about what happened?" I questioned. To be quite honest about it, her failure and the possession of past Heavenly Emperor had massively contributed to us occupying Q'ten Lo so easily.

"I couldn't move, but I remember everything. I resisted but hurt so many others—Lady Makina, the guards . . ." Shildina pressed her hands to her face, as though trying to hold in the crazy. "I can't believe Lady Makina would say such things."

"What did she say? Something before we got there?" I asked. Shildina nodded at my question.

"When I was trying to break free in front of Lady Makina, under the control of that strange pattern. When

I thought I was going to die—"

Her story went that, just before we arrived, Shildi-na—possessed by the past Heavenly Emperor—had Makina cornered when the patterns on her body had pushed her down and made her collapse. As she had already been resisting the past Heavenly Emperor, trying to prevent her from killing Makina, Shildina had tempo-rarily been rendered unable to move.

"Seriously," Makina had said, choosing that moment to spit some words of vile poison, thinking she had won, "so this is what it feels like to be bitten by your pet dog! If you'd just stayed in your place, I would have kept you around until the appointed time. All those sweet words of mine that you so easily believed! You foolish, idiotic girl. Raising your hand against me! Are there no limits to your idiocy?" Other key figures had also mocked the fallen Shildina. "It was so hard to hold in my laughter, seeing you believe in me, even defend me! You trusted me so blindly, heading off to die! What a wonderful little toy you were." Laughing at Shildina's struggles, Makina had gone on. "That's it! That's the face I've been want-ing to see! Hahaha! It's so funny I might throw up!" Makina had chillingly declared to the shocked Shildina after another bout of laughing, She reached out, still unable to believe this was happening. "That said, I don't need a silly fish that would dare to stand against me, dare to attack me. So die! You're so filthy I want to spit!"

Calling the killer whale therianthrope Shildina a fish, hah, what a comedian.

Then, as she tried to finish Shildina off, her body had been taken over by the past Heavenly Emperor, and that caught us up to when we appeared.

"What a total bitch. Just hearing the story gets me mad," I spat. Then she got herself killed and had the audacity to try and take Shildina's body. If we'd got there any later, she might have succeeded and managed to escape.

It was like hearing the exploits of Witch herself. She really was someone else, right? I almost couldn't believe it, but of course the timeline didn't match up at all.

Guess it just meant you could find bitches anywhere.

I looked down at the kid, his own eyes downcast, and placed a hand on his shoulder.

"She tried to run, leaving you behind, and our investigations suggest she was pretty involved in the past Heavenly Emperor's assassination. You don't have to feel bad about this—although I know that's of little comfort," I said to him and looked over at Sadeena.

"I mean, I remember her. She was really nasty to me too. I'd like to know more about these 'sweet words' she supposedly used," Sadeena remarked.

"I've encountered someone much like her in the past. She must have thought she could take advantage of people," I stated. After all, Sadeena was a pretty observant person, so the poisonous bitch must have thought it too risky to try and pull one over on her.

"You do sound as though you speak from experience," Sadeena said to me.

"Melty's sister has the exact same personality," I admitted.

"Ah, I see." She took that on board quickly, and then I turned back to Shildina and the boy. "I can only really imagine the hurt to your hearts, caused by learning the true nature about someone who was important to you. I have a complete understanding of being tricked, however," I told them. I'd been framed for a crime I didn't commit, after all. That definitely made me sympathize with feelings of having been tricked. "If she'd fooled you for so long, you should hear how she ended up and be happy about it. Give her a good 'take that,' you know?" I wanted to find Witch and give her the same treatment.

"After that, the past Heavenly Emperor who you

brought into yourself finished her off? That's correct?" I asked. Shildina nodded at my words.

"When I had first brought her out myself, back when I was much younger, she'd tried to take over my body and kill the ministers and Lady Makina. I managed to get her under control, and that was my trump card. Thinking about it now, she was trying to tell me who my enemies were the entire time," Shildina explained.

"So it was your dangerous last resort, potentially causing you to rampage," I surmised. Luckily, she had also proven herself to be something holy, attempting to extract the festering puss from this nation. Thinking over her fight with Raphtalia again, from one perspective it could be considered an extreme form of training. Like she was trying to teach her still inexperienced granddaughter a few useful skills.

"It means the teachings of the past Heavenly Emperor weren't a mistake. The boy isn't that bothered about you having killed her, right?" I said.

"Yes. I believed in Makina, but thinking about it now, there were a lot of strange things," she admitted. It really seemed like the boy just didn't know much but was quick to understand things once they were explained to him—that the Makina witch had thought she was tricking him, but he'd had some idea of what was happening all along. He didn't have a place to go now, so maybe I'd take him under my wing and teach him in my lands.

He might prove to be another Raphtalia.

"Shildina, you don't have to worry. Look up. Q'ten Lo is about to change, for the better. There's no one left here who can make things difficult for you. I want you to live your life freely," the child said and then looked at me and bowed his head.

"You seem to have quite a loyal following too. Any past wrongdoing will be overlooked. I really do want you to live as you please," I informed him.

"But still—"

"That said, you might find that difficult if we don't fix your sense of direction," I said.

"Oh my," Sadeena exclaimed. It was slight, but Shildina's expression seemed to have brightened.

"If you've only seen Q'ten Lo, you may not get a real sense of the scale of things. Come with this boy and try living in my village and country for a while. You can make the hard decisions after that. There'll still be time," I went on.

"Very well. Will you drink with me again? And play cards?"

"Yeah, there are lots of people who love games in the village. They'll all play with you if you teach them.

Of course, I'll join in too, if I have time."

"Okay. Very well," Shildina said, standing up from the blankets. She'd already recovered? She was tough, then, just like Sadeena.

"What should I call you then? Little sis? Or just Shildina? Now then, time to team up with your big sister and go punish those who started all this bother," Sadeena announced.

"Hah?" With a confused expression on her face, Shildina was dragged out by Sadeena.

"Oh my!"

"Yeah, go cut off relations with your dumb parents. I've no plans on letting this nation forgive the policies your clan has been following," I told them.

"Understood! We'll be back before you know it, little Naofumi! We do want you to come and see the village we were born in, too, when you get the time!" Sadeena announced.

"Sure, sure." A tour of the smoking crater, perhaps, after those two demons had finished with it.

"Oh! Naofumi! Oh my! Let go of me!" Shildina was protesting plenty as she was dragged away, but the two of them looked to be getting along just fine—with perhaps a bit too much magic whooshing and sparking between them.

"Shildina! Let's have a drinking contest later. Ah, maybe you need to be a bit drunk to get the juices flowing? Here's a little something that I recommend, then."

"Oh my—glug, glug!" Their voices were getting farther away, but I could clearly picture them both, in their beast transformations, laughing along together.

"Right. Back to the castle for us," I said to the boy.

"Yes. Thank you so much for everything," he told me.

"Hey, no need to be so tense, boy. There are loads of children in my village. I'll treat you just like them." I headed back to the castle, the child and S'yne in tow. Having taken a liking to the doll carried by S'yne, the boy made the biggest impression during the return trip by chatting happily with it.

Most of the adjustments had been completed, and I was out on the highest terrace of the castle, looking over the old city with Raphtalia. S'yne and the others were all inside, resting in their own way.

Finally, I had a chance to talk alone with Raphtalia.

The sunset looked especially beautiful, perhaps because the air was so clear.

The city was throwing what appeared to be a festival, once again, for our victory in battle and for defeating the Heavenly Emperor's forces. These guys really liked to celebrate.

"Phew. Finally we've ended this annoying conflict," I sighed.

"Yes, Mr. Naofumi, the battle had ended, but what do you plan to do next?"

"Huh? I'm planning on leaving the country to Raluva and the other leaders of the revolution from this side and getting straight back to the village. We've pretty much completely shut down the child Heavenly Emperor's forces, so they shouldn't have any major problems now." The defeated side was still causing the occasional ruckus, but they were few in number. With the presence of the dragon hourglass, Raphtalia could show her face when she was needed, and the country could run itself the rest of the time.

"Phew. This was all quite the commotion," she commented.

"Aren't you happy? You've learnt a lot about your parents. Not to mention getting to be a full-blown queen, throne and all," I said. There was no one who could assail Raphtalia's position now. She had become the highest representative of Q'ten Lo, a land that even Siltvelt had hesitated in trying to take over.

Reflecting on the chain of events, it really was quite

the success story. She'd gone from being a simple village girl to the queen of a whole country.

"I do want to learn more about the country that my mother and father used to live in. For me, though, I don't need to be the Heavenly Emperor of Q'ten Lo. Being a girl from that village, the village where everyone lives, and fighting as your sword, Mr. Naofumi—that's enough for me. Just being Raphtalia."

"You don't desire power, do you?" I asked.

"You're one to talk, Mr. Naofumi. You're the god of Siltvelt!" Yeah, good point. I certainly didn't desire power either. I just made use of everything I could make use of and didn't have a shred of intention to become the king of Siltvelt.

Raphtalia sat on the sill and looked at the sunset.

"Coming to Q'ten Lo, I've learned all sorts of techniques and ways to use my strength. I can't help feeling I need to get stronger, much stronger, in order to survive the future battles," she surmised.

"Yeah, I know," I sighed. When I thought about it now, Raphtalia did seem to have grown stronger through this battle. "Also, as Sadeena said, now I can finally have you wear that miko outfit without any further troubles." As I happily puffed up my chest, Raphtalia almost took a tumble from the sill, and I almost reached out to grab her. Falling from that height wouldn't be pleasant!

"After all this, that's what you're worried about?" she gasped.

"It's very important! It's the gear that suits you the best, Raphtalia." Putting Raphtalia in that outfit had been the start of all this, but I ultimately thought things had turned out pretty good. We'd punished the scum who had simply watched Raphtalia suffer and as a result saved Q'ten Lo from its festering corruption. Raphtalia's relative and Shildina both looked, for the time being, to be heading in a better direction too.

"Well, that means—heh heh heh—now both Siltvelt and Q'ten Lo belong to me!" I said.

"No, that's not what I want to say either," she groaned. Yeah, I knew that. But even if we weren't going to become supreme overlords, we had created connections in Siltvelt and Q'ten Lo. When it came to the crunch, we'd be able to ask for cooperation from them. "Seriously, Mr. Naofumi. You push forward so hard, so fast, it really is hard to keep up with you."

"That's quite the compliment."

"I'm getting tired of having to put you right. That's enough for now."

The sunset really was beautiful. Thinking that, we continued to watch the sun go down.

"Anyway, let's take a look later at your parents' possessions, Raphtalia. Their mementos, trinkets. You want to take a look too, right?"

"Yes. Sadeena and others from Q'ten Lo have told me stories, but now I want to know more about my parents for myself."

"Then let's take a bit of a break here. It's all been pretty crazy, so this looks like the perfect juncture to rest up a little. There are hot springs here too."

"If I can take a rest with you, Mr. Naofumi, then I'm happy to do so." Sakura lumina petals drifted gently into the room. The castle itself was made using sakura lumina lumber, and sometimes it appeared to glow a soft pink in response to Raphtalia.

"Maaaaaaaaster! Make your special food for me!" Another noisy nuisance returned. I did make that promise though.

"Hey, Mr. Naofumi. Filo has a job for you. Make your special food for her today, please."

"Okay, okay. I'll make it to celebrate Raphtalia finally being able to wear the miko outfit free of trouble."

"Why are you bringing that up again?!"

With that, we left the room. As we did so, I caught a glimpse of something—but it had to just be a trick of the sunset. For a moment, I thought I saw a man who looked like Raphtalia, and a kind-looking woman who also looked very much like her, waving gently after her as she departed.

Then, heading toward the kitchen in order to cook for everyone, I started down the steps, Raphtalia in tow.

The Rising of the Shield Hero Vol. 14
© Aneko Yusagi 2016
First published by KADOKAWA in 2016 in Japan.
English translation rights arranged by One Peace Books
under the license from KADOKAWA CORPORATION, Japan

ISBN: 978-1-64273-018-0

Written by Aneko Yusagi
Character Design Minami Seira
English Edition Published by One Peace Books 2019

Printed in Canada
1 2 3 4 5 6 7 8 9 10

One Peace Books
43-32 22nd Street STE 204 Long Island City New York 11101
www.onepeacebooks.com

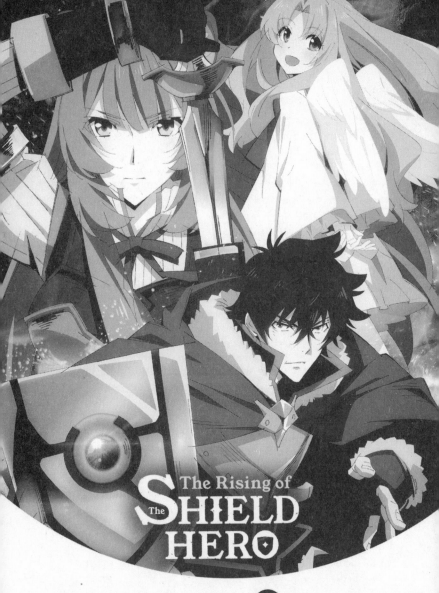